Kangazang!

remote possibilities

TERRY COOPER

CANDY JAR BOOKS · CARDIFF
2025

Editor: Shaun Russell
Cover: Terry Cooper
Editorial: Keren Williams

Printed and bound in the UK by
4edge, 22 Eldon Way, Hockley, Essex, SS5 4AD

ISBN: 978-1-917022-90-3

Published by
Candy Jar Books
Mackintosh House
136 Newport Road, Cardiff, CF24 1DJ
www.candyjarbooks.co.uk

To Nyssia, Finn, Mum,
Gary Bush and Barry J. House

And especially
Douglas Adams for providing so many
with inspiration and joy.

prologue

The Prophecy

Far out in the deep inky voidness of space, the imposing world of Emo Prime hung listlessly.

Its ring of asteroids encircled it, spinning and colliding enthusiastically, hundreds of miles above the mottled black-and-white surface of the planet. To the passing observer, it looked rather like the severed head of a panda bear, surrounded by a cloud of gnats. Only less furry, and not quite as disturbing to see.

Emo Prime wasn't, as its name might suggest, a place where emotions were of prime concern. In fact, since a couple of pale creatures crawled apathetically out of their pale primeval soup millions of years before, emotions were something of a nuisance, and not at all welcomed. During their early history, the Emo people had experienced many of the extremely damaging trends that advanced societies share – vicious, long-running wars that decimated the populations of both sides, followed by post-conflict population explosions, resulting in an overabundance of people who jostled and competed for living space and food, then starvation, unrest, violence, more wars, reality television, coffee shops on every street corner, and finally more general unhappiness for all concerned.

It was decided by the highest authorities on Emo Prime, that the source of all these self-replicating social problems was extreme emotion. Either hatred bubbled up unexpectedly like methane emissions in a bathtub, or joy reduced the minds of everyone to blissful nonsensical mush, resulting in carelessness and more of the aforementioned problems. Something had to be done. And so, they decided to totally revolutionise their society by banning one of the pesky emotional states. To ban both of these problematic feelings would have been difficult, as The Powers That Be weren't all that bright, and weren't sure what the remaining states-of-mind would be. So they held elections, surveys, local rate phone votes and population-wide referendums that would determine which emotion would be made illegal, thus saving their planet from further turmoil. The results were in. The mass of information was piled up in a large room and The Powers That Be stood and gazed up at it in awe.

In the end, they tossed a coin.

The public would never find out, it was a lot less hassle than sifting through the collected information, and they could all get home in time for 'Celebrity Substantial Sibling' on the telly that night.

It was decreed then, that happiness, joy, cheerfulness, glee, bliss and all other positive emotions would be outlawed and discouraged. As an additional measure, any music that was more than a droning dirge, or over thirty-five beats-per-minute was destroyed; colours were removed from clothing, paintings, foods and nature as much as possible. In theory, it was still possible to buy and wear a Hawaiian-style shirt, but only if you were prepared to wear it in one of fifteen identical shades of black.

A leaflet was drawn up to help the people of Emo Prime adjust to their new emotional status. It was a single sheet, folded twice, on black paper with grey text. The title:

LIVING: AS EASY AS ABC
(Apathy Boredom and Complacency)

This leaflet was filled with information about what was now considered illegal and how best to conform to the new governmental guidelines. It was widely distributed and accepted by the populace as the way things were going to be from that point on. Before long, the information in the leaflet was being taught in schools and displayed on billboards, and over the decades that followed, it was revised, re-written and amended until it became known as the Holy ABC: A tome of over five hundred pages, dedicated to ridding the planet of anything remotely concerned with enthusiasm or contentment. Even smiling was banned, under threat of rather nasty electro-shock therapy. (Of course, if one were deviant enough to enjoy such treatment, the alternative was too terrifying to contemplate. Legends tell of it involving a number of pigeons and the removal of one's clothing.)

Incredibly, this bizarre course of action had the desired effect on the people of Emo Prime. There were no more wars, because everyone was in a state of apathy, no new and exciting ideas to raise their pulse-rates due to ingrained boredom, and nobody wanted to change the way things were because of the general malaise of complacency that hung over the minds of everyone there. It was peace. Of a sort. In banning the positive emotions, the entire planet's populace was pushed into embracing the negative ones. And that worked rather well. To keep the threat of their society crumbling ever-present, they invented a prophecy of doom. It was vague enough to re-use and recycle countless times, and it could be rolled out every time they needed to rein the people in. The prophecy warned of the arrival of an 'Evil One' (always a good, non-gender-specific place to start), and their accomplice, (best to give them a sidekick, just in case) who would visit their planet (as some people used to, before it became the least enjoyable place to visit), and try to tell anyone to 'cheer up'. Heaven forbid.

The highest governing bodies of Emo Prime established a ruling class to ensure the compliance and strict adherence to the rules of the Holy ABC. A High Priest was elected, charged with the task of holding regular meetings, broadcast around the globe, that ensured the rules were stated, the people were sedated by fear, and control was maintained. The mood was, as intended, apathetic. Which was nice.

Deep down on the surface, beneath the sullen clouds, there stood a great cathedral. A towering, ornate behemoth of Gothic design, dark and foreboding, into which a steady stream of shrouded and dour figures shuffled, moaning softly to pass the time on their arduous pilgrimage.

The village meeting was in progress.

The High Priest, tall and spider-like, clad in elegant robes of the dullest colours, addressed the assembled throng of sour-faced listeners.

'Mood: Apathetic,' he called out.

'Mood: Apathetic,' replied the crowd in unison, both as an acknowledgement and answer.

Looking out over the hundreds of pale faces, each one framed by lank but shiny black hair, the Priest took a deep creaking breath, and began his sermon.

'To the Highest on high, the gods of Emo, and their desolate hearts, we send out praise. To uphold the principles of the Holy ABC – Apathy, Boredom and Complacency, we dedicate our pointless existences. This day, and forever, we yearn for the comforting solace of a dark and cold grave.'

It was a particularly cheery one, today's sermon. After all, the Priest had some particularly cheery news to tell. He swept a wrinkly pale finger across his wrinkly pale forehead to clear his eyes of limp black hair.

'Be thou warned,' he began, accompanied by some serious finger-waggage, 'That the Evil One and his accomplice are due to arrive… at any time, now that the planets have aligned. That he shall walk among us and spread the terror and fear that will end our lives.'

A visible shudder rippled through the audience; the desired response. He continued with vigour:

'That they will bring upon us the plagues and afflictions of Joy, Smiling and,' he paused for maximum effect, '…Laughter!'

The crowd began to mumble, clearly unnerved by the thought of happiness in any format. The Priest read on, with a weird grimace crossing his crumply-paper face.

'And when they arrive, we must be vigilant! We must prove to the Evil Ones that we SHALL worry! We shall NOT be happy! Only then will they tremble in fear of us! And only then will we do what must be done to purge the badness of their spirits.'

He took another final deep breath.

'WHAT WILL WE DO?' he yelled out to the crowd.

In unison again, the crowd called back:

'Complain! Condemn! Convert!'

The Priest was satisfied.

Justice will be done, he thought. *Our society is safe.*

But he was unaware that society as he knew it was about to change forever.

And it would take precisely four minutes and fifty-one seconds.

chapter one

The Man from Kangazang

Anyway.

Our story, like many unearthly stories, starts, rather predictably, on Earth.

Except for the previous part that didn't, obviously. You get the idea.

Jeff Spooner sat in the barber's chair, getting his bi-monthly trim. He looked around the faux-pine clad walls, and gazed at the flecks of mousy brown hair that slid down the apron in front of him. Haircuts seemed to be taking less time each month, he mused, while the percentage of silvery-grey seemed to be increasing. Surely they'd cancel each other out, at some point?

He looked up as far as he could without moving his head, and saw that his hairdresser was wearing an odd tie-pin that bore a penguin in a fetching shade of pink.

'Doing anything interesting this weekend?' asked Ray the Barber.

Ray was in his early forties, almost-but-not-quite portly, but still quite energetic. He sported a rapidly greying hairdo and matching goatee, which made him look a little like a jazz musician.

His hair looked like it was trying to evacuate his scalp and hide down around the back of his head, a sort of furry curtain. In his shirt, tie and white barbers' coat, he was always well turned-out, as are most barbers, and full of interesting yarns, many of which made no sense at all – again, as are most barbers.

Jeff looked up into the mirror, to see Ray snipping away effortlessly.

'Yeah,' replied Jeff. 'Organising me stag do, innit?'

Ray nodded.

'Oh yes. Big day coming up, isn't it? Two weeks?'

'Yeah. Hence the trim: Sarah wants a groomed groom,' said Jeff with a grin.

Ray smiled. 'Then her groom shall be groomed!'

Jeff looked a little dumbfounded. But he had other things on his mind. He wasn't usually an unhappy person, and Ray noticed the change in his usual bright demeanour.

'You look less than chipper, Jeff, if you don't mind my saying so. What's up? Worried about the wedding?'

'Well, sort of. I'm more worried about Sarah. Do you think women get the jitters, same as us men?'

Ray thought it was an odd question to ask. But then again, Ray thought the majority of Jeff's questions were odd. He racked his brain for an answer.

'I'm not sure. Depends on the curry.'

Jeff blinked, momentarily trying to connect the answer with his question.

'No, mate – You know, the pre-nuptial jitters. Second thoughts about going through with it, and all that?'

'Maybe,' said Ray, avoiding yet another social faux-pas, 'it's certainly a terrifying prospect. Why's that then?'

Jeff sighed sadly. 'I dunno. It's just that... well, she's been a bit... off, lately.'

'Off?' gasped Ray, momentarily freezing. 'Stale? Decomposing? Does she have that funny smell?'

'No, you nutter, you know! Distant. Not very chatty.'

Ray smiled. 'Oh, I see. You care about her a lot, don't you?'

'Yeah, I do. She's the best thing to ever happen to me, you know? I thought I'd never get married. Thought I'd be the perennial bachelor boy. All my mates got hitched and started families, but not me. Then I met her. She pretty much saved me from a rubbish life. But I'm worried about her. I don't see her smiling much, these days. Well, when I get home she is – but it soon fades, and then she goes to bed early without me.'

Ray saw that Jeff was in need of sage advice. Unfortunately he had very little idea about what to say to this particular customer. Still, he had to try.

'Oh. Well, perhaps you should try to cheer her up a bit? I'm not sure, but I read that women like gifts. Flowers, chocolate shoes. That sort of thing.'

Jeff raised an eyebrow.

'Sorry, Jeff,' said Ray. 'I'm not really an expert on women.'

Jeff looked at the pink tie-pin again, mentally confirming a suspicion he'd long held.

'No, didn't think you were. Flowers, though. Good point, that might work. Think I'll surprise her with some. Why not, eh? She's worth it after all. Maybe even a show. I'll pop into the theatre on the way home. *Cats*, I think.'

'When did they start selling cats in the theatre?' asked Ray, finishing up the trim.

Jeff blinked.

'No, mate... "*Cats*" – the play, you know,' he began, thinking that this might possibly be a wind-up.

Ray looked embarrassed and tried to make amends.

'Oh theatre! I thought you said... er... THE CATTER-y. Yeah, sorry.'

Jeff shook his head briefly, to wake up his senses a bit. The internal rattling didn't help. He decided to leave it at that. It was too early for surrealism right now.

Jeff had known Ray the barber for nearly ten years. They weren't exactly best buddies, but since Jeff met his fiancée, and found that she was very exacting in the way she wanted her future husband to look, he had to pop in for a trim – without fail – every two weeks. Thus, he and Ray had struck up the beginnings of a friendship.

Ray did have some minor eccentricities, when he thought about it. He was the kind of guy who never quite seemed to be on the same page as everyone else. But Jeff surmised that perhaps his barber had a sheltered upbringing. Perhaps his parents moved around before finally settling somewhere. Maybe his dad was in the army: being stationed in a long and confusing succession of different countries does tend to mix things up a bit for a child. Thus, Ray seemed a solitary sort of guy. For example, he refused Jeff's offer to come out for his stag weekend, and in fact he always declined an offer to go down the pub. When he thought more about it, Jeff had never seen Ray outside of his salon. Surely a barber can't be that busy? He seldom talked about his family, except to say that they were far away. And he charged next to nothing for his haircuts, as if he genuinely didn't need the money and was doing it just for the fun of it. *But each to his own*, thought Jeff. Nice to see a person who genuinely loves their job and takes pride in a task well done. Plus, with Sarah's demands for a 'groomed groom', he didn't fancy paying the best part of a tenner for a trim anywhere else. Yes, Ray was definitely cheap and cheerful.

The barber's skilful hands swiftly completed the job, and whipped the nylon apron off him like a matador.

'Cheers, Ray, what's the damage?' asked Jeff as he got up and out of the chair.

'There's no damage! It's quite neat! Look in the mirror!' said Ray in shock.

'Har har. What do I owe you?'

'That's um, one pound and… seven pence, please!' Ray seemed to have picked a random figure out of thin air, and opened his olde-worlde till with a push of a button.

Jeff paused.

'One pound seven? Have you put your prices down again?'

Ray smiled sheepishly.

'Well, yeah. Need to get some more customers. You know how it is…' he mumbled, looking rather embarrassed.

'I'm a fairy, my name is Nuff,' said Jeff, pulling out some coins.

Ray looked a little puzzled.

'No it isn't, it's Jeff.'

Jeff wasn't sure if Ray was really serious, so he let it slide.

'You really should charge more, mate. Seriously. The hairdressers down the road charge a minimum of seven quid for a dry cut. You won't be in business much longer.'

Ray seemed to agree, like it was a good thing.

'That's the plan,' he said cheerfully.

Jeff brushed a few specks of hair from his neck, and reached over for his jacket, which hung on a hook nearby.

'So, you're off on holiday, then? Or retiring?'

'A little from Column "A", and a little from Column "B", Jeff. Taking a trip, really. Going to... er... visit my family.'

'Oh right... where did you say they are, again?' asked Jeff, putting the jacket on.

Ray closed the till.

'Kanga... Er, Kanga-da. Canada.'

Taking a side step to allow another man to take the chair, Jeff nodded.

'Oh right. Canada. Bit nippy out there, mate, make sure you wrap up warm!'

'Well, I'll be on the beach a lot, if I can help it,' said Ray, 'Cheerio!'

'See ya mate,' called Jeff as he stepped out of the salon.

Hang a banger, he thought. *On the beach? In Canada? Brrr!* Then he chuckled to himself. Ray always was a bit of a peculiar one.

Inside the salon, Ray smiled to himself.

Jeff always was a bit of a peculiar one, he thought.

But in all honesty, it was Jeff who was closer to the truth: Compared to him, Ray was the peak of peculiarity.

So peculiar, Jeff couldn't even begin to imagine how peculiar.

Peculiarities, especially in this reality, are something of a paradox. This is because there are so many millions upon billions of peculiarities in each and every aspect of existence that they actually are the norm and not peculiar at all. So to be brutally honest (another paradox, incidentally), the most peculiar thing one could ever find is something completely normal. For example: if one were at a zoo, peering into a vivarium of stick insects, the sight of say, a Volkswagen Beetle, would appear to be the strange object.

But in the spirit of goodwill, progression and in the equally important spirit of 'moving-things-along-ness', we'll just assume that you share the narrow-minded human definition of peculiarity. Thought you'd agree.

In another part of the galaxy, hung the peculiar planet Orbitron. As its name suggests, it's not your common-or-garden planet. Resembling a gigantic ball-bearing or, to be more accurate, a chrome-plated Brussel Sprout, it was an entirely artificial, metal construction. Not a diabolical weapon of planetary destruction – 'Star of Death', anyone? – but a peaceful world that offered assistance, obedience and a local-rate technical assistance line to the countless peoples of the universe.

Orbitron was inhabited by – and indeed, built by robots. Or as they preferred to be known, Orbots. It sounded better, as they now had a place to actually belong, just like the 'fleshies'. Artificial beings of all shapes and sizes lived there, from minuscule nano-surgeons to towering Constructorbots. They lived in happy compatibility and prospered, being efficient and regularly upgraded, rebooted and defragmented. Where once, robots were created to serve, the Orbots had turned things around, and their reputation for efficient service became well known and respected across the galaxy. People would come from far and wide, often at great expense to get their computer systems, starships and robotic servants repaired by a race that didn't make mistakes or add a few quid to the bill when the customer's head was turned. The Orbots had integrity. In fact, their installed integrity was internally integrated. Interesting.

Of course, there are exceptions to every rule, and Orbitron was no different from any planet, in that it had its fair share of undesirables and non-runners. These unfortunate Orbots were known as the M-Classes. So named as they were designated "M" for malfunction.

Because the Orbots were a kindly and benevolent race, they tried to repair their broken brothers and sisters, until it became too expensive, but some just wouldn't be fixed. They tried installing newer operating systems, re-formatting their hard drives, and even the last-resort of disconnecting them from the InfoHEX – (InformationHyperEXpressway) entirely, but the source of the bugs still managed to elude them.

The M-Class Orbots lived in the lesser-developed areas of Orbitron, mainly on the surface. It was a sort of slum – albeit a spotlessly clean and organised one. The malfunctioning mechas went about their lives fending off meteor showers and magnetised space debris, while their more sophisticated cyber-siblings lived below the surface, running the server farms and doing all the techy stuff. It was on the surface of Orbitron where M4 and his female-designated cohabitant, M25 lived.

M4 was, for all purposes, a fine Orbot.

He had all his limbs and his programming was nigh-on perfect. Except – something deep and elusive in his software had a strange effect on his thought process. Everything he experienced seemed to be funny to him in some way. Humour and hilarity took over his operational matrix. He just couldn't take anything seriously.

Seriously.

No, seriously.

M4 was designed as a starship mechanic, built to humanoid specifications, loaded up with software that enabled him to repair almost any kind of spacecraft, and sent out to serve the Terran military forces in the Urff system. His placement was only semi-successful: On the one hand, he was extremely good at his work, and kept the morale of the troops high, with his penchant for seeing the funny side of life. On the other hand, the top brass were extremely irritated at his penchant for seeing the funny side of death. A tense military struggle in the far-off regions of the galaxy was no place for an Orbot that found everything hilarious. Military funerals seemed to lose some of their respectful sobriety when suppressed giggling kept coming from the back of the crowd. So finally, he was discharged from the armed forces and sent back to Orbitron, just as M25 was.

The Mainframes placed him in a small mechanical tool production unit near the surface of Orbitron, where he coped rather well. Or at least he thought he was coping well. It was only after he was jumped upon by his co-workers, who tried to batter him to pieces for laughing at the word 'tool' every single time it was said, that it was decided he was a lost cause. His superiors stamped him with an "M" and sent him up onto the surface because, quite frankly, they had had more than enough of his constant sniggering and jokey comments. In a world reliant on the solemnity of logic and conformity, there was no place for this annoying Orbot who laughed at anything, all of the time. You could understand their reasons. If you've ever worked in an office environment that had a person labelled 'the office joker', you'll know what I mean.

His cohabitant unit, M25, was perfectly fine with this. She thought it was sort of endearing and made him more human-like. M25 was created for the numerous roles normally reserved for female humanoids. No, not just the seedy ones, but across the universe, where humanoid life seemed to prefer the standard 'two arms, two legs and a head' configuration, the males of that species also preferred, and often demanded, a certain type of anthropomorphic attractiveness; long lower limbs, elegant bodily curves, pleasant demeanour and bright, attentive eye modules. M25 certainly had these upgrades, and was destined to do well as a waitress, hostess, child-carer, nurse, or any of the myriad tasks that female humanoids do so much better than their male counterparts. She, like M4, also seemed like a perfectly operational Orbot – a veritable Venus in white plastic and chromed parts. But one had to be very gentle with her – due to her phobias. This became a problem when they manifested themselves shortly after her Operation Day.

Most organisms, whether artificial or fleshy, learn to cope with irrational phobias, but M25 couldn't. Nor could those around her, as these phobias changed regularly. It could be oil that terrified her one minute, then her own feet the next.

M25 was unpacked from her factory wrappings a day after her Operation Day. Upon first activation, she was programmed with her designated task: that of running a pre-school nursery on the planet Woymalus. As any parent knows, a nursery can be a noisy, terrifying environment. More so for the carer than the child. The nursery was an ear-splitting racket of crying and screaming.

The babies were quite loud too.

The children of Woymalus are just like many other species, except the Woym species as its name suggests, are related to earthworms. Fortunately for them, they developed limbs to allow them to move about a little better than their earth-bound cousins, but when you throw a multi-phobic android into a room of young, enthusiastic (and truth be told, a little slimy) children who create a constantly changing environment of sound, sights, smells, textures and experiences, you really shouldn't expect peaceful harmony. The owners of the nursery were not happy. The parents complained.

The kids loved it, though.

Thus, M25 was shut down, stuffed back into the packaging and sent back to Orbitron for diagnosis and possible repair. Sadly, the diagnosis revealed that she had a similar problem to that of M4: not a physical problem, but her behavioural software contained a flaw that could replicate itself if threatened with fresh coding. Plus she'd added the fear of worms and bubble wrap to her list of terrifying things. In layman's terms, she was knackered.

The ruling Mainframes attempted to repair her until the cost of repairs exceeded the cost of her construction, and then they gave up – simply replacing her forehead plate with one marked 'M', and sent her up and out.

She was a nervous wreck when they dumped her on the surface, trembling at the sight of the starry sky, then wailing in fear at the arrival of M4, when he said "hello" (then burst out laughing) for the first time. But between them, they seemed to cope fairly well, and thus, they got on with life.

Their surface tasks were to repair and refuel docking spacecraft that passed by. Occasionally, M4 would crack a really terrible joke and laugh uncontrollably at his own humour, and M25 would run away, screaming in horror as a visiting ship's dog sniffed her silver leg, but generally they did OK. But they, like the numerous other M-Class Orbots, wished for something better, something really interesting and heroic to re-define their lives. The thought of a destiny, something spontaneous and random in their lives made them feel a little less like Orbots and a little more like humans. Who said that androids dream only of electric sheep?

They were about to get their wish.

And tenuous though the link may be, wishing is what brings us back to our rather un-peculiar and normal (well, relatively normal) human being called Jeff Spooner.

Jeff was in a bad way. He wished for a lot in his life, like everyone does, but tonight, he'd wished that he'd caught the later bus to Sarah's house. He wished he'd not decided to surprise her by turning up unannounced with the theatre tickets and medium-priced bouquet of chrysanthemums and various strands of overpriced posh grass.

But most of all, he wished he hadn't stood at Sarah's bedroom door to catch her in a rather compromising position with the local reverend. He may have stuck to his story about 'performing an exorcism', but that dog-collared deviant wasn't fooling anyone.

Although Jeff had a healthy respect for the clergy and the very good work they do, he felt it only right that he should perform his very own exorcism and try to beat the evil out of the vicarious vicar. In actual fact, it didn't go past the first punch, but for Jeff that was a bit of a victory, as he wasn't usually a violent man.

Thus, Jeff sat at the bar of the Red Lion Inn, and sniffed, watching his tears ploop into his un-sipped pint.

Jeff thought back on all the times he hadn't been there for Sarah; on the evening of their very first date, he'd made a complete mess of things. Sarah arrived at the local cinema on time, only to hang around on her own for over two hours. When Jeff did finally turn up, (due to his mate's car breaking down and an unreliable taxi driver with no sense of direction), he'd left his wallet at home, so he had to borrow money from Sarah to pay the cab fare, the cinema tickets, popcorn and drinks. To add to the confusion, the only film showing at that particular late hour was a rather distasteful slasher movie which didn't go down well with Sarah's aversion to graphic horror.

Surely that wasn't a reason to embark on an affair, was it?

Perhaps it was the time he'd forgotten her birthday completely: They just moved in together, and Sarah came home from a hard day at work. There on the living room table, was a large box which filled her with excitement. She'd talked about wanting a cute little Labrador puppy, or the latest fragrance and makeup set from Paris. Upon opening it, was a brand new home lager brewing kit. His offer of letting her taste the first pint brewed was of little comfort.

Surely even that was no reason to be unfaithful?

Maybe it was the afternoon he ran over her father's sandal-clad foot with the lawnmower. Or the day he slipped in the shower, grabbed the curtain rail and pulled the ceiling down. Or the time he turned up at her work's Christmas party, completely sozzled, and sang 'Especially For You' on one knee. To her boss. Minus trousers.

It could even have been the time he tried to fix the doorbell at her place, and made a complete canine's casserole of it, leaving the chimes hanging at eye level in the hall. Maybe he should've fixed that. Or perhaps it was the barbecue incident.

Whatever it was, he had to admit that he hadn't been a model boyfriend. And perhaps the sum total of his failings had been enough to make her seek comfort in the arms of another man.

'I'm sure he won't press charges, Jeff,' offered Glyn the barman. 'After all, it's not going to go down very well with his superiors, and it'd ruin his career for such a young bloke…'

To Jeff, this was hardly a comfort. He sniffed again and looked up with his watery blue eyes.

'It was her birthday. Birthday! I still can't believe she'd do this to me. I never two timed her, I never mistreated her, I never once hurt her!' he whimpered.

The barman stopped him there.

'Ah – that's not strictly true, is it? There was the barbecue incident.'

'That's not the same thing,' mumbled Jeff, as he took a tiny sip of lager-with-a-dash-of-tears-and-runny-nose-extract.

'It wasn't intentional. There was a wasp! I had a spatula! How was I to know she was behind me when I swung it?'

Glyn the barman suppressed his smirk. After all, Jeff was a valued regular. But the thought of Sarah with a triangular black mark on her forehead where the hot fat had branded her otherwise pretty face, did tickle him somewhat. He tried to offer more sympathy.

'You mustn't blame yourself, Jeff…'

'No, I don't…' he began calmly, but then Jeff shook like a long-dead volcano spurting into fiery activity.

'I blame her!! That evil cow! That unscrupulous, scheming sodding bint! That – that uncaring, unfeeling bloody… bloody… wench!'

Jeff never was very good at profanity.

He took a deep breath, and grabbed his jacket. Leaving his snot-infused beverage to the purple-nosed old soak at the bar who'd sat beside him witnessing the entire scene, he bid a mumbled, tipsy farewell to Glyn, and left for home.

To the crumpled old dipso, it was a lovely vintage, this one. Mmmm.

As he ambled down the high street, munching on one of Georgiou's Special Kebabs, Jeff wondered where his life was going.

It was going nowhere and fast. In fact, it was probably going in reverse gear, very fast indeed. He still loved Sarah, though. At least he thought he did. Who else would have given up smoking to be with her? Who else would have let her win on the games console so many times and make it look like he was trying? Who else would have bought her the Labrador puppy that she so wanted?

Alright, so he'd bought the puppy, but after stopping off in the Red Lion for a few afternoon jars, he got a little confused and ended up swapping the dog for a home brew kit. But he did buy the puppy to begin with. The thought was what counted.

And they did have some fun times together. Sarah loved Jeff for the hapless idiot he was. At least at first. Her plan was to take this feckless, unfit, very basic man and sculpt him into prime, neat, submissive, husband material. Needless to say it hadn't quite worked. Initially, she thought his absent-mindedness was endearing, so she accepted it. Later on, she found that he was rather naïve, and willing to go with any schedule, plan or suggestion that she came up with. This came in handy later on in their relationship when she needed him out of the way so she could embark on her quest to find a suitable replacement. One of the best ways of losing Jeff for an hour or two was to hand him a few pounds and send him off for a haircut. He'd invariably be tempted by the pocket full of change that was left over, and spend it in the local.

Thus, instead of ending their fatally-flawed relationship and looking like the villain of the piece, Sarah decided to keep him at arms length for as long as possible, while interviewing a few likely candidates in the meantime, until he called the wedding off. Jeff didn't call it off, though. He loved Sarah like a baby bird loves regurgitated worms. Alright, he wasn't perfect, but he had a deep respect for her: She was gorgeous. She was successful, and she was so much smarter, more ambitious than his other brief romantic encounters. To him, she was a princess, and in a topsy-turvy play of role reversal, she rescued him from a life of solitary drudgery. Anyone willing to care for a man who had resigned himself to a lifetime of loneliness was an angel in his mind.

This, coupled with his realisation that she had grown tired of him months ago, was the hardest thing to take. His princess had revealed herself as the wicked witch all along. What really hit him the hardest was the pain of seeing her satisfied smile when he pushed open the bedroom door and caught her with the reverend. She showed no remorse, only relief at the revelation. Finally – no more secrets and lies. Jeff was on the scrap heap, and that was that.

And so, Jeff needed to do some serious thinking about his directionless life, his empty heart and the one pound and seven pence that he'd spent on a pointless haircut that day.

Another peculiar thing (there will be many, so try to keep up) is that most people in this life (or the next, or indeed the previous), only ever make big plans, decisions or analytical forays into their own existences when they are either:

a) drunk, or

b) unhappy, or more often than not,

c) both.

These three physical and emotional conditions are quite possibly the very worst time to make a deep decision of this kind. Then again, it may be the best opportunity to be completely honest with oneself. Or not. That's the beauty of alcohol and melancholia-induced psychoanalysis – nothing (and indeed everything) is what it seems. Or maybe it isn't. But it could be.

Anyway, Jeff was no exception.

He sat down on the cold steel bench within the bus shelter, and fished out the long green chilli peppers from his kebab. Finding three, he flung them rather skilfully into the litter bin nearby, and wiped his vinegar-tainted fingers on his jeans.

As he munched on the vaguely meat-like shoe leather, he began to hum a tune. A tune which he at first thought originated in his lager-addled mind:

'Here's a little song I wrote,
You might want to sing it note-for-note;
Don't worry…
(bipidee bee boo beepdeedoo…)
Be happy…'

'Yeah, bloody easy for you to say, Muck-Ferret…' slurred Jeff, to nobody in particular.

He'd read somewhere that Bobby Mc Ferrin, the writer of the offending tune, (Also, singer, composer, conductor, multi-instrumentalist and eternal optimist) had topped himself in despair. After a little searching on the net, this had turned out to be a vicious, cruel and wholly inaccurate urban myth.

But right now, Jeff wished him dead.

'Don't worry, be buggered. Happy, my bunghole,' he spat.

'The day that song saves a life, they'll probably declare it a public holiday…'

It turned out that the song wasn't in his mind at all, but drifting out of a nearby window, not far away. Jeff crumpled up his kebab papers and dumped them into the litter bin. He walked toward the sound, mentally contemplating the gleeful strangulation of whoever seemed to be taunting him with the accursed happy ditty.

He turned the corner, and saw Ray's Gent's Salon.

The shop lights were on, and there was some definite activity inside. A party, perhaps? Ray's family were, so he said, all in Canada. More to the point, Ray once said he never touched alcohol, so why would there be music and life inside a barber's shop at nearly midnight?

Jeff crept closer to the window. Vertical blinds prevented him from getting a good view of the proceedings, but he could see Ray in there, dancing around with his brush, and a black rubbish sack, to the strains of Kylie Minogue's first hit single, 'I Should Be So Lucky'. Mercifully, Mc Ferrin had had his three minutes.

Jeff smiled. Dancing to Kylie? He'd never seen his barber with a woman and concluded that he must be a little 'light in the loafers', so to speak.

Those with the narrowest of minds prefer to tar others with the widest of brushes. But Jeff's rather narrow mind was due to be expanded laterally, not to mention exponentially from this night on.

Not that it was a problem for Jeff. He knew a few of the gay folk in the town, and didn't really mind what side their bread was buttered – so long as they kept their knives to themselves. And Ray seemed like the straight-acting type, which Jeff felt more comfortable with, such was his unevolved and rather fragile sense of masculinity. He concluded that his theory about Ray's tie-pin with the pink penguin was correct.

It was at that point that Ray stopped the CD of

eighties hits playing, and unlocked the salon door. He dragged the bin bag outside, and headed for the large lock-up garage adjacent to the shop.

Jeff took a few steps back into the shadows of the wall next to him, and watched as Ray unlocked the large chains that held the huge wooden door of the lock-up. In actual fact, it was an old converted hay-loft, as Ray's salon was an old farm house, a very nice place to live and work. How he could afford it while charging so little for a dry cut was indeed another mystery to add to the enigmatic chap.

To prematurely remove the mystery that currently surrounds our bizarre barber would be churlish, obvious and probably spoil things somewhat. But to shed a little light on the subject is probably a good idea.

Ray Scump (his correct title will be revealed to you in precisely one thousand, three hundred and sixty-two words), didn't really need the money, and coped rather well. But for the sake of maintaining an already implausible but completely factual dramatic narrative, I won't tell you much about it right now. But soon.

Jeff remained there for a few moments, wobbling in the shadows, watching the proceedings. He did quite well, until Georgiou's Special Kebab did an acrobatic leap within his stomach, forcing out the loudest gurgling ke-burp that he'd had ever created.

Ray spun around. He brandished his broom like a baseball bat. Jeff stepped out of the dark corner, both hands raised.

'Whoa! Whoa! It's me, Ray. It's Jeff!'

Ray remained keenly alert, almost guiltily stunned. He shook the broom, threateningly.

'Don't come any closer!' he said, still looking terrified.

Things would have probably gone a little smoother had Jeff not seen the spaceship in the garage behind Ray.

And thrown up everywhere.

Jeff Spooner wasn't the only person having a hard time coping with recent events. For example, Reverend Wilson, the young and sinful vicar who had recently exercised (as opposed to exorcised) Jeff's fiancée, was nursing a black eye. Jeff had surprised himself by being responsible for the black eye, as he wasn't a violent person by any means and didn't even hit the man. Well, not for want of trying.

The facts were these: Jeff momentarily lost control at the sight of his beloved in the arms of another man, and he did attempt to smite said vicar, in a moment of great vengeance and furious anger. He wasn't proud of it, but betrayal can be a terrible thing to push one to the darker side of the psyche. He took a swing at the vicar, and missed entirely.

Wilson, totally un-smited, thanked the Lord for the near-miss, and then decided to hand out a little smiting of his own. Jeff noticed this, and did what any red-blooded man would: he turned and ran. Wilson gave chase, flying down the stairs and bashed his face on a low-hanging doorbell chime – another DIY job that Jeff had failed to complete, hence his being solely responsible for the vicar's black eye.

Talking of which, the vicar was driving home in his little car, wondering if he was going to be bunged out of the priesthood altogether the next morning. *Surely*, he thought. *This is the work of the Devil?* The wicked temptress that cruelly seduced him, and his subsequent punishment. Or was it his act of mercy to such a pretty and needy woman that led Satan's follower (and the clanging chimes of doom) to exact such a terrible revenge?

Whatever it was, he'd have a lot of explaining to do in the morning. Hopefully, the Good Lord would provide him with a sign.

Jeff's ex-fiancée Sarah was also finding it difficult to come to terms with what had transpired only a few hours ago.

Lying in bed alone, she gazed out of the window, looking at the clear moonlit sky. But her face revealed a thin wry smile. Her concerns were for the slightly dented reverend who had been in her arms, and elsewhere, earlier on that night.

She smiled because she had managed to have her 'cake' and 'eat' it all this time, and now that her loser of a boyfriend had found out, she no longer had to deal with him. In all honesty, it turned out that Sarah really was an 'evil cow, an unscrupulous, scheming sodding bint, and an uncaring, unfeeling bloody... bloody... wench' to quote Jeff. But suddenly, the smile faded. A tear welled up in her eye, as she realised that all was not quite well...

Jeff still owed her fifty quid.

Another person having a lifestyle crisis at this crucial juncture in our tale was the evil dictator, Lord Rancydd of Skragg. Although he wasn't strictly anything to do with Jeff's troubled existence, he would soon set events in motion to make life a little more trying for our hapless human.

Approximately one hundred and thirty-five parsecs away, within the impressive cluster of youthful stars called the Pleiades, lay the Skraggi Empire.

The planet Skragg smouldered angrily like a red hot coal trying to stay lit. And like the hypothetical coal, the planet's leader was also smouldering, fighting to stay alive in order to maintain control over his gigantic kingdom, which had been ruled for millennia by a procession of vindictive and savage rulers. The latest in the line was Lord Rancydd, victor of countless battles, murderer of billions and fearful god of war to every nearby system.

And father to Kelvin.

Lord Rancydd, now just under a century old, lay dying in his jewel-encrusted golden bed, his only son at his side. Kelvin was a little under thirty, thin and nervous, and unlike his father, he wasn't really the vindictive and savage type. True, he'd read about countless battles, imagined insulting millions and tried to be a fearful god of war to the next door neighbours' pets. But Kelvin was about to inherit the title Lord Rancydd the Third, Overlord of Skragg. In all honesty, he would rather have been reading magazines of dubious subject matter outside in the garden shed.

On second thought, Lord Rancydd wasn't the one having difficulty in his life, as there was only about a minute left of it. Kelvin was the one going through the emotional mangle, buttocks-first. He sat beside the huge bed and watched the hours tick by as his ailing father took thin gasps of air. A tear welled up in his eye.

Oh, hurry up and go, you old git, thought Kelvin. *I'm missing my programme on the telly.*

Back on Earth, the hours had also ticked by. It was 2am in the morning, and Jeff Spooner sat inside the garage staring up at Ray, with an empty feeling in his stomach. The reason for this feeling was literal – his stomach contents was outside the garage, doing a rather convincing Jackson Pollock impersonation.

Ray had helped Jeff clean himself up, and handed him a strong coffee, which helped, but not a lot, because he was looking at a scene which was chock-full of mind-boggle-ation; his local barber, building a spacecraft, inside a garage (out of what looked like wool – what was that odd smell?), and a small army's worth of explosives piled underneath the shell-shaped ship.

Was Ray some kind of terrorist? Jeff had to ask to get this issue out of the way. Tactfully, too. It wouldn't do to upset him.

'Are you some kind of terrorist, Ray? Like, er… Al-Pacino… no, Al-Qaeda?'

Ray smiled warmly, rather unlikely for an AK-47-brandishing nutjob.

'No, of course not. Don't be ridiculous.'

This was a big relief. Jeff sighed and took a long sip of coffee as Ray continued.

'I'm an alien.'

Jeff's coffee left the way it went in, only twice as fast, accompanied by a spurty noise.

This had been quite a bizarre day for Jeff, all things considered and, if truth be told, also for the High Priest of Emo Prime; M4 and M25, the dysfunctional Orbots; randy Reverend Wilson; scheming Sarah; Glyn the barman; and the crusty old dipso, Lord Rancydd Of Skragg; and young Prince Kelvin. Even Bobby McFerrin, on the other side of the world, wasn't feeling so chipper at that particular moment, as he'd received a letter from his landlord, telling him that his rent was late and that he may have to litigate.

Only Ray seemed to be having a pretty normal sort of day. But at two in the morning, Jeff decided he might as well embrace the madness and go along with it. He resigned himself to the belief that, at some point, reason would soon slip back into the proceedings. Either that or a male nurse would top up his medication and re-tighten the straps.

Ray stood up and took a deep breath.

'I think it's time I explained myself,' he said, pacing around the odd mottled spacecraft, 'No, you aren't imagining all this. Yes, I am an alien, and this – well, this is my only way off this planet.'

Jeff could only smile weakly as coffee dripped from his chin. He looked at the insane craft and the deceptively sane barber. At this point, he could only assume that Ray had run through the crazy forest and hit every tree.

'Er… OK, Ray. But one question—'

'Only one?'

'Well, alright – a couple of million. How can you be an alien? I've known you for, well… at least ten years!'

Ray stopped pacing, and sat down on a wooden crate near Jeff.

'Firstly, my name isn't Ray. Well, it is, but that's only part of it.'

'Er… oh-kay then. So, what's the rest of it?'

Ray took another deep breath of fresh dignity.

'My name is Barbaray Sprambladack Fasstalon-Scump.'

Jeff couldn't help but snigger. Ray was prepared for this moment, thanks to his lungful of dignity, and so carried on regardless.

'I've been stranded here since the early eighties, when

my ship... this,' he indicated the craft, 'got severely damaged by the atmosphere. Most of the outer shielding got burnt up, and I've been repairing it ever since.'

'Repairing it? With what?'

'With this!' replied Ray, delving his hand into the black bin liner, and pulling out a large, itchy-looking clump of human hair.

'Keratin!' he exclaimed proudly. 'The finest trans-galactic insulation shielding known to lifekind!'

He sniffed the clump momentarily.

'Alright, so it smells a bit strange, but there's no denying its unique properties!'

Jeff suddenly realised the smell was this spacecraft, about the size of a Sherman Tank. It reeked of Brylcreem, shampoo and, well... hair. He had the weirdest urge to crack a joke.

'So this is your... haircraft?' he asked, with a big smug grin. 'Your... hairship?' he continued, beginning to smirk.

Ray looked tiredly at him.

'Yes, Jeff. Hairoplane, Hairliner, Hairodynamic Hairycopter. I've heard 'em all. Long ago. And they weren't that funny then. Did you have some more questions?'

'Er, yeah,' said Jeff. 'Is that a pile of explosives underneath it? And if so, what the hell for? Are you trying to kill yourself?' he asked incredulously, yet sensibly.

Ray stood up and pointed to the crates of highly explosive materials upon which the fibrous flying machine sat.

'These – are for initial thrust. I don't have the thrust capability to escape the earth's basic gravity field, so I have to use the crude explosive force of this material to get me up into the air, and from there, I can pilot it out into free space.'

Jeff widened his eyes. Each new answer managed to freak him out even more than the last.

'You mean to tell me, you're gonna get inside that – that thing, and blow yourself sky—'

'—Sky high. Yes! Exactly!' concluded Ray with a smile that defied sanity.

'Once airborne, the wondrous properties of Keratin take over, and whoosh! Off I go!'

He embellished the statement with a particularly enthusiastic hand gesture, meant to symbolise a rocket whooshing up into the sky. As he held his arm up, it kind of resembled a salute from the antagonists of World War Two, which did little to convince Jeff that the barber wasn't a beardy-weirdy.

To the casual observer, the spaceship looked like an oversized Brillo pad. Measuring about thirty feet in length, at least twelve feet high and about twenty feet wide, it was a finely-woven mass of thin hairs, twisted and thatched, with no visible means of propulsion or wings. It was pointed at the front end, so it sort of resembled an upturned rowing boat – only knitted from fine wool. Just beneath the outer layer of hair, there was what looked more like a conventional spacecraft – an inner shell of metal with glass portholes. A closer analogy would be an army tank in a tea-cosy. A small array of computers with the standard flashing lights graced the inner walls of the cabin. In all, it was the sort of impossible-to-behold sight that would get one carted off to the funny farm double-quick time, if one ever tried to tell somebody important about it.

Jeff quickly realised this, and shook the marbles inside his skull.

'Alright, hang on. Suppose you do actually get into

orbit – where the hell are you gonna go? Have you got oxygen? Warp-drive? A bog, even?'

He was feeling like a non-swimmer who had just been flung into the Mariana Trench.

Ray tried his best to explain.

'Look, it's quite elementary, to be honest: Keratin is made up of billions of cells that react to the vacuum of space and they form a nearly impregnable shield against radiation, cold and space debris. But the best thing about it is – it's like a living solar panel – I can sail on the solar winds indefinitely, at unimaginable speeds! No need to refuel, ever!'

'What about oxygen?'

'I have a recycling unit. Provides water, too!'

'The bog?'

'Chemical toilet, £27.99, Ebay.'

'Didn't you already have one in the ship?'

'I did. Broke it. Had to get a replacement.'

'Oh. That's... weird. Weren't you off to Canada though?'

'Not quite,' said Ray. 'Kangazang. My home planet. Lovely place, I'm telling you... beaches of pure chrome.' He sighed a little homesick sigh.

Ray had lived on Earth now for almost two decades. He had never intended to stay quite this long, and kept reasonably quiet, and in a state of social solitude. Only a stream of daily customers needing tonsorial trimmage kept him in touch with the ways of the world. He was an excellent barber though. His father had taught him the necessary skills, and this was to save him in the long run; his customers provided him with the supply of keratin that he needed, so the cheap haircuts guaranteed him a good supply, if only in small instalments.

Ray's solitude meant that he'd only had a basic understanding of the ways of Earth dwelling humans, their codes and conventions, and the history of the quaint blue planet. He made enough money to pay for his salon and lock-up in the first few years, while his spaceship's food replicator machine provided meals during this time. He lowered his prices regularly, to attract more and more customers. Then the replicator ceased to work, so most of his profits went on food and utility bills. After all, repairing the ship was of the utmost importance, and staying alone and relatively undetected was the cheapest way to live. His main source of entertainment was radio, as a barber's working life is set to a musical soundtrack. It was through radio that he gained a love for cheesy 1980s music: the pop hits that he'd first heard upon his arrival on Earth had become firm favourites, and his CD of the hits of that decade was one of his prized possessions. But now, it seemed like the time had come to leave Earth. And Ray felt a secondary type of melancholia. He realised that he'd grown fond of Earth, and would miss it once back home on the silvery sands of Kangazang. He decided that the least he could do to repay the humans for their hospitality, was to do a good deed for one of them. And poor, confused Jeff Spooner looked like a human in need of a change of pace.

Jeff had heard enough. He took a deep breath of fresh sanity, and smiled falsely as he stood up to face Ray. Or was it Barbaray Sprungdiddly Wotsit? Whatever. He wanted to go home and lie down for a bit. A month would do it.

'OK, well, cheers for that, mate. All the best with the big bang and all that,' he began, but Ray put a hand on his shoulder, which made Jeff want to soil his undergarments.

'Jeff, I must ask you not to tell anyone about me. In fact, why not come with me? I could do with the company.'

Jeff trembled. *This has got to be the part*, he thought. *Where Ray rips his skin off to reveal a bulbous pulsating monstrosity… hopefully on his shoulders.*

'Come on, Jeff,' said Ray, sounding like a bar-room buddy who wanted to get a round in. 'Think about it. You need a holiday. Why not take a trip to the stars and back? I can drop you off anywhere you like!'

Jeff considered it.

'Anywhere?' he asked.

'Anywhere – except Pluto, Ganymede, Tau Ceti, Emo Prime… and Swansea.'

'Why not Swansea?'

'Have you *been* to Swansea?'

'Oh, right. Fair point.'

'So – what do you say,' beamed Ray. 'Are you coming along? It'll be fun – and I'll throw in free haircuts! What have you got to lose?'

It was a tempting offer to a lovelorn, tipsy loser at nearly three in the morning.

Jeff had a quick think, and his conscience postulated some theories:

He could get space-sick.

He could get lost forever.

He could be killed by some alien menace.

He could die.

Then again, he could meet a nice bird for a change.

'Oh, what the hell? Let's go for it,' he replied.

chapter two

Space Flight for the Beginner

Jeff and Ray spent the next hour packing some essentials for the trip, with Jeff asking Ray a question every time one popped into his head. Ray answered each one patiently, to the best of his ability.

'Why did you come to Earth, again?' asked Jeff, trying to look busy, when in reality he was just standing around. Ray was packing a small suitcase with the few earthly possessions he had gathered; his *Top Hits of the Eighties* CD, his hairdressing equipment and various sentimental knick-knacks. He stopped packing momentarily to answer.

'Well, basically because of my parents. They kept on at me to get a trade under my belt, you know? Something that would keep me in steady employment.'

He continued to fold some clothes and put them in the case, as Jeff listened patiently.

'My dad was one of the most famous hairdressers in the galaxy, you know… After I left school, I took a year off to travel, popped over this end of the galaxy to see what jobs there were, and I was surprised to find that I could cut hair as good as my old man. That's when I learned that the job description was in my name – Barbaray, Ray the Barber! Crazy coincidence, isn't it?'

Jeff wasn't impressed.

'Nah, not really. I know a guy called Dave Van Berger – runs a burger van on the industrial estate where I work. Dave Burger-Van, we call him.'

Ray smiled.

Jeff paused for a second, deep in thought.

'Hang on a mo, work! What am I gonna do about my job?'

'Well, you're a painter and decorator, aren't you?' said Ray. 'Plenty of painting and decorating needed out there. I know of one planet where they don't even have paint! All the houses have bare stone walls – you could make a small fortune on there alone!'

This was good news to Jeff.

'Oh! Great! Should I nip home and get my brushes then?'

'No need, we'll get you a set en route to Kangazang.'

Jeff shrugged his shoulders. 'I am a fairy, my name is Nuff.'

Ray paused this time.

'You keep saying that. What does it mean?'

Jeff tried to explain, but Ray just couldn't grasp the concept of a fairy, which was ironic, as Ray's extensive knowledge of countless alien races provided him with an insight far beyond that of any earth man. But somehow, no matter how wildly he stretched his imagination, a tiny flying magical female, complete with tutu and a wand, was still inexplicable to him.

'No, I'm sorry,' said Ray, 'That all sounds a bit far-fetched.'

Finally, everything was packed and ready. The last thing to do was to bolt together the curved steel walls which went around the underside of the spaceship. These were designed – fingers crossed – to help focus the blast of the explosives upward, as opposed to sideways. Jeff and Ray set to work with a socket set each, tightening the bolts as best they could.

Ray paused.

'Jeff, can I ask you a question?'

'Yeah, go on,' said Jeff.

It was only fair that he did. After all, the sun was due up in a couple of hours, and most of the night was spent with Jeff's questions.

'What are you going to do about your fiancée? After all, I don't think she'd want to come with you on this trip. Do you want to see her one more time before we set off?'

'That's one thing I wasn't trying to think about, to be honest,' said Jeff, 'I don't think she's my fiancée any more, mate.'

Now that he was relatively sober, he felt a little guilty for hitting her lover. Maybe they'd both feel better if he gave their relationship some space. Pun intended.

'I think I should at least tell her I'm off for a while. Don't want her to report me missing to the police... That's if she even cares anymore.'

Ray walked around the ship and placed a fatherly hand on Jeff's shoulder.

'It's probably the right thing to do. We're almost ready to go. You go and see her, I'll be waiting for you to get back.'

'Cheers, mate,' replied Jeff, as he put his leather jacket on and made for the door, 'Don't go off without me, will ya?'

'Don't you worry, I won't,' came the reply, although Ray was a little bit worried that Jeff might think of returning with an army unit, or at least the nice young men in their clean white coats.

Sarah woke from her dream by the tap-tap-tapping of tiny stones bouncing off her window pane. She got out of bed, checked the time, and wrapped a dressing gown around her. She flung open the curtains, and opened the balcony doors, expecting to see the new man in her life, standing down below. Instead, she got Jeff.

Sarah sighed in disgust.

'I thought I told you to stay out of my life! What are you doing?' she hissed, trying to keep the noise to a minimum.

Jeff looked up with genuine sorrow in his eyes.

'I had to see you. I'm off, Sarah. I dunno when I'll be back.'

Sarah was not impressed at his timing, but quite pleased at the news. She yawned and adjusted her dressing gown.

'I really don't care, Jeff.' And she didn't. But she was strangely curious to find out whether this was just a bluff to inspire sympathy, or whether Jeff had indeed grown a backbone and taken charge of his life.

'Where are you going, anyway?' she asked.

'Canada,' said Jeff. He didn't want to lie, but felt it was the best thing to do, under the circumstances.

Sarah still wasn't impressed. This had to be a lie. After all, she knew that Jeff had only ever been abroad once, and that was to some god-awful desert, as a student.

'Canada. You don't know anyone in Canada.'

She looked again at the clock.

'It's half past four. Is that all you came to tell me?'

She was getting annoyed. But Jeff was feeling much in the way of regret.

'Yeah, well… no, I… Well, I wanted to tell you that I'm sorry about what happened earlier, and if you think we could work it out, then I'll come back sooner and we can talk.'

'Yeah? Well you should be sorry. He's a vicar, for God's sake!'

It was a fair point: he was indeed a vicar, and it was entirely for God's sake.

'How could you do that?' she hissed again.

Jeff took a step forward, holding up an index finger loaded with accusation, and pulled the metaphorical trigger.

'Hang on a minute, how could you do what you did to me? How long had you two been carrying on behind my back?'

Most of Jeff's sympathy had evaporated by now. Sarah realised it was getting ugly again and just wanted it to be over.

'Long enough to realise you were the biggest mistake I've ever made. Go home, Jeff. I don't want to talk things over. I'm happy now, and I don't want to see you again. Not ever.' She stepped back into her room.

Jeff watched her leave and as a parting shot, called out.

'You're a right cow, Sarah! I must've been insane to love you!'

Sarah heard the insult, and turned around. She went back onto the balcony for the last word.

'You still are! And you can drop my fifty quid through the letter box in the morning!'

Quickly, she went back inside, slamming the balcony doors to prevent Jeff from getting another retort out.

Jeff welled up, as he shuffled off in pain. But he was angry again, and even more determined to leave her, the town and the entire planet for good.

Meanwhile, Sarah picked up her mobile phone, and as a final act of defiance, accompanied by the same wry grin as before, she called her randy reverend. Classy.

Jeff stopped off at his flat to grab some belongings of his own to take on the trip. Three attempts at getting the front door key in the lock reminded him that he was still a little sozzled, and he second-guessed himself, wondering momentarily if he should go back to Sarah's house to apologise again.

No. She'd made it pretty clear that he wasn't wanted any more. He crept up the stairs to his first floor flat, aware that the two acidic pensioners who lived downstairs were light sleepers. He didn't turn any lights on, just in case. In his bedroom, he picked up his rucksack, stuffing in the bare essentials: socks, pants, spare jeans and his toothbrush and razor.

He saw a framed photo of himself with Sarah, in happier times, sitting together on a beach in the sun. The sound of his swallow was audible, and the following sigh was heavy with sadness. He picked up the picture gently and removed the back of the frame. For a moment, he thought of tearing it in half, but his hands just wouldn't comply. He folded the picture in half, and slid it into his back pocket. Grabbing his rucksack, he crept back downstairs, and made for the door.

By the time he got back to Ray's garage, it was nearly light. Ray came out of the salon with a kettle and two mugs, for in-flight tea breaks.

'Are you OK, Jeff?' he asked, noticing his friend's solemn expression.

'Yeah, I'm alright,' replied Jeff dumbly, 'I just can't get over how I could've been fooled by that two-faced, two-timing, good-for-nothing tart.'

Ray tried his best to sound sympathetic.

'Don't let it get you down. You know, there are plenty more tarts in the, er, oven. And now you've got the entire galaxy to fish for one!'

Jeff seemed to brighten up at hearing this horrendous mix of metaphors.

'What – you think I could meet a bird on another planet?'

'Absolutely! Birds, women, molluscs… The choice is yours! And most of them only have the one face, if that's what you prefer!'

Jeff felt a lot better, although he had to admit the prospect of getting off with some green and tentacled honey was still a little daunting. After all, he wasn't Captain Kirk.

He took the photo of himself and Sarah out, and looked at it, but now, all he felt was a smouldering anger. Stuffing it recklessly back into his pocket, he mentally resolved to start a new life – a life out among the stars. With a new bird. And if she was green, who cares? He was neither fussy, nor a racist. The tentacles might come in handy too. He'd just have to cross that bridge when he came to it. He took a deep breath, and slung his rucksack over one shoulder.

'Come on, Ray,' he called out. 'What are we waiting for?'

At the same time as this life-changing epiphany was taking place for Jeff, other things were afoot. Reverend Wilson had answered the early morning phone call from Sarah, and had turned his car around, heading back to her place. Sarah had told him about Jeff's decision to leave the country, and so he guessed that things were improving for him. Perhaps this was the sign from above that he was waiting for.

He parked the car outside the block, and got out. Looking up at the balcony, he saw the curtains in the darkened room ripple, then part, as Sarah stepped out onto the balcony, looking like a fairytale princess, with wavy long blonde hair and a wispy nightdress. She smiled a wide, welcoming smile, and threw down her keys. Wilson caught the keys and blew her a silent kiss. He excitedly went to the door of the flat.

Sarah, her mind already clear of any remaining thoughts of Jeff, greeted her man-of-the-cloth with a passionate embrace. She quickly got him out-of-the-cloth and they both retired to the bed. Wilson took a moment to thank the good Lord for his luck, as Sarah whispered to him.

'I told you it'd all work out. Good things come to those who wait…'

This may be so, but they also say, 'From above, the wicked shall receive their just reward.'

You'd do well to remember that.

Jeff climbed up into the spacecraft. He looked around

and was pleasantly surprised to see that it wasn't as cramped, or as hairy – or indeed as smelly – as he thought it might be. In fact, the subtle aroma of hair conditioning products was more like a built-in air-freshener. After all, it wouldn't do to be traversing immense galactic distances inside an armpit.

The ship was small but not as claustrophobic as it seemed from the outside. It seemed to be split into only two main areas; the main hold and living area, and the cockpit up front. The living area was bright and functional, with ceiling and floors in a silver material decorated in a hexagon pattern. At the rear of the ship he saw a small fridge and a set of tea and coffee making facilities, much like one would find in a hotel room. Beside it, Jeff chuckled to see the odd sight of a trouser press. This, he immediately told himself, had to have been stolen from a hotel room, as none had ever been seen in the outside world before. Still, for a neatly dressed barber, it kind of made sense.

There was a narrow wardrobe up against one wall, with a roller-shutter door on the front. He bent down and grabbed the bottom edge of the door, raising it up. The door slid open, to reveal the almost-new chemical toilet that Ray had mentioned. Although it was logical to have a toilet on board, for the life of him, Jeff couldn't remember a toilet in any science fiction movie. Ever.

He dumped his rucksack on the zebra-skin patterned seats beside some of Ray's boxes, and went up front to the cockpit area.

He took a seat next to what looked like the pilot's chair. It was a converted barber's chair, naturally, and as it had been recently outfitted with seatbelts and a number of control panels, it really looked the part. Jeff secretly hoped that he wasn't left alone to pilot the thing at any point in the near future. He reached out in front of him, and touched the thick glass windshield. It seemed to be gently vibrating, as if the ship had a slight pulse deep inside.

He still didn't understand much about this crazy ship, or indeed about his new travelling companion, the man from Kangazang. Just when you think you know someone, they turn out to be completely enigmatic.

Just then, the walking enigma entered the craft.

'So, what do you think of her then?' beamed Ray. 'Splendid, isn't she?' he added, obviously very proud.

Jeff looked at Ray with mock disdain.

'What a piece of junk!!' he whined, trying to sound American. The pop-culture reference was lost on Ray, and he looked clearly upset.

'Well... well, that's a fine way to start the trip! I did my best! It wasn't easy, you know, collecting hair for over a decade...' he trailed off.

Jeff realised his faux pas.

'Luke Skywalker said that, didn't he?'

Ray looked a little concerned.

'Oh great. This is supposed to be a secret! Who else did you tell?' he sniffed, turning and heading over to the outer door of the ship. He grabbed the inner handle, and pulled it as hard as he could. It clanged shut, followed by a thin hissss sound, as the oxygen recycler kicked in.

Ray returned to the cockpit, and took the pilot's seat. He looked over at Jeff, who sat next to him, strangely silent and not blinking very much.

'You alright, Jeff?'

'Yeah, suppose so. So – this is it then?'

'Yes indeed. Er… This is what?'

'We're actually going to take off in this thing? And not just fly, but you know… get out there. Outer space?'

Ray smiled, remembering that Jeff's species had not done a lot of intergalactic space travel. In fact, Jeff had only ever boarded a plane once, so to him a long drive was a pretty big deal as far as traversing great distances went.

'Oh yes,' replied Ray. 'You'll enjoy it. It's as safe as houses. Well, tiny thin metal houses with a bubble of air in, amid an endless void of airless nothingness.'

Jeff attempted to swallow, but it felt like someone had lodged a small hedgehog in his throat.

Ray strapped himself in, and Jeff followed suit, still caught somewhere between terror and wonder. He stared dead ahead, going whiter by the second.

'It'll be alright, Jeff,' said Ray, as soothingly as he could. 'It's just like riding a bike.'

He pushed a button and a countdown timer illuminated in red digits on the panel in front of him.

Jeff remained staring and still. A bead of sweat ran down his forehead.

'I… can't… ride… a… bike… Ray,' he muttered through tight lips.

Cold, heavy seconds dripped by, as Ray checked a variety of switches and lights around him.

Jeff cracked.

'Oh, just get on with it!' he finally blurted. 'I'm crapping in my pants!'

'I am a Fairy, and Nuff is my name,' replied Ray in victory, and pushed the throttle lever forward. The ship began to vibrate, accompanied by a low rumbling, like distant thunder.

Underneath the spacecraft, a timer on the pile of explosives began to tick down. It read: Ten.

Ray counted down the seconds aloud.

'Nine... Eight... Seven...'

'Is it too late to change me mind?' asked Jeff.

'Oh, absolutely! Here we go...'

'Three... Two... One...'

Jeff squeezed his eyes shut tight. Ray looked rather tense too.

Nothing happened.

They waited a few more seconds.

Still nothing.

Jeff kept his eyes shut.

'What's happening?' he pleaded.

Ray, for once, didn't have the foggiest. He checked the instruments around him.

'No, not that, that's ok... So's that one... Erm...'

Jeff opened his eyes and released his vice-like grip on the armchair.

'So... It's not working then?' he correctly deduced.

Ray unstrapped himself, and went to the rear of the ship.

'You stay there, I need to do something back here.'

For a couple of minutes all was silent. Ray was still down the other end of the darkened craft, and Jeff was beginning to get bored. He flicked the tiny furry dice that Ray had hung up on the ceiling.

'Ray?' he called. 'Do you need any help back there?'

'No thanks, I'm fine, Jeff!'

'What are you doing anyway?'

'If you must know, I'm having a dump!'

'Oh. Sorry!'

Jeff smiled. Then chuckled to himself. Twisting around in his seat, he called back to Ray.

'Save me some paper, will you? I might need to go –'

BOOM.

Out in the street, a lone policeman was knocked off his feet by the shockwave.

He looked up to see the roof of Ray's lock-up shatter into millions of matchsticks, and a thirty-foot Brillo pad shoot up into the air like a cannonball.

The spaceship was airborne.

At the same moment, Sarah and Reverend Wilson were having nocturnal fun and games, and the deafening noise made both of them squeal with delight.

'Jesus Christ!' gasped Sarah. 'Was that the earth moving?'

'Blasphemer,' purred Wilson, as he kissed her again, glad of the sign from above.

Inside the now floating spacecraft, Ray wailed in shock and terror, as he raced back to the pilot's chair, holding his trousers up. He wrestled with the controls and punched buttons all around him frantically. Jeff screamed like a five year-old on the Ghost Train. With real ghosts.

'We're up! It's working!' shouted Ray in triumph.

'No kidding,' screamed Jeff. 'What happens now?' he added, still in his infantile octave.

Ray swung his control pad over to the left, then to the right. He stabbed at a couple of buttons above his head and then the ship stopped shaking. It floated gently upwards for a few hundred feet, and then settled, bobbing softly. This was just one of the miracles of finely woven, electronically stimulated Keratin.

'Now we prepare to leave the solar system,' said Ray with a smile. 'But first, I need to clean up back there.'

He ran back to the toilet cubicle.

Jeff called again.

'Don't be too long mate. I think I need to go really soon.'

He leaned forward as far as his seatbelt would allow, and looked out of the front windscreen. The ground bobbed up and down – or rather the ship did, and Jeff put a hand over his mouth as a precaution, as a feeling of vertigo came over him. It was like standing over a model village after downing half a bottle of some insanely strong drink.

A few moments later, Ray returned to the cockpit, and made his apologies. Jeff hurriedly accepted them, and unbuckled himself so that he could avail himself of the lavatory too. He had done an admirable job of not soiling himself (from either end) in the last five minutes, and wanted, if at all possible, to remain that way.

As he sat in both mental contemplation and bodily evacuation, he looked out of a small porthole, and noticed that the sun was just coming up over the horizon. It looked awesome. And the sunlight bathed the interior of the ship in a golden glow, which warmed the air, and reminded Jeff of his youthful Sunday nights after a bath, his newly washed mullet smelling of shampoo.

Ray called out to him.

'Are you finished? We need to get moving before somebody spots us and gets the air force out!'

This was the weirdest feeling – to actually be the

occupant of a flying saucer. Perhaps someone down on the surface was already taking blurry video footage of the strange craft currently hovering a couple of hundred feet in the air above the town. But who'd believe it?

Jeff stood up, and re-buckled his belt. As he stepped out of the toilet cubicle, he noticed the crumpled photo of himself and Sarah on the floor. It must have fallen out of his jeans as he sat down on the throne.

He thought for a minute. Then he checked his wallet for currency.

'Ray? Can we make a quick stop?'

Over at her flat, Sarah pushed the balcony doors open, and stepped out to see the sunrise. Her new man, Wilson, joined her, wrapping his slightly flabby arms around her. It was a new dawn, a new day, a new life... and they were feeling good. As the song goes.

Sarah turned to face him. She smiled her wide smile of contentment.

'This was a perfect night. Thanks for coming round.'

'It was my pleasure entirely,' said Wilson.

'We've weathered the storm. Only good things ahead for us from now on.'

They kissed tenderly.

'Nothing in the world could spoil this moment.'

Suddenly, the princely sum of fifty pounds dropped out of the sky, rolled up with an elastic band around the notes. Sarah picked it up, and then looked up to see where it could have come from. All she saw was a small cloud with a vague dark spot within.

From a few hundred feet above them, Jeff emptied the chemical toilet.

'From above, the wicked shall receive their just reward.'

And so they did. Here endeth the lesson.

A hundred and thirty five parsecs away lay the smouldering, black and red rock that was the planet Skragg. It looked angry, and bitter, much like its current ruler, who lay in bed, dying. Really slowly. Lord Rancydd, ancient dictator and leader of the feared Skraggi Empire looked, for all intents and purposes, like he'd died months ago, and was already embalmed, mummified and beginning to turn to dust. So, not good then. He was four hundred and ninety-six years old by the Skraggi calendar, and the time of his passing was long overdue. But he refused to shuffle off. Why? Because that's the kind of selfish git he was. It made him all the more evil.

Lying upon his bejewelled death-bed with the water-filled mattress (which he insisted on having installed during his younger, more virile days), he coughed a pathetic cough, and his eyelids flickered open a tiny amount. Through watery, semi-cataracted eyes, he looked upon the face of his only son, Prince Kelvin.

Kelvin sniffed again. In part, due to his sorrow at the imminent passing of his old man, and partly because he was trying to work out what the awful smell was.

'Father?' he asked tenderly, 'Father, can you hear me?'

'More's the bloody pity,' replied Lord Rancydd, in a feeble whisper. He'd dreaded this day: the day when his glorious reign would come to an end because it would be utterly ruined by the inauguration of his idiot son. He'd had hamsters that were more evil than Kelvin. A pet slug that was more driven. And now, this embarrassing flaccid tool, this immature damp tissue of a boy, was soon to be hailed as the Supreme Overlord of the Mighty Skragg Empire. Oh, the shame of it! At this point, he smiled – at least he'd be dead and gone, and not have to live through the humiliation of it all.

Kelvin saw the smile, and took it as an indication of love from his dad. He leaned a little closer, cleared his throat, and said his well-rehearsed piece.

'Father, I… I… well, I just, er… just want you to know that when they, I mean, when I become Overlord, I'll do my best – I mean my very best, that is, er… to be a great ruler like what you was.'

So much for the speech. First thing he resolved to do in the morning was fire the royal speech-writers. He carried on in his own words.

'Dad, this isn't easy for me. I mean, I don't think I'm cut out to be an evil overlord like you and Grandad, but I have learned a lot, and I can see the rewards, um, if only in the tax reliefs.'

Lord Rancydd smiled again. And again, Kelvin took this as a sign of his dad's approval, when in actual fact the thought that accompanied it was, *Ah… won't be long now… Hurry up, you scythe-wielding bonebag, I'm ready to go.*

He coughed, then spoke.

'Kelvin, just remember this, and you will do well. Every time you make a decision, listen to what your heart tells you… Then ignore it and do the complete opposite – cough – only this will ensure the Empire's future. Don't fail me son, or I'll be back to haunt the crap out of you forever.'

Kelvin nodded sagely, wringing his thin hands. He had one more question.

'Father – where's the family fortune hidden?'

Lord Rancydd exhaled in despair. Dust came out.

'Spent the lot. I'm not having you waste my money – cough – on toys and flowery shirts. If you want to be a success, seek the Universal Remote. Then you can rule over everything and everyone. And for Bod's sake, don't make a mess of it.'

Kelvin took his father's twig-like hands in his own.

'I'll find it, Dad. And I'll make you proud, you can count on me.'

He stood up, to show his determination and resolve.

'I'll rule the Empire as well as anyone! Entire star systems will cower in my shadow, as I make the power of my anger known. Races will fall, and… and…'

He suddenly looked at his father, motionless and quite dead.

'Oh bugger.'

Inside Ray's hovering Shredded Wheat, Jeff was in tears. Not tears of pain or sorrow, but immense hilarity. He thumped both his fists on the arms of his co-pilot's chair, as he giggled insanely.

'Oh, God! That was just perfect! Absolutely top banana! Ah – ooh, me sides! Oh, you should've seen them, Ray! Ker-splatch! And they had no idea what happened! I bet – hee hee! – I bet they thought – haha! – I bet they thought it was a massive seagull!'

He went into fits of laughter again.

Ray was smiling. At least Jeff had cheered up, but he did think that dousing one's unfaithful partner with three litres of chemically-treated human sewage was a little excessive.

He sat back down in the pilot's chair, and buckled up.

'Come on, then – let's make tracks.'

Jeff had lost most of his fear by now, and was really looking forward to the trip.

'Wahay!' he exclaimed, 'Say goodbye and good riddance to that pointless armpit of a town, Ray! It's margaritas on the beaches of Shangalang from now on!'

Ray considered correcting him by reminding Jeff that his home planet was called Kangazang, but thought it best not to spoil his mood, and so he let the Bay-City-Rollerism go uncommented on.

He waited for Jeff to wipe the tears from his eyes, and then punched an array of buttons, and moved a thick lever forward. The ship bobbed up and down twice, and then began to pick up speed.

'Here we go, Jeff. Full throttle!' announced the pilot, and with a satisfying dose of G-forces, the entire planet seemed to drop away beneath them, and become a speck in the distance.

'Welcome to outer space, Earthlet!' declared Ray grandly. He received no answer, as Jeff lay slumped in his chair, having fainted moments earlier. Ray wiggled his directional control stick from left to right a few times and this managed to rouse Jeff from his unconsciousness. He opened his eyes slowly, saw the blue horizon of his planet out in front and screamed effeminately.

'Stay with me, Jeff!' urged Ray. 'Don't go all slumpy again! Breathe! That's it, breathe... Breathing good.'

Jeff did as he was told, and found it to be good advice. His heart rate settled down to a steady minor panic, and he took a moment to wrap his cerebral cortex around his new status: 'Jeff Spooner, Painter and decorator of the Galaxy!'

The ship turned around and pointed its nose toward

the moon. Ray pushed the throttle and they began to pick up speed.

Just as they left the earth's outer atmosphere, they were nearly hit by another small spaceship going in the opposite direction. Ray swerved his craft just in time, and yelled obscenities at the careless pilot.

'That was a close one!' gasped Jeff.

'Rush hour,' said Ray.

Back on the surface of Earth, in a city called London, a schoolgirl walked through the park. She noticed the small ship, as it came down, and crashed not too far from her. But that's another story entirely.

Ray's airborne hairball flew onwards at sphincter-clenching speed. Soon, all they could see was a black velvety expanse, dotted with twinkling diamonds. Up, down, left and right – there was space. Infinity. Endless void. The temperature in the ship went down by a few degrees, and Jeff noticed this with a shiver.

'Forgot me gloves. I guess this is the cold of deep space. Is it going to get much colder?' he asked.

Ray shook his head.

'No, I just put the air conditioning on. Can't drive without it, to be honest.'

Jeff raised his eyebrows – air con! He was impressed.

'Do you want to see something interesting?' said Ray, pointing to a grey speck out in front.

Jeff nodded.

'What's that, then?'

'We're approaching the moon. Press that orange button in front of you.'

Jeff searched for a moment, then pointed to a small square orange button that looked like a Liquorice Allsort.

'This one?'

Ray hummed a sound like a 'yes', as he piloted the ship nearer to the grey ball.

Jeff pushed the button. The windscreen of the spacecraft became active, as a grid divided up the previously clear glass. Ray touched one of the squares, and it grew larger, magnifying the view by a few hundred times.

Jeff stared in awe, almost entirely speechless. He uttered a soft 'Blimey Charlie!', as he realised he was the first human being in nearly forty years to look upon the moon's surface with the naked eye. The dusty craters, the craggy hills and meteorite-scarred plains were laid out before him as if they came from a top Hollywood special effects company.

Ray pointed to a large area of relatively flat ground.

'The Sea Of Tranquillity,' he declared proudly. 'Site of Mankind's giant leap.'

Jeff squinted.

'Hang on… that can't be it. There's no flag or landing craft. You must be on the wrong side or something.'

Ray shook his head.

'No, that's definitely it. Trust me.'

Jeff was aware that he was debating this with an alien space traveller – he was a little out of his depth, to be honest, but he stuck to his guns.

'No, mate. They left a plaque, too. The flag fell over, I remember reading about that, but there should be a lunar rover-buggy thing, and some other stuff… Wait a minute!' he exclaimed in shock. 'Are you saying that those myths are true? That we didn't go to the moon at all?'

Once the shock subsided, his heart began to sink. After all, Jeff was born in July, 1969 – a week after Armstrong's legendary speech. It felt like he'd been betrayed. Lied to all these years by his teachers and that bloke on the telly with the monocle.

He was even more shocked by Ray's answer.

'No, of course you got to the moon. All the stuff you left there is still on the surface, but it's over on the dark side. Let me show you.'

He banked the ship around, and they orbited the moon, until they entered the shadowy, hidden half of the moon. Ray put some spotlights on, and there, in a rocky canyon, was a twinkling pile of NASA's finest technology, and some early Russian probes. Lunokhod 1, the pressure cooker on pram wheels, was there too, untouched and still relatively shiny.

Jeff tingled with excitement. He got even more electrified to think that this was only the useless old moon. How was he going to cope with seeing a completely new planet that you could walk upon, breathing the air, and meeting the people?

He turned to Ray.

'That's nuts! That's un-flipping-believable! How did all this stuff get over there?'

'Moonies,' replied Ray nonchalantly.

Before Jeff could picture a group of crazy religious cult members in space, Ray explained.

'The Moonies are the inhabitants of the moon. They live beneath the surface, and usually don't come out unless there's something to do. They weren't too happy to see all this junk left behind, so they tidied up a bit. It's a sort of museum-cum-scrap yard now, but I have heard that the leader of the Moonies wears a pair of silk, star-spangled boxer shorts!'

Ray chuckled to himself. Jeff slumped back in his seat, breathless.

'That's mental.'

Ray agreed.

'Yes it is. I'd never wear that flag so close to my nether regions!'

He returned the screen to its original configuration.

'I'll show you some more things like this as we pass the planets, but we can't see them all – it's a long way to Tipperary, as they say in er… anywhere. Except Tipperary.'

He flicked some switches, and the ship began to accelerate. It was moving at speeds much faster than anything on Earth did, but in the blackness of space, it felt like they were floating calmly in a barge.

The remaining planets of the Solar System loomed. As they passed, Ray divulged what few interesting facts he knew about them, to a mostly silent and astonished Jeff Spooner.

Mars, for example, was another scrap yard. And there was water there, lots of it – but it was in red powder form. Just add Hydrolectin Sulphamite.

Jupiter – its mighty Red Spot is actually a thriving market, run by enterprising Martians, who sold powdered water.

Saturn was just as it looked: uninhabitable and hostile. Apart from its beautifully impressive banded rings of ice crystals, it was, frankly, a bit rubbish.

After a while, they approached Uranus. Jeff made all the usual jokes, but was surprised to learn that it was composed entirely of sewage from the inhabited planets that they'd just passed. Hence the name. It's smell was detectable as far away as Jupiter. It was, quite literally, a crap planet. Planet of crap.

Pluto was, or so the legend says, the huge skull of a fallen warrior from Ursa Minor. He'd got his head chopped off and sent into orbit around the Sun, as a warning to any other would-be planetary barbarians. That showed him.

Now, it was just an unrecognisable pitted and ice-coated rock. Since Earth astronomers disputed its status as a bona fide planet, it was demoted to the sad status of 'dwarf planet', which essentially was the same as calling it a 'floating stone'. Thus, it was even less interesting, despite its mythical origins.

Soon, even Pluto was a faint speck in the distance. Jeff stood at the rear of the ship, looking out as his Solar System faded away into the void. Here he was, covering more interplanetary miles than most of the deep space probes, and he didn't even have a space suit on.

'Mental!' he said again to himself, thinking of old black and white footage of American astronauts in their fat suits.

Suddenly he looked down at his feet.

'Ere, Ray,' he called. 'Why aren't we weightless? I was really looking forward to that bit.'

Ray turned in his seat.

'Gravity field. Look around the walls and floors.'

Jeff did as he was told, and noticed that the floors and walls had tiny round discs embedded into them, about the size of small coins.

'What? So these things stop stuff from floating then?'

surmised Jeff eloquently, pointing to one of the discs.

'That's right,' said Ray. 'They continuously adjust and balance out the molecular densities of everything contained within the matrix of sensors. It's quite simple really. Without them, the G-forces experienced by our sub-light speeds would crush us to paste.'

Jeff was just a tad disappointed. He wanted to bounce around the cabin in slow-motion like the NASA guys. Who wouldn't?

'Can't you turn 'em down for a bit? I'd really like to see what it's like.'

Ray tried to protest.

'Space travel isn't a game, Jeff. It involves balance, physics and complicated calculations, you know.'

Jeff felt a sulk coming on.

'Aww, please? Come on! It's just that weightlessness is probably the coolest thing about space travel, y'know?'

Ray gave in.

'Oh, for Bod's sake! Alright! But only for half an hour, OK?'

Jeff beamed and clapped his hands quickly in front of his chest like a kid who'd just unwrapped a shiny bicycle.

Ray remembered that Jeff was good enough to accompany him on his interstellar voyage, and a little fun would keep his guest in high spirits. He operated a few switches, and brought the ship to a complete stop, which took half an hour to accomplish because of their incredible speed and no brakes to slow them down. He unbuckled his seatbelt and joined Jeff who was standing in the middle of the cabin, still beaming insanely.

'Ready?' asked Ray. Silly question, really. Jeff was born for this moment, if nothing else.

'Whoop! Hold on, Ray. I'd better clip the toilet lid down.'

'Good thinking,' replied Ray.

As soon as Jeff came back to the middle of the cabin, Ray reached up to the ceiling, and opened a small hexagonal hatch. Inside was a T-shaped handle. He turned the handle anti-clockwise and the gentle hum which was audible in the cabin shifted down in pitch. As it did so, Jeff was filled with the strangest feeling. His cheeks – both pairs – began to rise up, free of their weight.

His spine felt less encumbered, and his small-but-perfectly-formed beer belly gurgled as it began to float. He looked down, and watched as his feet lifted off the floor gently. Ray had begun to float also, his white barbers' coat billowing up around his head.

With a whoop of joy, Jeff pushed himself off a wall and floated across the cabin, trying to spin as he went. This was rather boring to Ray, so he pulled out a paperback and just hung in the air, turning the page every minute or so.

Jeff was squealing with childish delight as he boinged from wall to floor and floor to ceiling repeatedly. He flew down to the boxed provisions and grabbed a can of cola, opened it and giggled as he spent ten minutes pretending to be a shark, chasing and gobbling up wobbly droplets of liquid. There wasn't much in the way of fun that could compare to the sensation. Except perhaps that one time at his twenty-first birthday party, with the surprise strip-o-gram and the squirty cream.

Ray had reached the end of one particularly amusing chapter in his book – something about mice and towels

– and decided that it was time to recommence the journey.

'OK, Jeff,' he called out. 'That's enough for now. Maybe later you can play some more, but now it's time to get going again.'

Jeff protested with an immature, 'Awww…', but Ray was resolute. He grabbed the handle, and slowly twisted it clockwise to its original position. Both men floated gently to the floor again. This too, was a weird feeling – just like lying in a bath of water while the plug is pulled: everything slowly becomes infused with its correct weight again. Try it.

Jeff watched keenly as Ray did this, and Ray noticed it.

'Don't go playing with this control, Jeff,' he warned. 'I'm serious. Turn it too far, and we'd be pressed into the floor as if we were made of lead. So no touchy.'

Jeff held up his hands.

'Hey – I gotcha. No touchy.'

Ray went back to the pilot seat, and started the craft in motion once more. Soon the stars were whizzing past the portholes again. Jeff sat on the closed toilet lid and relived the past thirty minutes in zero-gravity. He grinned foolishly. Looking around, he called over to Ray.

''Ere, Ray? Does this ship have a name then, or is it just a hairship?' he asked, thinking that he might get the opportunity to suggest a title for the fibrous flying machine.

Ray continued to pilot the ship but leaned his head back.

'Yes, actually, it does. I named her after the family pet back home.'

'Well, what is it then?'

'I call her the "Marshmallow Penguin".'

Ray pointed to his pink penguin-shaped tie pin.

'Marshmallow Penguin?' repeated Jeff, in total incredulity. 'That's a stupid name for a pet, let alone a spaceship!'

'No, you misunderstand,' continued Ray. 'Our family pet was a Marshmallow Penguin. They're common on Kangazang. Similar to penguins on Earth, I suppose, only pink and yellow in colour. Very smart animals. Very loyal. Very sweet.'

'So what was your pet penguin's name then? Something equally mad I bet.'

'Of course not. We called her Tania.'

Jeff threw his head forward into his hands and let out another big sigh of astonishment mixed with a giggle of amusement. He was fast realising that everything he'd ever learned up until now was a tiny crouton, floating in an endless tureen of undiscovered knowledge soup.

The thought of soupy croutons made him remember that he was feeling a little peckish.

'Erm... is there any grub on board?' he called. 'I haven't eaten since last night's kebab, and most of that ended up on the floor.'

Ray called back, his attention still on the view ahead.

'Yes, there's a box over to the port side. Have a look – there should be some provisions. Bring me a snack too, there's a good chap.'

Jeff looked around, and found the box. In it were a number of oversized toothpaste tubes, in silver, with twisty caps at one end. Jeff smiled. He'd read about astronaut's food, and now he'd get to try it. Finding a good, tightly packed tube, he unscrewed the cap. He squeezed an inch of deep red paste out of the tube and sniffed it. No actual smell. Judging by the colour of it, he hazarded a guess.

'Must be steak,' he surmised.

Beside the box was a larger box with some 'proper' food in it: two loaves of bread, some cutlery, tins of assorted food, and a small tub of margarine. *Mmm… sarnies,* he thought. Sitting cross-legged on the floor of the spaceship, he quickly knocked together two thick steak-paste sandwiches.

He stood up, and went over to the front of the ship, stuffing a sandwich whole into his mouth, and had a go at eating the thick gooey stuff. At first, it had no taste at all. Then he paused, giving his taste buds time to report to his brain. It was cold. It was sticky.

It wasn't steak. That was for sure. Maybe he'd get used to it.

Jeff handed a sandwich to Ray.

'What's in it?' asked the barber cautiously.

Jeff chewed the viscous, glue-like concoction, in order to swallow a large part of it. It wasn't easy. Finally, he had enough room in his mouth to answer.

'Steak paste. From the tube. It's not great though, to be honest.'

Ray looked up with as much tenderness as he could muster in his eyes.

'That's not food, Jeff.'

Jeff stopped chewing.

'It's burgundy hair dye.'

Jeff started choking. He ran back to where the chemical toilet was, and spat the remainder of his sandwich into the bowl. He coughed a few times, but wasn't able to throw up. Wailing in disgust and shock, he tried to push a finger or two down his throat, but only succeeded in choking himself a bit more. Finally he gave up. Ray set the ship to drift along on its own, and walked back to see his poorly crewmate.

He found Jeff looking into a small shaving mirror.

'My bloody teeth are purple!'

Ray tried his best to be comforting.

'Sorry, Jeff. I should've said something. I packed my hairdressing stuff to show my parents when we got home.'

A terse silence greeted the comment.

Ray tried a feeble grin.

'For what it's worth... It's a good look on you.'

Jeff spun around, angry for the first time since they'd taken off.

'A good look?! A good look? I'm gonna die of food poisoning, my corpse will have purple teeth, and you tell me it's a good bloody look?' he roared.

Ray took a few steps back. He'd never seen Jeff angry before. He stepped on the discarded silver tube, and looked down at it. Picking it up, he quickly scanned the small printed label on the side of the tube. He showed it to Jeff, who was still fuming.

'Here you go – it's non-toxic. And the colour washes out in six shampoos.'

Jeff, who was actually very relieved to hear this, rooted around in his rucksack for his toothbrush and some toothpaste.

'Water!' he barked.

Ray nodded quickly and ran to the wall. He unclipped a small metal canteen from its cubby-hole in the wall panel, and went over to the water/air recycling unit. Pushing a blue button, he filled the canteen with freshly reconstituted water, and handed it to Jeff. Snatching the canteen from Ray, Jeff sat himself down on the floor, and began to brush his teeth thoroughly, spitting purple froth into a coffee mug.

Ray leaned over in sympathy.

'I'm sorry, Jeff...' he began, but Jeff wasn't in the mood to talk, nor could he, as he had half a tube of toothpaste and a brush in his mouth. Instead, he just grunted, and glared at Ray.

Ray put both palms up in acceptance.

'I'll go back to the cockpit, I think.'

He backed away, then turned and sat back down in the pilot's chair.

Jeff kept scrubbing away at his teeth, until his gums bled and they felt like they were vibrating. He took another swig of water and checked his teeth. The purple dye had mostly gone, but there was a faint violet hue to them, along with a weird, chemical taste. He huffed in resentment, and decided to stay there on the floor for a while. At least until he cooled off. He lay back, lacing his fingers together behind his head, and closed his eyes. The humming of the spacecraft's internal systems soon made him drift off to sleep.

chapter three

New Life, New Civilisations

Jeff awoke feeling a bit strange. He'd rolled across the floor of the ship, and ended up lying face down, against the wall, like a piece of skirting board. But that wasn't the weird bit. He'd had a particularly vivid dream involving Kylie Minogue and a tin of fruit cocktail – the stuff of many a young man's desires. Well, his, at any rate.

As his senses flooded back to him, he could hear music. It was Kylie again, inside the ship. Well, not literally, although he wished it was. He should be so lucky. Lucky, lucky lucky. Ray was playing his *Top Hits of the Eighties* CD again, and had piped it through the sound system.

He got to his feet and shook his head a few times to wake his brain up. Once it had awoken, he commanded it to take him to the cockpit to see where they had got to.

Up front, Ray was bobbing up and down in his seat to the music, which was a little too loud for Jeff.

'Where are we?' called Jeff. This startled Ray, who let out a scream in alarm. He turned the music down.

'Ah, Jeff. Had a good sleep? How are the teeth?'

He noticed they were slightly whiter.

'Oh, good, good. We're passing through the constellation of Profania Minor, about six light years from the sun. Take a look!'

Rubbing his bleary eyes, Jeff took the seat next to Ray, and looked out. Spread out in front of him was a fantastic sight: a colossal, smoky nebula in clouds of blue and purple. Trillions of stars were scattered among the clouds, looking like an explosion in a sequin factory. He gasped at the wonder of it all.

Ray stared ahead, unimpressed. Jeff stretched his arms and yawned.

'How long was I sleeping?'

Ray looked at his watch and squinted.

'About two hours. I could do with a rest myself, to be honest.'

He unbuckled his seatbelt, and stood up, arching his spine, which clicked and crunched unceremoniously.

'These long drives certainly take it out of you,' he complained. 'Not far to go now, though. About another ten light-years and we'll be on Kangazang in time for fruit and cocktails!'

Jeff suddenly remembered his dream and felt dirty.

'Er, how long will it take us in earth hours?' he asked.

'Oh, let me see...' pondered Ray, pacing the length of the ship. He mumbled to himself.

'Ten... turn right at Bellatrix... swing through the Corriton field... I'd say about two days, depending on traffic.'

Jeff slumped in disappointment. He'd had nearly enough of being cooped up in this flying toupee, and was getting restless. Never mind the fact that he was now the only human being ever to have travelled out of the Solar System, or the only man in existence to have seen Pluto with the naked eye. Never mind the fact that his hairdresser was a real living and breathing alien. He was hungry and grumpy. There was plenty of time to be astonished by the wonders of the universe once he'd had a decent meal, a bath and maybe even a...

'Oh my God!' exclaimed Jeff.

Ray heard, and ran quickly back to the bridge of the ship. Looking out the windscreen feverishly, he scanned the stars for danger.

'What? What is it, Jeff? What did you see?' he asked in panic.

Jeff explained the severity of the situation.

'No, no, it's nothing out there. I just realised something. Something really important.'

Ray was getting worried. He held his breath and bit his lip. What could it be? He saw Jeff's concerned expression, the wringing of his hands and the fear in his eyes, and prepared himself for the worst.

'Where am I going to get a pint?' asked Jeff in über-seriousness.

Ray exhaled loudly. Then he turned and walked away again. Jeff followed him.

'I'm serious, Ray. I don't think I can last without a couple of pints a week. I should've packed some cans, a bottle of wine. Even gin, at a push!'

Ray looked exasperated.

'I might've guessed. What is it with you earthmen and alcohol?'

Jeff tried his best to explain.

'Well, you gotta have a pint now and again, haven't you? It's like... well, it's one of the reasons for going to work – so you can get bladdered on Friday, innit?' Then he remembered that Ray never went to the pub. He was obviously one of those boring, teetotal nerds who hated the whole booze culture that made Britain great. (Which, in all honesty, it didn't).

'You don't drink, do you? I forgot,' said Jeff. 'I suppose it's poison to you aliens. Makes you shrivel up or something?'

Ray shook his head.

'Not at all. I can drink it. I could probably drink you under the table, if I wanted to. But I never touch the stuff.'

'Why?'

'Because it makes you act like a twat.'

Jeff was a little insulted by this. But he didn't want to act upon his offended feelings, as the only person who knew how to operate this fibrous flying machine was in front of him. He tried another tack.

'OK, you're a control freak, I'm a free spirit. Each to his own. But seriously, Ray – is there anything like beer on your planet?' Behind his back, he crossed his fingers to try and influence a positive answer.

'Of course there is!' came the answer, positively.

Jeff grinned. His life was complete now. Nothing else could dampen his spirits once spirits were dampening his liver. Ray continued. And it was sweet, sweet music to Jeff's booze-ravaged hepatic organ.

'The best drinks in the universe are out here. There are lagers that drive you temporarily insane and leave without a hangover! Wines that don't make you wince with the first sip! Stout that would make a leprechaun weep!'

'Enough! enough!' exclaimed Jeff, jumping up and down like a five year-old. 'Where can we get a drink?'

'Alright, OK,' said Ray, giving in. 'See that group of stars over there?' He indicated to the right.

'Services. We can stop off, get some food, I can stretch my legs and you can have your flipping drink.'

Ray steered the Marshmallow Penguin over to the left, and headed towards a relatively small solar system – well, smaller than the only one Jeff knew, at any rate – and approached a greenish moon, a lot smaller than the earth. Beside it, at a distance of around a million kilometres or so, was a huge sandy-beige world shrouded by clouds. Ray and Jeff buckled their seatbelts as a crackle came over the ship's sound system.

'Unidentified craft! You are in violation of Profanian Space. Identify yourself immediately!' said a voice. It was crackly, but it sounded vaguely female.

'What was that?' asked Jeff.

'I dunno,' replied Ray in confusion. 'The last time I was here was over twenty years ago, and it was free space, then! Perhaps there was a war or something!'

He looked ahead and saw two larger spaceships, fish-like and agile, heading towards them. They were more like the type of spaceship that Jeff expected to see, silver and aerodynamically designed (although aerodynamics is a little pointless in space). At least they weren't hairy. They glided to within a few hundred metres of Ray's ship, and held their positions.

'I think we should get out of here!' said Ray, feverishly strapping himself in and stabbing buttons on the console.

Jeff did the same.

'Who are they? And why do they want us?' he yelled.

The voice came through again.

'We can hear you, you know! I'll say it again – you are in violation of Profanian Space. Identify!'

Ray and Jeff looked at each other.

'I suppose we better had,' said Ray.

Pulling on the small microphone mounted above his head, he cleared his throat.

'Er... Profanian authorities, this is Barbaray Sprambladack Fasstalon-Scump, Captain of the Marshmallow Penguin. I'm trying to make a quick stop on your second moon, to rest and get some provisions. Is that alright?' Then he added, 'Over...?'

There was a short crackle. Then the voice came back.

'Marshmallow Penguin, we have scanned your vessel and see that you are accompanied by another person. Identify!'

Jeff stared at Ray, his eyes revealing terror. Ray mimed an 'I-dunno-what-to-do' kind of shrug accompanied by what he thought was a fitting facial expression.

He leaned into the microphone again.

'My passenger is from Earth. Um... His name is Spooner. Listen, if it's all the same to you chaps, we'll be getting out of your, er, hair, so to speak, so if you'll just let us pass, we'll be...'

'Desist! You are unarmed, and we are quite capable of destroying you in an instant! Therefore we will dictate in this situation. You are now prisoners of the Profanian Empire, and will land on the surface. Any attempt to escape will be met with your immediate destruction! That is all!'

'Oh, bugger,' said Ray.

One of the silver spaceships led the way, while the second one followed after Ray's craft. They descended through the atmosphere of the beige planet, and were directed to a landing platform near one of the major cities.

Jeff tried to get a look at this, his first proper alien landscape, but there wasn't much to see. Just a load of rocks, mountains and the odd clump of greenery. It reminded him of his trip to Tunisia, back in his student days. Even the sky wasn't some exotic shade; just the standard blue with fluffy white clouds. But over to the extreme right, he noticed movement. Far off in the distance, he saw a multitude of bright orange dots kicking up dust as they moved along. It was a herd of exotic animals, possibly kangaroos. He watched the animals settle for a moment, then bounce along again.

Once the ship had settled, Ray and Jeff looked out of the porthole, and saw two armed soldiers approach their ship.

They were clad in gleaming gold and silver armour, with headgear that looked rather like motorcycle helmets, except for plumes of yellow and white hair that flowed out of the top, and went down the back of the soldier.

As he looked further, Jeff saw that the soldiers had proportionately longer legs than was normal. Not freakishly long, but just longer than average. Long enough to make him wonder…

Then he saw the heels.

These soldiers were women! They wore high heels, almost too high to walk comfortably in, but they seemed to manage well enough. This must be some kind of warrior race, like the Amazons. Either that or a troop of cabaret dancers.

'Please, God,' he muttered. 'Don't let them be drag queens!'

Ray pushed the ship's door open, and clambered out. Jeff followed, climbing down and out of the ship as calmly as he could. This was scuppered by his abruptly falling over as he took the last step down. So much for impressing the birds, then.

He jumped back up, brushed off the dust, and acted like nothing had happened.

Ray went to his side, and whispered out of the corner of his mouth.

'Just follow my lead. Don't make any sudden moves.'

This impressed Jeff.

'What – you've got an escape plan?' replied Jeff, in the same edge-of-mouth whisper.

'No, I just don't want you to get me killed.'

'Charming,' said Jeff.

The soldiers raised elegant but deadly pistols at the stunned travellers. One of the soldiers stepped up, brandishing two pairs of metallic manacles.

'Hands!' exclaimed the soldier.

Jeff looked up into the tinted visor, trying to get a look at the person inside, but all he saw was his own distorted reflection. Both he and Ray offered their wrists, and the manacles were quickly clamped on.

Ray thought he had better open the lines of communication. He quickly thought of a few statements, such as 'We are a peaceful people', 'We come in peace', and the good old favourite, 'Take me to your leader!' but in the end, he settled for a more fitting and important demand.

'Please don't kill me! Please! Please! I'm only a lowly

hairdresser! I'm worthless! I'm too young to die!' He dropped to his knees to look especially penitent.

Jeff was visibly shaken by this pitiful act, but thought it best to follow Ray's lead, as instructed. He fell to his knees beside Ray and also made a shocking display of himself.

'Show mercy! Please! We're unarmed! Don't hurt us!' An act of defiance it wasn't.

The soldier was unimpressed.

'Get up!' she barked.

Ray did as he was told, as did Jeff, who got up a little slower, so as to get a good long look at the frankly stunning legs of his captors. It was like a gold-plated lap dance.

The two helpless and hungry captives were marched briskly across the dusty path until they got to a large doorway, surrounded by what looked like a fortress.

The soldier banged three times on the door with the handle of her pistol, and the door clanged and rumbled as it began to slide upwards. As soon as it got to about six feet, it stopped and the prisoners were shoved under it.

The inside of the fortress was dark, cold and a little smelly. Jeff whimpered in trepidation at the thought of ending up as a cliché, chained to some dungeon wall without his skin. Up ahead was a source of light, which indicated that not every room was dank and dreary. There was literally, but not figuratively, light at the end of the tunnel.

After what seemed like an eternity of being marched through winding corridors, Jeff and Ray came to what resembled a pair of elevators. Pushed apart by the soldiers, they were directed into one each.

A voice bellowed out through wall-mounted speakers.

'Kill the parasites!'

Transparent doors slid closed in front of them, and both men looked on in horror as strobe lights flashed violently at them for thirty seconds. Ray and Jeff screamed in fear, then stopped in momentary confusion. They realised that they weren't being killed, or in any pain, and they apparently weren't the parasites being referred to. Suddenly, their clothes began to dissolve, broken down into their component molecules by the lights.

The screaming resumed.

Up above, in one of the opulent towers, was a throne room. Looking somewhat like a Roman palace, it was draped in silks and the walls were decorated with life-sized statues. Large marble pillars at each corner supported the domed roof, where a fantastically intricate and colourful stained glass design let the daylight through.

On a raised dais at the far end of the room, was a huge throne. This was as luxuriant and ornate as any other, except it was in a delicate shade of pink. There were feather boas, draped around it, and the air had a floral fragrance to it.

Sitting on the throne was a beautiful woman. In fact, to say that she was beautiful was probably an insult. She was possibly the most physically perfect woman in the galaxy. It was almost impossible to determine her exact age, as she looked youthful and pampered, but in actual fact, her vanity (and a liberal amount of cosmetic adjustments) hid the fact that she was nearer forty than twenty.

Taller than her subjects, finely upholstered in all the right places, but just enough muscle tone to give off the impression that she could kick some serious bottom. Eyes that were glossy and blue enough to have been cookie-cuttered out of a summer sky. Her perfect golden skin bore little make up, except for dark smoky eye-shadow and glistening red lipstick that looked like strawberry jam. Her face was a divine sculpture, framed by a lush, silvery-white mane of wavy hair, which was decorated sporadically with tiny gold beads and tubes. She was wrapped in a glittering golden toga which showed off just enough neck, cleavage, leg and calf to drive any red-blooded man wild with desire. To complete the look, she bizarrely wore huge, chunky Army-style boots with thick soles.

A handmaiden entered from a side door, saluted her queen and made her report.

'Your majesty! The two trespassers have been captured.'

The queen spoke, her voice like sun-warmed honey:

'I know. Sod off.'

Scratch that. Sun-dried pie and mash.

The handmaiden quickly retreated. The queen watched as the door opened, and the two prisoners, now in strange white loincloths and nothing else, were sent in.

Jeff took one look at the gorgeous vision in front of him, and instantly forgot Kylie. He moved his manacled hands down to cover his shame. Ray was one step ahead of him, already embarrassed to be wearing a nappy.

The queen stood up. Although she was on a dais, she would have towered over both men easily. She smiled with an air of superiority briefly, before addressing them.

'What'choo fink yer playin' at, eh?'

A thick cockney brogue spewed out of her mouth, totally contradicting her elegance and grace.

'This is our bleedin' patch, awlright? No place for you bleedin' men. Don't you know who I am?'

Jeff didn't mind the accent. He, like many thirty-somethings from Earth, used to carry a torch for Lorraine Chase, the actress who shot to fame in the late seventies, for her stunning good looks and working-class twang. In fact, if he had a couple of 'Campari Sodas' right then, he'd definitely give her one.

Ray decided to keep it simple.

'Uh, hello.'

Good start. He accompanied his greeting with a weak grin, as if she were a next door neighbour.

'I don't believe we've met. I'm Ray Scump, and this is Jeff.'

Jeff found his tongue at last.

'Spooner. Jeff Spooner. How's it going, babe?'

Connery would've been proud.

The queen stepped down from the dais, still towering over them by over a foot. She walked up to Jeff, whose face was exactly the same height as her chest. It was close enough to sniff.

So he did.

The queen slapped Jeff across his cheek. Hard. He spun and hit the deck.

'Dirty git!' she exclaimed. Then she turned to Ray, who whimpered and cowered, covering his face with the manacles. She leaned close to his scrunched up face.

'Scump! You got a bladdy cheek, showin' yer 'airy mug round 'ere!'

Ray was dumbstruck. Although not as dumbstruck as Jeff, who was literally dumb and struck.

He needed answers.

'Erm… I've never been here before, your worship-titude. I think you must be mistaking me for… Argh! How do you know me?'

The queen returned to her throne. She eyed Jeff, who was still on the floor, undecided whether to get up or not.

'On yer feet, you bladdy wimp!' she bawled. Jeff got up quickly, rubbing his red cheek.

'I know you, mate, because of what yer old man did,' she began, pointing an immaculately manicured finger at Ray.

'I dunno who that muppet is,' the finger went to Jeff. 'But your daddy declared war on all of us 'ere.'

Ray was totally confused.

'I don't understand, your, er, highness-ness. My father was a humble hairdresser, just like me! I'm sure he never declared anything! On anyone!'

The queen glared at both of the nappy-clad men.

'Does the name Bakerloo mean anything to ya?' she asked.

Ray shook his head dumbly. So did Jeff.

'Michelle Bakerloo?' she demanded.

Ray's face visibly changed from confusion to surprise in an instant.

'Michelle Bakerloo? Shelley Bakerloo? I have heard of her, actually! She used to go out with my dad, just after my parents divorced!' he said with a smile. Finally, they were getting somewhere.

'Did you know her?' he asked in a pleasantly social manner. The queen glared once again, but kept her temper.

'You could say that. Whadda you know about 'er?'

Ray relaxed a bit. He began to pace around as he talked, which frightened Jeff a bit.

'Shelley Bakerloo... My dad met her when he was hairdressing for a living. She was a bit younger than him, but they got together and went out for a while. Gorgeous looking woman, by all accounts... Pretty as a picture, but really vain. Hard work, was Shelley. Then it went a bit pear-shaped. She was trying to make it as a model, and went to him for a top notch hairdo. Unfortunately, he got nervous and overdid the peroxide. All her hair fell out, and it never grew back. Well, suffice to say, he dumped her. She freaked out and went off across the galaxy. Nobody ever saw her again. Dad couldn't handle being with a baldie, I s'pose...' He chuckled for a second.

At this point, the queen strode right up to Ray, and grabbed him by his goatee. Ray squealed in pain as she pulled him close to her face.

'Got it in one, mate. Who'd wanna be seen with a bird who looked like that? A bird who looked like this?'

She ripped off her silvery locks and threw them to one side. Her hairless scalp shone in the sunlight.

Jeff gasped in amazement.

'Ray! I think she's Shelley Bakerloo!' he whispered.

The queen raised an eyebrow.

'Quick, innee?' she said dryly.

'Queen Shelley, ruler of the Slargs of Profania to you, mate!' she roared, still in Ray's face.

'And you're gonna pay dearly for what your daddy did to me, I can tell you that for nothing!'

Jeff looked over at Ray.

'Nice one, mate,' he muttered. 'It'll be fun, you said.

Beaches and cocktails…' he huffed in disappointment.

The still bald (and frankly still beautiful) monarch released Ray's beard, and walked over to Jeff, who began to flinch and twitch uncontrollably, as he was expecting another slap or possibly much worse. Shelley snapped her fingers, and another handmaiden hurried to her side, carrying a golden tray on which rested another wig – this one straight and black, like Cleopatra. The handmaiden helped her place it back on her ruler's head and hurried away, scooping up the discarded blonde one as she went.

'OK, babe,' she said with lashings of sarcasm. 'You're a big strong man, I'm gonna make you a deal…'

Jeff swallowed and croaked out a reply.

'Uh, OK… what kind of deal?' he said cautiously.

'Glad you asked,' said the queen, as she strode around the terrified travellers.

'I could, should an' would have the both of you executed immediately, but I think I can make some use of you… How fit are you, little man?'

Jeff decided not to try either charm or wit again, so he answered simply.

'Er… pretty fit, I'd say… Why?'

Queen Shelley stopped pacing when she got to Jeff again. Once again, he flinched, which made her smile.

'Well, I could do with some entertainment round 'ere, so 'ere's the deal. You take the trials. If you succeed, you spend the rest of your useless lives as eunuchs, serving me around 'ere, or you can refuse to take 'em, and end up as 'eads on sticks outside the palace. Your choice.'

Admittedly it wasn't much of a choice. Either way, they were destined to lose their lives. Jeff put his hand up.

'Excuse me, your majestic-tastic-ness… What if I take these trials and fail?'

This made the queen laugh.

'Oh, you'll know if you've failed, 'cause you'll be dead anyway, and Scump 'ere will face death by humiliation.'

Ray flinched this time, and frowned in despair. Jeff looked at him quizzically, and Ray just replied to the look with a simple, 'you don't want to know.' He didn't.

Ray stepped forward, gathering all the courage he had. Which wasn't much.

'Take me, your wondrousness. Not Jeff! He's an innocent in all of this. Let me do the trials!'

Shelley considered Ray's sickening plea, and shook her head.

'Nah, you wouldn't last a minute, Scump. Anyway, I want you where I can see you.'

She clapped twice to summon her guards.

'Take 'airy over 'ere to the dungeons, and take this one out to prepare for the trials.'

Ray was manhandled out of the throne room, protesting feebly, while Jeff was pushed and shoved in the opposite direction, through a side door, and into what looked like some kind of armoury. The queen sat back on her throne. She picked up a small pink hand mirror, and ran a finger through her fringe.

She sighed. 'Ah, revenge or power. I just can't lose.'

chapter four

The Trials of a Hero

Jeff, still nervous, and still shaking, was shown into the armoury. He assumed that he was to be a gladiator of some kind, and was being primed for combat. The guard handed him some basic clothing: rough linen trousers, a baggy overhead shirt and some simple leather plate armour. He put them on, and slipped on a pair of boots which resembled wellies made of brown leather.

Taking a look around the walls of the room, he saw a large collection of various weapons, from short daggers to savage-looking axes. But before he could decide on one, he was grabbed by the arm and led out. He was escorted to a small chamber with a marble table, upon which rested two plates of exotic-looking, but appetising food.

The thought of a hot meal was welcome, but would have been a little more welcome if he hadn't remembered the old Earth tradition of giving a condemned man one last hearty feed before he was put to death.

He was directed by his guard to sit at the table, which he did, and the guard backed off, to leave him in peace while he ate. The plates were filled by a multi-coloured assortment of odd-shaped vegetables, two thick orange steaks, some smaller chopped plants (possibly chips?), and the whole thing was surrounded by a thick purple sauce that looked rather like puréed blackcurrant jam. It smelt vaguely of lavender, with a hint of nutmeg. Weird, yes, but not so off-putting that he'd refuse it. Grabbing the two forks provided, Jeff tucked in, first hacking off a chunk of orange steak. It was a little chewy, but for all intents and purposes it could have been beef. Perhaps this meat came from the wild animals he saw as they were coming in to land. Having renewed confidence in the strange food, he began to eat with more vigour, trying combinations of different things.

At that moment, the door opened again, and Ray was shown in. He was in a plain grey baggy overall and manacles, looking like a lifer.

Jeff turned to see his friend.

'Ray! Am I glad to see you! Did they torture you?' he asked.

'No,' replied the bedraggled barber. 'Not really. Although the music in the lift wasn't pleasant.'

He sat in front of Jeff, and began to eat.

'I've found out what these trials are. Do you want to know?' said Ray, through a mouthful of orange meat.

'Well, yeah, course I do,' said Jeff, munching away.

'It's a tradition on Profania – The Three Difficult-But-Not-Impossible Tasks.'

Jeff listened intently, realising that this may be his only help for a long time.

'The queen will set you three tasks to carry out – a mental quest, a physical test and an endurance challenge. They get harder as they go on. The first one is difficult but not life-threatening, the second is deadly, and the third one – Bod help you! Of course, you have to pass all three to save us both.'

He thought for a second.

'Well, I say, "save", but we'll end up as royal eunuchs. It's probably a fate worse than death.'

Jeff put his forks down.

'I'll do me best, Ray. Don't worry about me, you just think of a way out of here, and I'll try and get through the trials. Then we'll make our escape, OK?'

Ray was taken aback. This was a heart-warming show of bravery on the human's part.

'You're a good man, Jeffrey Spooner. Bod bless you.'

The two friends shook hands and finished their meals.

As soon as they had finished eating, the guards separated the prisoners and took them to their own individual cells for the night.

Darkness splattered over the planet.

Jeff paced the dusty floor of his cold cell, wondering what would become of him. He sat in a corner, looking at the moonlight poking through the iron bars of his window.

Half-heartedly, he stood up, and grabbed the bars. He tried shaking the bars on his window, and to his surprise, the mortar crumbled, and they came out easily. Perhaps this could be his chance for freedom!

He jumped up, hanging onto the window ledge. Then he pulled himself up, until he could lean the top half of his body out of the window.

Looking down, he saw nothing. Nothing but a perfectly flat wall. He was over three hundred feet above the ground, so unless he had about two hundred bed sheets to tie together, he wasn't getting out that way.

Which he didn't. In fact, he had no bed sheets. He twisted his head and neck around as far as possible, and looked up. Nothing again, except more flat wall. No drainpipes, ledges, cracks or flagpoles to climb. Sighing an utterly defeated sigh of defeat, he cursed his luck.

'Oh, God!' he wailed, 'I'm doomed! Absolutely bloody doomed!'

Just then he heard a reply.

'Cheer up!'

Jeff looked to his right and saw Ray, thirty feet away, hanging out of his own cell window in the same way. He looked rather in pain.

'At least you're not stuck in a window.'

When the morning came, it arrived far too early and not at all welcomed by Jeff and Ray. They were violently woken by the sharp clanging of soldiers' boots bashing against the steel doors of their respective cells.

Ray was dragged whimpering out of his cell and down the left corridor, while Jeff was dragged in a similar fashion to the right. The tall, golden-clad and curvaceous soldier said nothing as she pulled him by the shoulder, and together they marched down the longest of corridors, until they were outside the rear of the palace. A huge sandy courtyard, surrounded by a wall of at least twenty feet in height, stretched out in front of him.

For the first time, he realised that he didn't even have Ray at his side to provide him with facts and figures and good old-fashioned moral support; he was alone, about to fight for his life on an alien planet, ruled by a completely insane cockney bird who made his devious ex-fiancée seem like Mary Poppins.

Talking of the lunatic Amazonian, Queen Shelley watched the terrified human as he waited for his first challenge, up in a large balcony above the courtyard.

Behind her, Ray was manhandled in, still wearing the manacles. Turning around, the queen, in yet another exotic hairpiece, a lush red number, smiled a false smile of welcome.

'Mornin', Scump!' enthused the queen sarcastically. 'We're gonna 'ave a right ole giggle today, watching yer little chum take the trials, and when 'e pops 'is clogs, I'm gonna giggle a bit more, watching your noggin get the chop!'

Ray clamped a hand around his neck protectively. He feigned bravery. 'Your overconfidence is your weakness.'

The queen looked back at him with a sarcastic grin. 'Your faith in that muppet is yours.'

Still, Ray continued to goad her.

'That "muppet" down there is my friend. A man of honour. Of intelligence and wisdom, with a nerve of pure steel. You won't break him,' he declared proudly.

'Is that right?' said the queen, looking down at the lone figure below. 'So why has he just wet himself, then?' she asked.

Ray's head sagged in despair.

'Oh my Bod...' he whispered.

The queen looked out at the sandy courtyard. Addressing the hundreds of women – the Slargs of Profania, lined up atop the walls, she called for silence.

'Shaadaap! Let the first trial commence!' she roared, greeted with cacophony.

Down on the sandy floor, Jeff swallowed hard as the jeering and shouting shook him to the very core. Three soldiers approached him, each one brandishing an ornate glass bottle. Inside each of the bottles was a rolled up piece of parchment.

He looked at the bottles, and realised that he had to choose one. As soon as he picked the middle one, the soldier smashed the bottle over his head.

Jeff yelped in agony as the bottle broke and showered him with green glass. Dazed momentarily, he wobbled on his feet, and noticed the piece of parchment was still on his head. Picking it off his head, he unrolled it, and read the words, 'Mental Test'. This didn't bode well.

On the other side of the paper, further instructions were written.

If you are to live, then here's what you do:
Teach us something that we never knew.

Jeff had a think. This was a pretty advanced civilisation, with laws, politics and knowledge. What could he possibly teach them, that they didn't already know?

He racked his brain, but couldn't think of anything at all. Stumped, he resigned himself to his fate. This was a planet totally inhabited by women (as far as he knew) – what would a woman never previously know? What fact, what tiny nugget of information could he impart to a civilised race?

Just then, the spark of logic suddenly burst into life, somewhere deep in his synapses.

Eureka! He turned around, and looked up at Ray, who looked down nervously.

Jeff smiled broadly.

And then he explained the Offside Rule in football.

One down, two to go.

*

As a historical note, the star system of Profania is one of the oldest in the galaxy. It is a smallish solar system, surrounding the star Profania Major. The planets in the system are six in number, and are named thus: Bluddyel, Saudorf, Boolsheet, Haulysheet, Scrooyu and the largest, Profania Alpha, which is the planet upon which our intrepid heroes find themselves fighting for their liberty, ideals and gonads, if not their lives. Profania Alpha is in fact populated by three distinct species. These are the Slargs, the Yobs and the indigenous animal species called the Hoppas.

The Slargs are a race of female warriors, as we have seen. Legend tells of a small band of physically perfect cloned women who set up their domain centuries ago. They only use men for the purpose of reproduction, and rather like the mating habits of the Earth spider, they eat the unfortunate male once he has served his purpose. To establish the viability of the male in question, they created the trials known as 'The Three Difficult But Not Impossible Tasks'. The man who survived these tasks would be decreed fit for use in the siring rooms, helping to breed as many more Slargs as possible. (The chance of any male children being conceived is reduced by precise radiation treatment to remove any X chromosomes form the source. It's not pleasant.)

Once the male is, shall we say, used up, he is cleaned, stripped, rolled in breadcrumbs and served up with various large fruits occupying his bodily orifices, and in certain occasions, chips.

For thousands of years, the Slargs have been at war with the Yobs. Much like the Slargs in their extreme beliefs and fanaticism, the Yobs are another warrior race, composed entirely of men. A similar legend tells of a foolhardy band of space pirates, marooned on Profania, who slowly devolved into mindless thugs, with no compassion, intelligence or pride. So, football fans, essentially.

A notable difference between the Slargs and the Yobs is that when the Yobs procure a suitable female for breeding, they strive to choose one of extremely low intelligence, so that the resulting offspring do not grow up infected by the curse of rational thought, and overthrow the entire race.

The Slargs embrace beauty, art, poetry and the colour pink, whereas the Yobs embrace anything with a pulse. But unlike their female enemies, they lack manners, grace, witty repartee and soap.

As for the third race on the planet, the animal species known as the Hoppas – you may recall Jeff Spooner watching a herd of them as they arrived on the planet. We shall learn more about them when the time is right. Which it isn't.

Jeff stood victorious in the arena, having successfully passed the first of the trials. Reluctantly, Queen Shelley had to give him the thumbs-up sign, to approve of his win.

Beside her, Ray cheered as loudly as he could, at least until he received a slap around the back of his head from the irate ruler, who turned and left the balcony in disgust, leaving Ray to jump up and down in celebration.

As he turned to see this, and cast a beaming grin back at his manacled comrade, Jeff received the instructions for his second challenge in the form of another bottle smashed over his head. This time, he fell to the floor, garnering a round of applause and laughs from the baying crowd. He stood up, getting annoyed.

'Pack it in, will ya?' he yelled.

The soldier who assaulted him simply handed him the rolled up piece of parchment which said 'Physical challenge' on it. Again, the reverse had some more information in a particularly inane verse:

Strength of a man will be laughed at in jest
When pulling against our mighty and best.

Jeff knew what this meant. A long rope was thrown into the arena at his feet. It was to be a Tug Of War contest. Yes, like many men before him, he had to pull a Slarg.

The soldier holding the challenge bottles stepped aside, and from behind her came the champion of the Slargs. The strongest and most physically perfect of the women. Tall and imposing, she was clad in golden plate armour which clung to every impressive curve, and this armour was accented with pink feathers. The champion wore a reflective chrome mask with carved features which made her resemble a six-foot movie trophy.

Jeff gulped. She was obviously a lot stronger than him, and to make matters worse, a rumbling sound coming from the ground shook any courage he had left right out of him. In gaseous form.

The ground opened up to reveal a chasm between the combatants. Six feet wide and hundreds of feet deep. The rope lay across the fissure, indicating that the loser of the contest would be pulled into the hole, and fall to his – or her – death. (Who are we kidding? There wasn't much chance of 'her' death in this one.)

The Champion picked up her end of the rope, and pointed to Jeff, indicating that he did the same. Jeff bent down and grabbed the rope, wrapping it tightly around his waist. With an unblinking stare, and trembling in terror, he looked across the pit into the reflective gold visage of his opponent. *This'll be the end for one of us, and no mistake*, he thought.

From up above, Ray bit into his knuckles in trepidation, fearing for both his friend's life and their collective family jewels.

'You can do it...' he uttered.

Jeff, in a similar state of trepidation, felt the rope tighten, and set his feet wide apart, in preparation for the immense physical ordeal upon which his life depended.

The rope became taut, and a horn blasted out a note from somewhere in the crowd. The Champion lowered her stance, and with a superhuman heave, she pulled Jeff completely off his feet and into the air.

His grip had held, which was unfortunate, as he found himself sailing over the wide trench. Events seemed to slow down for him, as he twisted in mid-air, glimpsing the utter matt-blackness of the bottomless pit.

Ray fainted.

The next thing Jeff was aware of was the Champion, as she twirled around on her heels, like a shot-putter, still bawling out her throaty grunt of exertion. Jeff passed her, still flying, and as she turned, he managed to swing right around her head, the rope forcing her arms to her sides. As he came around, his flight path gave in to gravity, and he hit the ground at her ankles. But he still had a tight grip on the rope, and his momentum pulled the Amazonian warrior off her feet and she spun around, tripping over him and falling head first into the trench with a wail of terror.

The crowd gasped. They had never imagined that such a relatively small and puny man could have defeated their greatest fighter. But Jeff had no time to gloat – his opponent also had a tight grip on the rope, and her weight pulled Jeff toward the edge of the trench.

Somehow, his heels found purchase in the dusty ground before he reached the edge. The rope around his waist took the weight of the Champion, who dangled helplessly against the sheer walls of the pit.

The crowd stood up in unison. A chorus of 'Kill! Kill! Kill!' broke out. For a moment, Jeff thought of obliging them – after all, he had no doubt that, were the situation reversed, his goose would have been well and truly cooked. But he was a better man than that. And he wanted to prove to this race of bloodthirsty feminists that not all men are from Mars, despite what the book said. So he yelled out at the top of his voice:

'AAAAAAAAAAAAAAAARRRRRRRRRRGGGH HHHHH!'

It wasn't exactly what he had planned to say, but he was, after all, in considerable pain. At least it silenced the crowd. Composing himself after the scream, he tried again.

'Listen, you bunch of nutters! I'm not killing anyone, you hear me? Forget it! All I wanted was a rest, some grub and a pint! And you can tell your mental-case of a queen that I've passed two of her stupid tests, and I can pass the third, alright? Bring it on!'

He looked down the trench at the Champion, still

hanging on for dear life. The defeated warrior tore her mask off with one hand, revealing Queen Shelley, exhausted and wigless, dangling by one hand.

'Fair 'nuff, mate! Now 'elp me get outta this 'ole!'

Jeff, although immensely shocked at the discovery, allowed himself a smile. For the first time in years, he had the upper hand with a bird, and he was going to savour it.

'Promise me,' he began. 'That if I pass the third test, you'll let me and Ray go free. Swear it!'

He loosened his grip on the rope for a split second, to underline his point.

'Alright, alright!' came the reply, 'I swear it – you can 'ave yer freedom!'

'Nuts too!' added Jeff.

'Nuts too, alright!' called the queen.

Jeff heaved and slowly began to pull her up and out of the hole. He fell to his hands and knees as soon as the queen had climbed out, utterly exhausted.

The queen walked over and held out her hand. Jeff took it gingerly, still expecting a judo throw or something sneaky, but instead, she pulled him to his feet. Jeff noticed a new-found respect in her eyes. Or at least he would have, had he been looking at her eyes. Instead he got cleavage again. And it was a welcome reward for the victor.

Ray had witnessed this amazing turn of events, having regained consciousness a few minutes earlier. He closed his eyes, clasped his hands and whispered a silent prayer of thanks to Almighty Bod.

For a momentary respite from the proceedings, it's

probably a good idea to explain a bit more about the galaxy to you, as this is after all, a voyage of discovery for both you, the reader, and our hero, Jeff.

You may have noticed that Ray seems to be mispronouncing the word 'God' a lot. This is, in fact, not true, as he is a follower of the largest intergalactic religion. This religion is known as 'The Holy Unity Of The Prophet Known Simply As Bod', or more simply, Boddism. Boddism is a belief system based around a holy trinity of deities, much in a similar way to Christianity. The deities are called Famabalimo, Antflo and the holiest of the three, Bod. Again, many Earth religions have similarities, as the Boddist movement is incredibly popular, and when the earliest settlers came to Earth from the farthest reaches of the universe, they brought Boddism with them. Over thousands of years, the religion became diluted, blurred and entangled with other religions. Hence the confusion: God – Bod, Buddhism – Boddism, etc.

The Book Of Bod tells the story of a young child, known simply as Bod. This holy child, like many others in religious tales, was also hairless. (Hair does seem to crop up a lot in this story, doesn't it? Weird.)

> *'And lo, the child didst have two protectors, neither parents nor siblings, but Famabalimo, the grower of food and all things edible, and Antflo, the carer.'*
> (Book of Bod 12:20)

There is another prophet in the tale, that of Peeseekoppa, the lawmaker, but this being is usually discarded in favour of the freer, nurturing aspects of the other two.

'And it is written that Bod didst walketh upon the world, with feet splayed akimbo, discovering the ways of people and learning to accept his role as omnipotent being and force of all that is good and colourful.'
(Book of Bod 3:42)

In the tales of the Earth Bible, the story of the chosen one includes a large amount of tragedy and pain, but one of the reasons that Boddism is so widely practised, is that it is centred around positivity and happiness. It's not a religion that hangs over you, threatening you with eternal damnation if you so much as think about sinning, but Boddists live in happiness, knowing that Bod will forgive and smile at you, regardless of your transgressions:

'As like Bod, thou art all innocent learners in thy lives. Worry not if thou hast transgressed, for thine mistakes are necessary if thou art to grow.'
(Book of Bod 2:21)

A place of worship on Earth, for example, would have the priests and higher religious leaders dressed in robes of severity and seriousness, but Boddist practitioners dress in simple, brightly coloured garments, and in place of a doleful and oppressive dirge emanating from a pipe organ, Boddist places of worship are filled with dancing and smiles as they leap about in spiritual contentment to a jaunty piccolo-orientated number.

This is only a beginner's guide to Boddist beliefs, but an appendix at the end of this story will attempt to tell you more, should you be tempted to convert. But at least you know a little more about the workings of the universe.

Now, back to the business of Jeff and his third, and final, trial…

Jeff was escorted out of the arena by two guards and the queen. Soon happily reunited, the two friends shook hands vigorously.

Ray beamed in delight and admiration.

'Well played, Jeff! Well done indeed!' he gushed.

'Aww, it was nothing,' said Jeff, feeling his cranium.

'Well, apart from these two sodding lumps on me 'ead, that is.'

Queen Shelley returned wearing a lilac Afro wig. Again, on any other mortal in the universe, it would have looked ridiculous, but accompanied by silver eye-shadow, lipstick and eyelashes, the queen still managed to look utterly glamorous.

Ray regarded her with defiance in his eyes.

'Hasn't he been through enough? Let us go. You've had your fun.'

The queen contemplated this for a moment. Then she tilted her head to one side.

'You're probably right, Scump. But Jeffrey 'ere demanded to do the third trial, and who am I to argue, eh?' She smiled. ''Owever, seein' as he did beat me fair an' square, like… I've got somefing a little less deadly for him.'

Shelley snapped her fingers and her guards grabbed Ray and dragged him, whimpering uselessly, out of the room. Jeff struggled, but the queen held him back – with one hand. It wasn't difficult.

'Hold yer horses, Jeffrey boy! I need you for the next trial, mate.'

Jeff had no idea what she was playing at.

'If you hurt Ray, you can forget about me doing anything for you! Bring him back!'

The queen feigned a yawn.

'Don't be so dramatic, Spooner. He'll be alright. After all, I did promise. But – you still have to do something for me, remember?'

Jeff tried his best to believe her. He nodded suspiciously. Shelley paced over to the window as she spoke.

'See, I was gonna stick you in the fightin' pit with an 'undred Yobs to deal with, but instead, I'll give you a new deal. Find something for me, bring it back, an' we'll call it quits. Both of you can sod off, scot-free. Wodja reckon?'

Jeff stepped forward.

'Find what, exactly? The Holy Grail or something?'

'Yeah, pretty much.'

'Fantastic. What is it then?'

The queen raised a hand, and snapped her fingers. A lowly maiden hurried up and handed her a small flat box, rather like a slate blackboard. It had a screen on the front, and two control knobs at the lower corners. Jeff wondered what she was going to attempt to draw with the etching toy. She handed it to him, and the screen displayed some information, maps and graphics.

"Ave a butchers at this. We know it's on the planet, and we know it's somewhere in Yob territory. They nicked it from us yonks ago. It's up to you to get yer 'ands on it, and bring it back to me. Then I'll let you go. No, 'ang on... Not only will I let you go, I'll give you anyfing you want. Deal?'

Jeff's dormant libido suddenly woke up.

'Anything?' he hinted.

Shelley cottoned on to his lewd intentions and drew herself far too close to be decent, brushing her impressive shirt-potatoes across his chest. She brought her silvery-glittery lips to within microns of Jeff's trembling cake-hole, and breathed, 'Any… fing.'

Jeff trembled at first, and then found himself nodding enthusiastically.

'You got yourself a deal, your hottiness!'

Shelley smiled disturbingly, and beckoned for a guard to open the doors. Jeff bounded out of the hall, and down the corridor.

Queen Shelley looked at her handmaiden, still humbly standing at her side.

'You know,' she began, examining her manicure, 'even though he's tiny, he could probably do me a bit of good, d'you know what I mean?'

The handmaiden asked for clarification.

'You mean, you actually like him, your majesty?'

'Nah, not like that,' replied Shelley. 'I just fancy some chips. Stick the fryer on.'

After a bath, a decent, albeit orange, meal, and a change of clothing, Jeff was reunited with his still complaining companion and they were led out of the palace. They stood at the front gate as a gigantic portcullis was raised. The voice of Queen Shelley came from internal speakers.

'Good luck, fellers! And come back in one piece, Jeffrey – I've got plans for you, sonny Jim!'

This made Jeff feel special. He'd never pulled such a gorgeous woman before, and this one was royalty!

Result!

The thought of living it up in a kingdom of subservient totty really appealed to him. Well, it did – until Ray, being the intergalactic know-all and on this occasion, spoilsport, explained what 'plans' were being made for him upon his return.

'You WHAT? Eat me?' exclaimed a bewildered Jeff.

'Oh yes. You'll get your lusty little pleasures first of course – I dare say it'll last for the best part of ten hours, but after that, it's dinner time, and Jeff's on the menu.'

Jeff couldn't believe it.

'Say that again?'

'You'll be on the menu,' repeated Ray.

Jeff shook his head. 'No, no, no, no… Did you say TEN hours? Fantastic!'

He grinned the grin of a crazy person.

Ray hung his head in despair. They began their journey, kicking up dusty clouds and wandered off into the direction of the sunset.

Ray looked over to his comrade.

'If we could make our way back to the palace, under cover of night, maybe we could overpower some of the guards and escape this place.'

Jeff mulled it over.

'Nah.' He sighed. 'It'd take us all night just to get back, and we'd be so knackered that the guards would mash us to a pulp without a fight.'

'Hmm,' hummed Ray. 'You're probably right.'

'Mind you…' Jeff went on, 'If the queen fancies me, I might get off without the beating and move straight on to the lurving!' he said with a grin.

This made Ray frown.

'You'll still be served up with chips later, though. In

places where chips shouldn't go. Big chips. Possibly crinkle-cut. Or had you forgotten that part?'

'Oh... yeah,' said Jeff as his heart flushed like a toilet, any remaining thoughts of lurving quickly draining away.

'I hate your dad, Ray.'

The two weary travellers had been walking for what seemed like hours, so they decided to have a rest. Ray paced the plain and sighed again.

'I can't believe this. All I wanted was to go home. Why, oh why, is nothing simple anymore?'

He looked over at Jeff, who was contentedly playing keepie-uppie with a small pebble. The game ended when he forgot that it was a pebble and tried to head it.

Ray sighed again.

'Why, oh why, aren't most things simple anymore?'

Nightfall closed in on the dusty plain like a velvet tablecloth, shrouding all in dense blackness. As there were no major cities to illuminate the horizon, nor street lights, the stars were the only source of light. Pin-sharp and twinkling, they gazed upon the two lost souls.

The two lost souls gazed back. They had found a small hill, at the base of which lay a number of huge boulders. The boulders sat in an almost perfect semi-circle. Ideal for shelter from the dust-laden winds.

Both Jeff and Ray lay on their backs and looked up at the stars. Even Jeff had to admit that he was feeling a little homesick. Not for Earth, but just to be out there, flitting carefree and cavalier, among the infinite planets. He made a concerted effort to try and get some sleep, curling up foetus-like against a large rock.

Ray couldn't get comfortable. For some bizarre reason, the thought of being violated, skinned and devoured by attractive, over-evolved cannibals wasn't conducive to a good night's rest.

He looked around for a weapon of some sort, so that in the event of the ambush, he might defend himself and his friend. Picking up a nearby stick, he swished it to and fro a couple of times, and then, noting that it was four inches in length, dropped it with a whimper of despair.

Looking over at Jeff snoring away, he noticed a faint blue glow near his leg. He walked over and gently took out the digital slate pad that the queen had given him. It occurred to him that he hadn't even been told what it was they were sent out to find.

Somewhere in the recesses of Jeff Spooner's sleeping synapses, Kylie danced for him. He found himself seated in the front row of a deserted theatre, where the delectable Miss Minogue was treating him to a private pole-dance, in which the diminutive antipodean saucepot swung, shimmied, writhed and twisted her lithe frame around a highly polished chrome pole, to the strains of her hit, 'Confide In Me'.

Like a spoilt child, Jeff clapped enthusiastically. The dance progressed, and then it took an odd turn. As his fantasy woman began to peel her scant clothing off, rectangular strips of her skin peeled away too. But far from being raw and bloody, underneath showed that she was made of chrome, like the pole. Her silver shoulders glinted in the spotlight, as she seductively crawled toward her bemused spectator. Jeff's eyes widened in amazement, as she closed in on him, almost close enough to touch. Then with a flourish, she grabbed her nose and whipped her face off, to reveal a polished silver visage.

This would be enough to frighten most men, but Jeff being the strange little man he was, found it even more of a turn on. He remembered his bedroom wall as a teenager, upon which he had a poster of a chrome female robot, expertly airbrushed by a Japanese artist. It made him feel... funny.

Just as the dance was coming to it's (for want of a better word) climax, the scene painfully exploded into a million stars and Jeff felt a dull ache at the back of his skull.

He awoke to find Ray squatting in front of him, holding the digital pad.

'Ow!' cried Jeff, suddenly putting two and two together.

Ray looked hard at him.

'You idiot! You know what you've done, don't you? You've sentenced us to death!'

Jeff sat up, rubbing his freshly-bashed bonce.

'What are you on about?' he asked, genuinely in the dark, both literally and figuratively.

Ray brandished the pad in front of Jeff's face, so that he could see the diagrams on the screen.

'This,' he admonished, 'is the fabled Universal Remote.'

Jeff looked at it the only way he knew how: dumbly.

'So?' he replied, equally dumbly.

Ray bashed him on the head again with the pad.

'It's "fabled", Jeff. Mythological! It's never been found and it never will! To most sentient species in the universe it never even existed!'

'So, what you're saying is we don't have much of a

chance to find this thing then?' He flinched as Ray waggled the pad again in a threatening manner.

'Well done, Einstein.'

Jeff looked up at his barber friend sulkily.

'You don't have to keep twatting me with that thing.'

chapter five

Ruling with an Ironic Fist

Across the galaxy, young Kelvin, newly appointed Evil Overlord of the Skragg Empire, took his father's throne for the first time. It was a magnificent chair, assembled entirely of bones and skulls of vanquished enemies, and lovingly coated in gold, silver and ebony. To a human, it looked like H.R. Giger had thrown up all over it.

Unfortunately, where it previously did a good job of accentuating the sinister presence of Lord Rancydd, it had the opposite effect on Kelvin, dwarfing him and making him look like a small doll within its bony embrace. He'd placed a small cushion under his royal bottom to help alleviate the pain of his uncomfortable position. It helped a bit, but he had to wonder if sitting for hours on a bone-throne in considerable discomfort was what made his late father the bad-tempered dictator that he was.

He'd been in office now for just over an hour, and already hated it. On a regular basis, peasants and various military leaders were brought in front of him, and all he had to do was give the thumbs-down, and they got carried off and thrown into the razor-crab tanks. It was boring and repetitive, and as he hadn't inherited Dad's lust for blood. It wasn't even any fun to watch. He'd rather be watching cartoons on the telly, but was advised by his dark ministers that such behaviour was unbecoming of the Evil Overlord.

As tedious as that was, he was due a visit from the Intergalactic Tax Inspection Office. He'd been told that the position of Evil Overlord brought with it not only a phenomenal wage packet, but some attractive tax benefits, a handsome pension scheme, and regular deliveries of clean monogrammed socks.

The doors to his throne room swung open, and a trio of suited, balding men with briefcases walked in, a little hesitantly.

'Speak!' called Kelvin, trying to get into the spirit of things.

'My Lord, we represent the Intergalactic Tax Inspection Office, and are here to pay tribute to your late father, and also to ensure the fiscal stability of your reign, which we humbly wish to be as long and fruitful as that of—'

'Silence!' interrupted Kelvin. Being the most feared man in the galaxy had its plus points – one didn't have to be concerned with manners, small talk and most of all, sycophantic, waffling bean-counters. Looking down at the arm of his throne, he noticed a small round button, with a skull engraved into it.

Things just got interesting.

'Tell me,' asked Kelvin. 'How is the company doing?'

One of the trio of pin-striped lackeys stepped forward, opening his briefcase.

'My Lord, the Empire is uniquely positioned to reap enlarged and substantial financial rewards in the next quarter. Further to that, exports and imports are steadily providing additional monetary stability...' he went on for at least another minute in vague multi-syllabic prose, until Kelvin had completely lost track of the sentence's original subject.

'Silence!' he yelled again. He pressed the button on his chair. Instantly, the man was turned to grey dust with a bright flash.

Pointing at one of the other taxmen, he tried again.

'You! Tell me – are we making money? And try to be concise, for Bod's sake!'

The stuttering man, still dusted with the ashes of his late colleague, tried to explain to the best of his ability, but when you're a scholar of the finest mathematical teaching, and faced with a patience-less, ruthless, and quite frankly, clueless dictator, there's always going to be a little language barrier.

'My Lord. Shares are up, and are set to flourish annually, developing into a considerable...'

'SILENCE!' Another flash, another pile of dust. It wasn't going well.

The last of the accountants realised it was up to him to provide a clear answer.

'My Lord,' he began, shaking visibly. 'You're, er, loaded. Filthy rich, to be honest.'

Kelvin smiled. Finally someone was talking in a language he understood.

'What can I afford?' he asked, rubbing a pair of sweaty palms together in greedy anticipation of the answer.

'Anything!' replied the little man, mopping his

perspiring brow with a handkerchief, allowing himself a little smile of relief.

'Anything?' said Kelvin. 'What about a house? No – wait a minute – a city! A country! Can I buy a country?' he asked, frothing over with excitement.

'My Lord, you can buy planets! Entire systems, if you desire!' The accountant was getting more confident. All he had to do was remember to translate his thoughts into a more readily understandable dialogue, and things would go swimmingly.

Kelvin bounced up and down on his throne in the manner of a young child approaching the seaside in their parents' car.

'Oh! Oh! I want one! How do I go about it, then?' he gushed.

'Well, first you need to release the considerable equity, currently withheld in your portfolio of –'

'Silence!'

Flash, bang, dust... silence.

Kelvin sat back in his chair. This dictator lark wasn't as bad as he first thought it'd be.

chapter six

Remote Possibilities

The sun of Profania Alpha finally saw fit to crawl up above the horizon. As Ray and Jeff, newly-appointed artefact hunters, walked along the desert trail, Ray read up on their quest, using the slate-like computer that the queen had provided them with.

'It says here,' began the sweating tonsorial trimmer. 'That for over a hundred generations, the Slargs have been searching for the Universal Remote – literally, a remote control for the universe.'

Jeff was listlessly booting his keepie-uppie pebble along the trail, only half-listening. Ray went on regardless.

'Apparently, whoever holds this thing has control of the universe's workings – literally. You know, my father once told me about this, he said it's the thing that empowered the most advanced races. To create, to destroy, conquer, alter space and time…' He added a little gasp of awe.

Jeff took an almighty punt with his foot and the pebble flew off the trail. With nothing trivial to occupy him, he looked at Ray.

‘Uh? What – so you’re saying that this thing is like a magic wand or something?’

Ray switched the slate off.

‘Yes, either that or an atom bomb. It’s true what they say: “With great power, comes—”’

‘—Great responsibility, yeah, I know,’ interrupted Jeff. Ray was impressed.

‘I’m surprised you knew that saying, it’s from the book of Bod, chapter ten, verse ten.

‘Oh? I got it from Spider-Man,’ mumbled Jeff flatly. ‘Book one, chapter four. Where are we supposed to find this thing, anyway? We’ve been walking for hours!’ Like his tongue, his adventurous enthusiasm had totally dried up, and tasted unpleasant.

‘Well, we’ve followed the map so far, we should be entering Yob territory any time now. I suggest we be careful. These Yobs make the Slargs look like children’s television presenters by comparison.’

The two weary travellers reached a narrow pass between two towering mountains. Jeff stopped to crouch down at a small pool of water that had gathered in the shade of the rocks. He delved into it with cupped hands and drank. It was a bit warm and tasted a little coppery, but it refreshed him suitably. He hadn’t slept all that well, and was still tired.

For a non-believer, Ray certainly seemed to be more enthusiastic about finding the lost artefact, this morning. Not so much the fact that it would make them both famous, but more likely because it would just allow him to get home at last.

‘This is the gateway to the village of the Yobs,’ proclaimed Ray. Jeff stood up and shuffled over to the gap in the mountains. In the dusty haze, he could make out a wide flat plain, dotted with crude, conical wooden huts that resembled bonfires. Right in the centre of the village was a tall, thin tree that was at least a hundred feet in height.

'You said these Yobs are dangerous?' he squinted, looking for signs of life among the huts.

Ray stroked his goatee, trying to look deep and thoughtful.

'That, my friend, is an understatement. In fact, I'd go so far as to say you will never find a more wretched hive of scum and villainy,' he mused. 'Except for Swansea,' he added.

'Well, firstly, how do we get in there to look for this non-existent... thing, and secondly, how do we escape without being killed in the process?'

'No idea,' replied Ray, still trying – and failing completely – to maintain some dignity.

'Well that's just brilliant! We're naffed before we start then!' exclaimed Jeff in a fit of newly-generated despair.

Ray turned to Jeff looking annoyed.

'Don't you put the blame onto me. You're the one who thinks with Mister Johnson and decided to go on this quest! You try and think of something!'

Jeff had to admit that it was mostly Mister Johnson's fault, and the guilty expression he wore showed it. He stepped forward and looked out at the village once more, watching faint plumes of smoke waft upwards from the huts.

'I suppose we'll just have to improvise, then. Make it up as we go. Otherwise we'll never find the Universal Remote. As long as we're not discovered, we'll be...'

Just then, a scratching, scuffling noise came from out of the rocks. Jeff and Ray looked at each other in terror. They had been discovered!

Overlord Kelvin sat in his throne room, bored rigid. To pass the time, he'd surveyed his lands, made some laws and raised taxes. Twice. That had been fun, but now he was feeling a bit jaded.

He stood up, and walked over to the door on the far side of the court room. Just as he reached the door handle, both the doors swung open, making him scream in shock. It wasn't conduct becoming of the new Overlord of the Empire.

Standing at the doorway was another trio of bureaucrats, only this time, they didn't look afraid of Kelvin in the slightest. Because they weren't.

This was no ordinary group of bean-counters. They were Galactic Tax Inspectors, ready to do a complete audit of the Skragg Empire and put to right any wrongs that they found in the process. That included deposing and replacing the Overlord if need be. They weren't to be messed with.

Kelvin knew this. It wasn't the first time he had seen these imposing, sinister men. He'd heard tales of their previous visits to his father, and knew that it was only these men that could make his dad look afraid.

The Tax Inspectors stepped into the room, and Kelvin scampered back to his throne as fast as he could, trying to regain his regal composure when he got there.

One of the men spoke, a rasping, emotionless hiss.

'Overlord of Skragg, we come to perform a full inspection of your Empire. We wish to know all that you have planned for the coming financial century.'

Kelvin thought as fast as his noodle would allow. Coughing a little to clear his dry throat, he began to stall for time.

'Ah, yes. Well, in the coming months, I plan to er, expand. Yes. Expand the Empire by er, by conquering! Yes, conquering those worlds nearest to us that need to be – well, conquered, I suppose.'

'Is that it?' asked the Inspector.

'Yes. Well, no!' said Kelvin, beginning to wobble.

'I plan to do more, of course. Like erm…'

He was beginning to crack up under the pressure of the unblinking beady eyes focussed on him. He had to think big. Bigger. Biggest, if entirely possible.

'Like conquering the entire Universe!' he declared loudly, standing up in his most noble pose, looking out into the middle distance.

It had the desired effect. Kelvin heard a faint gasp of astonishment emanate from one of the inspectors.

'Erm… If that's alright with you chaps?' asked the Overlord, sitting down again.

The lead inspector looked suitably impressed.

'Excellent. And how do you intend to achieve this?'

He watched as Kelvin's previously confident expression gave way to befuddlement.

Suddenly, Kelvin remembered his father's last request.

'I will, er… conquer the Universe because I will use the legendary Universal Remote! Yes, that's it! That's the thing!'

The chief Inspector raised a tenth of one of his eyebrows, which signalled interest. Kelvin bluffed onwards.

'And I plan to rule the universe with an iron fist.

Mightier than that of my father. He may have been a great ruler, but I promise you this – the universe will cower in terror at the very thought of my mighty fisting!'

The inspectors looked at each other speechlessly, then filed out the door.

Kelvin ran over to his throne. Pushing the communicator button, he leaned into the microphone.

'Get me the Royal advisers, pronto!'

Jeff and Ray stood backed against a stony wall, gasping at the sight that greeted them. It wasn't that they were in any mortal danger, and it wasn't that they had been surprised as such. It was the fact that they found themselves talking to one of the planet's indigenous species – a Hoppa.

Now, two things went through Jeff's mind at boggling speed: First, that this articulate, intelligent and very alien alien was something he'd seen before: his childhood 'spacehopper'.

Secondly, he felt guilt at realising he'd eaten the animal's ancestors recently – the orange meat served up with every meal.

Yes, here he was, light-years across the Galactic disc, and he was talking to a living, breathing, and surprisingly nutritious bouncy toy. He rubbed his eyes. The Hoppa noticed.

'Is friend alright?' it asked Ray.

Ray was thankfully more composed.

'I think so. It's probably a little cosmic culture-shock. Did you know that on his planet, they have toys that look just like yourselves? I hear it. Not planet, but toy.' The Hoppa looked sullen as it bounced a little closer. 'Many years, are hunted for meat, skin taken for fun of Slargs and Yobs. Skins sent to many places because of this.' It pointed at Jeff with its antennae. 'Friend had one as child?'

Jeff spoke out. 'Well, I had one, but it wasn't made out of your skin, it was rubber. All over. It didn't have any of that fur on it or real eyes or anything.'

'Ah, cheap one. That OK. So he not bad human?'

Ray shook his head. 'No, not at all. He, er, good human.'

The Hoppa cheered up considerably at this and changed the subject. Bobbing up and down in a similar way to a dog wagging its tail, it continued.

'You here to find Universal Remote? I hear you talking.'

'Yes, that's right. But it's impossible. Either it's down in the village over there,' said Ray, pointing to the smoking huts. 'Or it doesn't even exist! Either way, we're both dead meat!'

Jeff thought of the term 'dead meat' and looked at the bobbing orange creature with renewed pangs of guilt. He nodded in agreement.

'Impossible.'

'Impossible?' snorted the Hoppa. 'Pah! Not impossible, not non-existent. We know where it is!'

It was pleased that it had impressed the humans, and skipped back a few feet.

'You come out now, they good humans!' it called, seemingly in the direction of the rocks. From behind the rocky outcrops and large boulders, twenty more Hoppas bounced tentatively out. Some were older, looking more leathery and beginning to grey around the whiskers, and some were little more than football-sized babies, bobbing energetically at the excitement of meeting two other beings that didn't want to skin and eat them.

Jeff looked around at the orange crowd of bouncing admirers. It was like one of his more surreal dreams. But at least they had information, allies and some sense of purpose now.

'Town meeting tonight!' called the Hoppa. It beckoned to Jeff and Ray with its curly antennae.

'You come with us – hop on!'

Ray, then Jeff, approached a Hoppa each – rather sheepishly – and straddled the orange blobs. Jeff mumbled a rather feeble apology, as he got on, and gripped the antennae. Then the entire herd of Hoppas, led by the two humans, moved off.

Jeff wobbled as he bounced, remembering his childhood days of boinging around the garden, and it soon came back to him. Minutes later, the plain echoed to the sound of ecstatic whoops and laughter as he felt the wind in his hair and bounced higher and further than he'd ever done as a child.

The convoy of Hoppas finally bounded into their town just over an hour later. It was more of an open-air commune; basic beds of grass and leaves, a washing pool, and the entire settlement was circled by a small collection of boulders for protection. Having no hands, just dextrous antennae, the Hoppas weren't equipped to build anything particularly useful or complex, but there was a satisfying sense of a close-knit community. It seemed strange to Jeff that reasonably intelligent, speaking creatures like the Hoppas should live so primitively, but then again strangeness and astonishment was fast becoming a regular thing in his life.

After dismounting, Jeff went over to Ray, who was discussing the forthcoming meeting with the head of the tribe.

'What's the plan then? Do we just pick up this remote-thingy and go, or what?' he asked, crossing two fingers surreptitiously, in the hope of a simple answer.

Ray turned around to face Jeff, and the Hoppa bobbed away.

'Not exactly, Jeff. You remember the Yob village that we saw?'

'Yes...' said Jeff, cautiously. He found himself uncrossing his fingers, as it was obviously not working. Ray continued to explain.

'Well there was that really tall tree in the middle of the village, remember? The Universal Remote is hidden at the top of the tree. In fact, it's not exactly hidden. You could probably reach it if you had a really, really long stick or something...'

Jeff shook the marbles in his cranium around for a second.

'Hang on a minute,' he began, pointing for added emphasis. To be honest, it was a rather well-observed point, which was proof that Jeff was beginning to find his metaphorical feet in this new life of his.

'Hang on a minute,' he repeated. 'If the remote is only at the top of the tree, why don't the Yobs just climb up and get it? Or saw the tree down?'

Unfortunately for Jeff, though his logic was sound, there was a rather noticeable absence of logic in the answer.

'They don't know how to climb and they like the tree too much to cut it down.'

Jeff rearranged his mental marbles again, to help clarify the answer.

'Don't know how to climb?' he said in astonishment.

Ray took Jeff by the shoulder and walked around the Hoppa village as he tried to explain. It became apparent that the Yobs were of extremely limited abilities – mental, logical and physical. Their opposable thumbs had regressed to sub-primate standards generations ago, hence the inability to climb, and their unimpressive brains had long-since withered away to something resembling a ladle full of mushy peas. (Except that mushy peas, when tested under strict laboratory conditions, could at least recognise the fact that they were mushy peas, and consequently not get ideas above their station.)

In fact, the mental capacity of even the highest ranking Yob was so underdeveloped that he thought a myth was a female moth. The only thing the Yobs worshipped more than alcohol and violence was their incredibly tall tree, which to them was a kind of totem pole. It was also the only thing they had in their settlement that hadn't been vandalised. Head butted, chewed, danced with, urinated upon, worshipped, vomited over, even amorously molested, but not vandalised.

Ray and Jeff had strolled away from the middle of the village. In front of them was a large crater, almost a hundred metres in diameter. On the floor of the crater were pear-shaped rocks of different sizes, arranged in straight lines. It looked like a giant solitaire board. Around each of the stones were small yellow flowers that grew wild on the plains. Neither Ray nor Jeff had seen anything like it, and it dawned on them that what they were looking at was a cemetery.

Over to the left, Jeff noticed a little female Hoppa bounce into the crater, with some more yellow flowers held firmly in her antennae. She slowly and carefully bobbed around the stones until she came to a stone that was bigger than her. Leaning forward in a sort of bow, she placed the flowers at the base of the stone. Jeff saw a glint of light in the eye of the little creature that revealed a teardrop.

The little Hoppa bobbed up again, then turned around and solemnly moved away, heading for the edge of the crater. She hopped up over the ridge, and sat there looking at the stones, just like Jeff and Ray.

Against his better judgement, Jeff walked over to the little Hoppa and crouched down. Ray remained standing at a respectful distance.

'Hello there,' said Jeff. 'What's your name, then?'

The Hoppa looked up at Jeff.

'Me Pon-Pon. Me go see mother. She have stone there.'

Jeff was touched. Although the thought of having a tender conversation with a space hopper was about as cubist as it could get, he did feel for the little orange child.

'Are all these stones to remember someone?' he asked gently.

Pon-Pon nodded.

'All Hoppas remembered here. Yobs come, Slargs come. Each time, take many, kill all. Hoppas live on in head. Not forgotten.'

Jeff put a friendly hand on the little Hoppa's head.

'I'm sorry. I don't know what I can do to help, but I'll do whatever I can, alright?'

Pon-Pon smiled weakly.

'You good human. But more Hoppas die. Always die.'

Jeff swallowed in determination. 'Not if I can help it,

little 'un,' he vowed.

Pon-Pon smiled up at the strange human, then she skipped off, heading for the village. Ray came over to Jeff and they watched the little orange thing bounce away.

'What was that all about?' asked Ray.

Jeff looked more solemn and serious than Ray had ever seen him.

'These Yobs – and the Slargs – they've been killing hundreds of Hoppas every year. We've got to do something about it.'

Ray tried to explain.

'Well, it doesn't seem right, I know, but in all honesty, they're kind of dumb animals – like cows, for instance. Or chickens. They're beasts of burden, a source of food. What can we do?'

'These are intelligent, caring things. That makes them a little more than dumb animals. We've got to stop this somehow,' said Jeff with new resolve.

'Come on,' said Ray, 'let's get back to the village. We'll see what the situation is and how we can best help.'

The sun was beginning to set, sending golden beams of warm light through the clouds that cast soothing deep brown shadows across the desert plains. Jeff and Ray could smell the welcome aroma of cooking food and campfire smoke, and they headed to the town centre in the direction of the sights, sounds and smells.

The village was a friendly place to be when the sun went down. Jeff and Ray sat on clumps of dry grass and watched as the villagers prepared a humble but varied banquet. The males hopped in, laden with fish that they'd caught in nearby rockpools, and the females cooked them over small fires. Jeff had wondered how these oddly-shaped creatures coped without proper limbs, but he noticed that their head antennae were incredibly prehensile, and to add to that, they had tongues that were split twice, forming three crude digits, that could grasp objects or form into scoops for eating their favourite soup.

Barbecued fish was followed by a thick vegetable soup and small, antennae-made bread rolls. Jeff was all the more impressed by these little orange aliens after seeing how talented they were, and he strengthened his resolve, there and then vowing silently to do his best to free them from persecution.

The Hoppas had all gathered in what seemed to be the town square – in actuality a roundish, relatively empty patch of ground. Ray was offered a place at the front of the crowd of orange bobbing villagers, and was soon supping from his second bowl of vegetable soup. He beckoned Jeff over to join him, as Chief Fnar-Fnut, the oldest and wisest of the Hoppas bounced up onto a small mound of earth to address the gathering.

'I wonder if the queen is missing us?' said Jeff.

Ray took a final slurp of soup and wiped the stray drips from his beard.

'I doubt it, Jeff,' he replied, rather matter-of-factly. 'I'd even go so far as to say she thinks we're both dead already. Which is fine with me, because I really don't want to go back there, but there's a slight problem.'

'Isn't there always?' muttered Jeff sadly.

'The Penguin,' said Ray. 'We've got to get back to her to get off this planet, and that means taking the Universal Remote back to the queen first. But that's still no guarantee of her letting us go. I appreciate that you want to help, Jeff, but let's face it: it's hopeless, Jeff. Hopeless!'

He dropped his head forward in a shameful display of melancholia.

'Cheer up, Ray,' urged Jeff. 'At least the Hoppas are going to help us get the remote. That's a start, innit?'

He nudged Ray with his elbow, and nodded towards the chief, who was about to begin. Jeff was surprised to hear that Chief Fnar-Fnut had what sounded like a Brummie accent.

'Dear Hoppas, many time I speak of old tale. Legend say thing that make big changes get stole by Yobs. Legend say too, of two-legs that come to Hoppas and help. Here humans, and now time come for big fight. Yobs many and strong. Hoppas few but quick. Hoppas win big fight, get remote back.'

Hearing this, the excited Hoppas began to chatter loudly, bobbing up and down quickly. At the front of the audience, Jeff and Ray looked at each other, clearly not as excited. The word 'fight' was terrifying enough to both of them, but when preceded with the adjective 'big', it became seriously worrying. Jeff had only won one fight in his life and that was with Reverend Wilson. And if truth be told, that only counted as a victory because Wilson hadn't fought back. So, alright – it wasn't even a fight then.

Ray was having similar thoughts. He too, had only been victorious in a combative situation once, and that was an hour-long, sweat-stained ordeal of mentally and physically exhausting battle against a medium-sized bluebottle that had invaded his shop a week ago.

Had Ray not been armed with a newspaper, a can of

'Bug-zap' and a water pistol, the outcome might have been very different indeed.

The Hoppa chief waved his antenna in a gesture that effectively quietened the enthusiastic throng.

'When remote back, humans fulfil legend. Take to old-young-old ones, far away.'

Things had got to a point in Jeff's head where the questions outnumbered the answers again. He stood up, drawing gasps of what sounded like shock, but was actually reverence from the assembled townsfolk.

'What legend? What old-young-old ones? What in the name of Bobby McFerrin are they talking about?' Clearly, he was fighting for adequate phraseology.

'Don't worry,' said Fnar-Fnut, 'be happy!'

Jeff groaned.

'Big fight tomorrow,' continued the orange blob, 'Yobs no match for Hoppas and humans. Get remote, all well again.'

'And the old-young-old ones?' asked Ray, who was feeling a little left out. 'Who are they?'

The chief seemed surprised that Ray, being one of the saviours of the Hoppas, hadn't heard of them, but he thought it best to explain anyway.

'Old-young-old ones come from big far away. They make remote. But remote stolen. End up here. But now must go back. Methuselah – place to take it. Old-young-old ones make safe then.'

Something flicked a lightbulb on in Ray's darkened mind. He spun around, grabbing Jeff by the shoulders.

'Methuselah! I remember now! Jeff – I've heard of the Methuselans – a race of immortals! They're known as the wisest of all the life-forms in the universe!'

Jeff looked weary.

'And on the other end of the stick, are us, Ray – the stupidest life-forms in the universe. What chance have we got? Tell me that then?'

Ray's new-found enthusiasm briefly got lost again. He frowned as the truth sank down over them both like a duvet.

'Well… I'm not sure. It could be a long and terrible conflict. But let's see what we can do, eh? Like I always say, "Improvise – until something miraculaculus happens!"'

'You mean miraculous,' corrected Jeff.

Shaking his head, Ray explained.

'Nope – miraculous is pertaining to miracles. Miraculaculus is a fine blend of a miracle and calculus! We'll overcome this problem, my friend, and we'll be back in the Penguin, heading to Kangazang, before tea-time tomorrow. Just you wait and see!'

Jeff had to admit that Ray's optimism was infectious, and it made him feel a lot better. The Hoppas showed both of the legendary bipeds to a small cave which was padded on the floor with soft straw, and they soon crashed out, trying to clear their minds of the impending battle the next morning.

A huge circular table in a huge circular room displayed a disappointingly small and square map to Lord Kelvin of Skragg. He had brought his royal advisers in to locate the whereabouts of the Universal Remote, and in just two days of sleepless researching, it had to be said that they'd done well for their new ruler.

The great book repositories and libraries of the entire

planet were scrutinised and examined meticulously for any clues leading to the fabled item, and with a little searching on the InfoHEX net, they had narrowed it down to one of two locations, both of which were on the surface of Profania Alpha.

Kelvin stood up from his chair, causing a Mexican wave of flinching to ripple around the advisers seated at the immense table. When the shuddering had died down, he proceeded to walk around the table, as he'd seen his father do, stroking his rather pointy chin – he had no impressive beard as yet. He did a rather impressive job of looking knowledgeable as he strode elegantly around the room, but underneath the thin show of bravado was a lost cause. He had no idea how to read a map whatsoever. But that, he theorised, was what the Royal advisers were for.

'Tell me,' he began, 'what's the name of this planet again?'

The bravest and highest-ranked of the advisers cleared his throat.

'My Lord, this is Profania Alpha. Seventy light-years from the Skragg Empire, situated two thirds of the way across the Galactic disc, en route to the Bellatrix system.' The adviser decided to stop there, as he could see Kelvin's eyes glazing over.

'Ah, good, good. Do we own this planet?' he said.

The adviser shook his head.

'No, my lord. It is self-governed by the dominant species, headed by Queen Shelley of the Slargs.'

'Oh. Is that going to be a problem, do you think?' said Kelvin, chewing on a fingernail.

'Not really, my lord. Although the Slargs have a

formidable military presence, it is fortunate for us that the Universal Remote is not located there with the Slargs. We have searched the archives for all the available facts, and have reason to believe it lies with the secondary species known as the Yobs. Erm, that might pose a slight, er, problem-ette.'

Kelvin was experiencing three simultaneous emotions by now. Boredom, confusion and worry. He felt that the time had come for actions, because words had clearly become too tiresome for him.

'Mobilise the troops! Prepare the planet destroyers!' he declared.

Another adviser cleared his throat.

'Erm, we don't actually have planet destroyers, my lord.'

'Really? What about galactic blitzers?'

'No.'

'Oh. Um, what's the name of that really big ship then? The red one. It's got that nice tower on top and the big guns at the front?'

'That's the Skraggi Imperial Battle Cruiser, my lord. Your Father's ship.'

'Ooh! That one then! Load it up and let's get going!'

Kelvin clasped his hands together in satisfaction and grinned maniacally.

The advisers rose from the table and began to make for the exit.

'Wait!' called their Overlord and master. 'There's something I haven't done yet.'

The advisers looked around at each other. They'd surely dotted all the I's and crossed every T. The researching and planning was perfect. Kelvin pointed at the shortest of the advisers with a thin index finger.

'You!' he called. 'You displease me!'

The short adviser jumped and began stuttering in fear.

'What have I done to upset you, your worshipfulness? I've served you faithfully for years – er, days!'

Kelvin realised that the short man had a point.

His eyes roved around the room. Finally they stopped on a half-drank cup of tea that the adviser had left to go cold. Vindictively, Kelvin pointed to the cup.

'You offend me with your blatant refusal to finish the Royal tea!'

As the unfortunate adviser continued to shake and protest, Kelvin made his way over to the throne. He jabbed the button on the arm of the chair, and the all-too-familiar flash and bang reduced the adviser to a small pile of dust.

'Let that be a lesson to you!' yelled Kelvin to his assembled nervous audience. 'Now – let's go to war!'

Morning came on Profania Alpha. The sun was just creeping up over the horizon, and the village of the Yobs was slowly coming to life.

One particularly foul brute lay crashed out at the foot of their tall tree, surrounded by the sticky orange remains of a Hoppa kebab. The Yob looked like the result of a gene-splicing experiment involving a gorilla, a wrestler and a rhinoceros. Only hairier. His large body was topped by a thick neck and on top of that was a small head with a sloping forehead that indicated the absence of a particularly large brain. Fleas bounced gaily over his hide, and flies circled the unconscious lump, no doubt basking in the stomach-emptying stench that pervaded his very skin.

Drooling from the side of his mouth, the thuggish moron twitched. Something had begun to rouse him from his alcohol-induced stupor. He grunted and broke wind loudly. This provoked one eye to open, but opening the other proved to be too much of an effort, so he settled back to sleep.

Then, a distant rumbling woke the Yob once more. Dragging himself into a sitting position, he looked down at his stomach. Must be hungry. He grunted and scratched his personal areas, sniffing his stubby fingers after each scratch.

But the rumbling persisted. Not only did it persist, but it grew louder. The Yob looked around, to see other Yobs emerging from their huts in equal puzzlement.

One of the Yobs grunted and ran to the edge of their settlement, pointing wildly at the horizon, in the direction of the sound. His eyes widened and the ugly face froze as the information took time to crawl from his eyes to his miniscule and rarely-used brain.

Out of the sun came an incredible sight. A thousand Hoppas poured forth, an unstoppable orange mass, accompanied by a thundering drumbeat generated by their bouncing movements.

Right at the front of the charge were Ray and Jeff, wearing crude vests that had wooden plates attached for armour. They hung onto the antennas of the biggest Hoppas, and swung large wooden clubs over their heads. Jeff swore he could hear the classical strains of 'Ride Of The Valkyrie' in his head, whilst Ray hummed 'Holding Out For A Hero' as the soundtrack to the epic scene.

The Yobs may have been stupid to the point of insanity, but they knew an attack when they saw one.

Grunting and yelling frantically, they raced around, grabbing clubs and stones for use as weapons. Some had crude swords made from scrap metal. The Yobs formed a rough line facing the oncoming stampede.

Jeff shouted over at Ray.

'OK, this is it! You take your lot around to the right, and I'll sort this lot out!'

The bouncing horde split into two groups, confusing the Yobs even more. Behind Jeff, the whooping and hollering group of Hoppas swung double clubs around their heads from their antennae.

The first wave of Hoppas ploughed into the Yob line like a tidal wave into a sandcastle. It was inconceivable to the Yobs that the timid orange bouncy things could ever pose any sort of threat to them, but generations of mindless slaughter can do great things to motivate the meek.

The Yobs scattered as the Hoppas attacked, swinging their clubs into the heads of their lifelong enemies. Blood, sweat and drool sprayed into the air with every impact. Every now and again, one of the Yobs would manage to hit a Hoppa, and it would scream out loudly as it deflated and died, leaking its marmalade-like blood. But this only served to enrage the fallen one's comrades, and the attack grew in ferocity.

Ray took his group around the side of the village, effortlessly dispatching any retreating Yobs that ran from the onslaught. He fought a way to the tree at the centre of the settlement, and began to circle it, keeping any Yobs at bay with a dizzying barrage of swinging clubbage.

Meanwhile at the front of the village, the Yobs were putting up a good fight. They had broken up into smaller groups, and each group successfully coordinated their defences, picking off a few Hoppas every few minutes. Jeff stopped his ride, and leapt off, adrenalin surging through his veins as he ran screaming into the Yob defences.

One of the Yobs spun his huge frame around to see the unnatural sight of Jeff, a human on the side of the Hoppas. He swung his log-like arms around, catching Jeff on his shoulder, and knocking him off his feet.

Jeff went tumbling across the dusty floor. The wooden plate armour only made it more painful as it jabbed him all over. He looked up to see the dust clear, and the sun was eclipsed by the huge Yob standing over him. It was all over.

The giant Skraggi battle cruiser Furious Anger came out of hyperspace into the Profania system. Looking like a barnacled red shark, it powered along using multiple nuclear fusion drive engines toward its goal. Hanging in front of them was the small blue planet of Haulysheet.

Overlord Kelvin stood at the top of his ship's observation tower, surveying the journey. In his right hand he held his father's sceptre of office, a thin bejewelled cane that concealed a deadly electrified spike. In his left, he held an equally bejewelled paper sick bag, already half full. Light speed travel didn't agree with the poor boy.

He looked at the bag, considering a top-up, but noticed his wrist chronograph that showed him the date. This reminded him of how urgent his quest was.

A uniformed navigator stepped up. He looked nervous as he eyed the sceptre.

'My Lord! We've arrived at the Profania system. The

planet we seek is ahead, just past Haulysheet. There…' He indicated the small blue one out of the window.

'Excellent. How long will it take us to arrive?' asked Kelvin.

'Well, once we plot a course around this planet, we should…'

'Go through it, idiot! Let nothing stand in our way!' Kelvin was getting power-tipsy.

The navigator gulped, expecting to be zapped at any moment.

'Through it, my lord?' he stammered.

'Yes! Blow it away! Open fire!' yelled Kelvin, pointing dramatically at the blue unsuspecting globe.

'At once, my lord!' The soldier saluted and turned to leave.

'One more thing—' added Kelvin quietly.

'Yes, my lord?' said the soldier, preparing for disintegration.

Kelvin handed him the puke sack.

'Take this away will you? There's a good chap.'

Outside, the people of the planet Haulysheet had picked up the approaching intruder, and panic set in. But it was far too late. The Furious Anger lived up to its name, sending a salvo of trillion megawatt laser pulses into it.

The last collective words from the people of Haulysheet were the name of their planet.

The battle cruiser moved on, gliding effortlessly through the maelstrom of debris and newly-created asteroids.

Jeff lay on the dusty ground, breathlessly looking up at

the huge Yob standing over him. The Yob grunted in disgust and raised his club. It was all over.

It was all over for the Yob, as a small orange Hoppa flew through the air, and hit the man-mountain smack in the temple.

The Yob lost consciousness immediately and hit the dirt like a wardrobe full of bricks, and laid there motionless and silent, save for a small escape of bodily gases.

'Leave human alone, big stinky!' said Pon-Pon in defiance.

Jeff sat up and saw the little Hoppa balancing proudly on the fallen Goliath's chest. With renewed vigour, he swept his little friend into his arm and rejoined the fight.

Ray was standing beside the tall tree, and had also dismounted. The remaining Hoppas kept the last few Yobs at bay easily, while Ray looked for a way to get the remote from the highest bough. No amount of shaking or vibration would dislodge it. There had to be another way.

He looked across the square and saw Jeff racing towards him, club in one hand and Pon-Pon under his arm.

'Over here, Jeff!' he yelled over the cacophony of shouts, bounce-thumps and battle cries.

Jeff looked up at the tree.

'It's massive!' he shouted. 'We can't reach that! We'll have to cut it down somehow!'

Ray waved his hands, shaking his head.

'No! We can't risk it! If the remote gets damaged, it's useless! Besides,' he added sheepishly, 'nobody thought to bring a saw.'

Jeff quickly looked up again at the top of the tree. Then he crouched, putting Pon-Pon down on the ground.

'Alright, little 'un, you've saved me. Now it's your turn to save us all. Round up the rest and bring them back here.'

The little Hoppa bounced off eagerly. Ray looked confusedly at his friend.

'What can she possibly do?' he asked.

'Leave it to me. Let's get back to twatting these twats first!'

He ran over to the nearest Yob, who was engrossed in battling an older Hoppa, and smacked him as hard as he could on the back of his ape-like noggin. The Yob spun round, half-dazed, and Jeff followed it up with a penalty kick of astonishing force right between his legs. A pitiful high-pitched yelp from the Yob told Jeff that he'd hit the jackpot. The thug crashed to the ground so fast, that Jeff had to dive to one side to avoid being crushed by the massive frame.

Ray was also getting into the fighting spirit. He'd found two clubs, each with leather straps on the end, and he quickly tied them together, forming an over-sized pair of nunchaku. Ray moved off into the battling hordes, swinging his new weapon of choice into any Yob skull that he came across.

It was a good ten minutes before the battle died down. The remaining Yobs had decided that enough was enough, and began to gallop away as fast as their thick and stumpy legs could carry them. Jeff and Ray stood among a sea of bodies, mostly Yobs. It pleased Jeff to see that there were few Hoppa fatalities. Most were unconscious, but occasionally, the terrible sight of battered and lifeless bodies, both Yob and Hoppa, greeted his eyes.

At the tree, Ray called Jeff back. The Hoppas had congregated around the base of the tree, and Ray was trying to organise them into a sort of cone arrangement, so that one of them could get to the top of the tree.

'That's it... steady now,' said Ray, trotting from side to side, trying to keep the formation in place with words of encouragement. But soon, the very nature of the Hoppas' anatomical construction meant that the structure was never going to be solid enough to support its own weight. The lower Hoppas began to compress and squash, and the Hoppas on top wobbled and tumbled down.

Ray looked at the collapsed pile and tutted.

'This'll never do, come on – let's try again!' he called.

'No, forget that,' Jeff chipped in. 'It'll never stay solid enough, and anyway, there aren't enough Hoppas to get even halfway up there!'

'Hmm, you might be right. What do you suggest?' asked Ray in near-total befuddlement.

'Watch.'

Jeff arranged the Hoppas in a long line running from the base of the tree to as far back as they would go. Ray looked on, a blend of amusement and pride crossing his face as he watched this particularly normal human find a solution to an almost impossible problem.

'Alrighty, then!' Jeff beckoned over to the little Hoppa who'd previously saved his life.

'You ready, Pon-Pon?' he asked.

The Hoppa nodded.

'Me ready. Fly like bird, save all!'

Jeff led Pon-Pon along the lined up villagers, and as he passed each one, he instructed them to start bouncing up and down on the spot. Soon the entire line was like an undulating orange snake, again accompanied by a thundering beat. Jeff and the brave little Hoppa got to the end of the line. Pon-Pon took a deep breath.

'OK!' Jeff shouted above the noise. 'Once you've done your bit, get around to the other side as quick as you can!'

Ray took a few steps back. He still had no idea what this crazy plan was, but he imagined it might involve him getting pummelled to paste if he wasn't careful. And in all honesty, he was right.

Pon-Pon leapt into a long bounce, landing on the end Hoppa. The timing was perfect – the two Hoppas compressed at exactly the same moment, and the resultant bounce was double the height of the first one. She came down again, but further along the line, where another Hoppa caught her, and sprung her up even higher.

The Hoppas at the end of the line furthest away from the tree, quickly hopped around to the other side, and watched intently, as Pon-Pon continued to gain altitude every time she landed on another in the line.

Jeff stuffed a knuckle in his mouth in tense concentration, mumbling, 'Come on… Come on, you can do it!'

Pon-Pon was halfway along the line, and already she was bouncing over half the height of the tree. All the now-redundant Hoppas had gathered near Ray, and watched.

This was it. The final bounce. There would be no room for error.

Suddenly, Jeff realised that the last Hoppa in line was the chief – the oldest one from the village. The momentum wouldn't be enough, and it might even kill the old chap. Jeff called over to a group of three of the biggest Hoppas he could find and directed them over to the chief.

Pon-Pon was making her penultimate descent.

With milliseconds to spare, the three larger Hoppas bounded in, knocking chief Fnar-Fnut out of harm's way, and took his place, knotting themselves together by their antennae. Pon-Pon came down fast, and with a loud smack, she bounced up again, higher than the tree itself. It was an astonishing sight.

Travelling through the air, hundreds of feet above the ground, the little Hoppa gasped. No other Hoppa had done what she had, and she was rewarded with a breathtaking view of her land. From the twinkling golden castles of the Slargs, far off near the horizon, to the Hoppa village just past the mountain range – it was awe-inspiring. The wind whistled past her and even a bird flew by, with a rather confused look on its beak.

For just one brief moment, she was one with the gods.

Looking across to her village, she saw the cemetery, in its solitaire-board arrangement. Pon-Pon picked out the stone that served as a memorial to her mother and smiled. 'For you, Mother,' she whispered.

She flew over the top of the tree at the apex of her leap, and she could see the Universal Remote sitting in a bough beneath her. Gritting her teeth, she curled up as best she could, and turned a somersault, which allowed her antennae to grasp the metallic remote as they passed it.

Down on the ground, the rest of the Hoppas had arranged themselves into a crash landing pad. Jeff and Ray clung to each other as if their lives depended on it, both with tears in their unblinking eyes.

Pon-Pon came down like a meteorite, still clutching the lozenge shaped remote control.

But something went wrong. In this unique case, what comes down must go up, and she hit the group of villagers as planned, dropping the remote. But then she rebounded up again, flying way past the huddled group.

Jeff and Ray gasped in terror as they watched Pon-Pon crash into the ground hard and skitter off across the rocky surface, rolling and half-bouncing until her little body ground to a stop. Everyone raced over to the fallen Hoppa, and gathered around, looking in with grave concern. Jeff pushed through to get to her. He knelt at the little one's side.

There was no sign of life. Little Pon-Pon had suffered terrible damage upon landing, and her body and face were marked with numerous cuts and grazes, each one leaking clear orange blood. More awful was the fact that she was half-deflated, which was never a good sign for a Hoppa.

The crowd saw this and a sigh of sympathy rang out. Some of the Hoppas began to weep. This little orphan had become the greatest of all Hoppas in her short life, and would no doubt be honoured as such.

Jeff sniffed, wiping his eyes with the back of his hand. He gently cradled the little one in his arms and stood up. He looked around the scene, and was surprised to realise that it was probably the saddest event he'd ever witnessed. The Hoppas hung their antennae in sadness as he spoke.

'I'm responsible for this. It was too much to expect from a young child. I only hope that you can forgive me, and honour the memory of Pon-Pon here, because she's saved not only me and Ray, but your village and your way of life. Remember her forever. Get your biggest stone and place it with her family.'

Ray's bottom lip twitched uncontrollably.

The Hoppas looked down at the ground, in an unspoken minutes' silence. All that could be heard was the desert winds howling around the mountains.

Then there was a gentle hiss. Jeff looked down at the child in his arms and saw that Pon-Pon was re-inflating! He looked on in astonishment, as the little one's eyes flickered open.

'No... stone for Pon-Pon yet,' gasped the child weakly. 'Me want to celebrate victory.'

Jeff whooped in joy as the Hoppas all realised that their little hero was still alive. Ray threw his head back and wailed loudly, the emotional rollercoaster becoming too much for him.

The group moved off, heading back to their village. It was going to be a great celebration.

About an hour or so later, a huge shadow moved over the devastated Yob village. Hundreds of feet up in the sky, the terrible shape of the Furious Anger moved in, like some evil vulture, circling for scraps.

'Bugger!' screamed Kelvin. 'We're late! Heads will roll for this!'

And roll they did.

The following morning, after the joyous party, Jeff and Ray stood at the edge of the Hoppa village, preparing to return with the Universal Remote to the kingdom of the Slargs.

The eldest Hoppa handed Ray the remote, and Ray accepted it carefully, looking at the strange and revered object. It was a flattened, torpedo-shaped thing, pretty much resembling a remote control as one would expect, except that it was larger and had only a small number of golden buttons. It definitely looked alien, at least other-worldly construction.

Jeff regarded the object.

'Well, now we have it, what does it do?' he asked.

The old Hoppa looked serious. Or at least as serious as an orange, bouncing pear-shaped thing with antennae could look.

'Remote fixes things. Changes. Alters. Very powerful and very dangerous. Only old-young-old ones to use it. Please deliver safe.'

Jeff nodded, not quite understanding the old chap. Ray put the remote into a small shoulder-bag that he had been given. It looked like a ladies' handbag, but he had no other options.

'OK then,' said Ray, stretching his arms out in preparation for the trek back to the distant city, 'time we went, I suppose. Thanks for everything, old chap.'

He patted the Hoppa on his head and began to walk. Jeff didn't.

'Come on, Jeff,' said Ray, slightly confused.

'Not yet. Look,' answered Jeff, pointing to a number of approaching Hoppas.

From the village huts, the rest of the villagers emerged. At the front of the group were the three big Hoppas that helped in Pon-Pon's giant leap, and they carried a crude hammock-cum stretcher, inside which sat their little hero.

Pon-Pon still looked a little weak and battered, but she was smiling and on the road to recovery. The Hoppas reached the humans and raised the hammock up so that

Pon-Pon could address them.

'Thank you, humans,' she began, 'Hoppas safe from Yobs now. Never attack again.'

Jeff shook his head.

'No, you guys have saved us. And hopefully now you'll have a real future for once.'

He looked at the other villagers around him.

'You've got Pon-Pon to thank for this freedom, never forget that.'

Pon-Pon beamed at Jeff.

'They know. Me village chief... er... When me grow up.'

Jeff smiled.

'And a great choice too, little 'un.' he kissed Pon-Pon on the forehead and set her gently back down into the hammock.

'Come back soon! Don't forget Hoppas!' said Pon-Pon.

Jeff nodded.

'We will. See you soon, all of you,' he replied. In the back of his mind was one unsolved problem. The Slargs had also been guilty of persecuting and slaughtering the Hoppas. How were they going to be safe from them?

The Hoppas watched as Jeff walked off. He turned and waved, and then caught up with Ray. A few steps later, they were both cheered up to hear a rhythmic rumbling of the Hoppas bouncing up and down on the spot, as if applauding their new friends.

chapter seven

In and Out Quickly

The tall towers of the Slarg castle loomed over the desert plain. A pretty yet muscular lookout, in her golden armour, noticed two dusty, bedraggled figures trudging into view.

'Inform Her Majesty! The men have returned!' she called, grabbing a long golden bugle-trumpet. She blew a mighty blast, which echoed out all around the kingdom.

Inside the throne room, Queen Shelley, wigless and semi-dressed, was receiving a massage, manicure and pedicure simultaneously from her aides, when she heard the siren.

She got up, dismissed her servants and strode over towards the nearest window, grabbing a red flowing wig on the way. The report was true. She was impressed to see the small dusty figures of Jeff and Ray approaching the city walls. They were alive, and more importantly, carrying a handbag, which could only mean that they had succeeded in their task. The Universal Remote was finally in her grasp! She allowed herself a smug grin.

'Oi! Open the bleedin' gates!' she called.

The city gates slowly rumbled open, allowing Ray and Jeff to enter. They were dusty, tired and bruised from their battle, but their spirits were high. Unfortunately for them, they'd still not been able to think of a way to escape from the Slargs and their domineering headcase of a queen, despite having been talking about it for hours during the trip.

Jeff pointed over to the landing platforms, upon which stood the Slarg ships and among them, the Marshmallow Penguin. Both men sighed in despair.

'We've got to get to her somehow,' said Jeff.

'Oh, it's hopeless, Jeff. Let's face it!' whined Ray.

'Will you please stop saying that?' retorted Jeff. 'Whatever happened to, "Improvise until something miraculaculus happens"?'

Ray looked weary.

'Oh, I dunno any more. I'm never going to get home, am I? We've used up all our miracles I think,' he continued sorrowfully.

'Well, try and think of something, alright?' said Jeff desperately. He noticed the guards beginning to pour out of the palace and head their way.

'Here comes the welcoming committee.'

The metal-plated amazons formed two lines, between which Jeff and Ray walked. At the end of the lines stood the queen. Regal, centred and mouth-wateringly attractive in her best red satin dress, she faced the travellers. Jeff noted that she was wearing sparkling ruby lipstick to match her glittering locks. He grinned a little, and nudged Ray with his elbow.

'Now there's a sight for sore eyes, eh?'

'Yes. Lovely,' replied Ray, coldly.

Jeff remembered something suddenly. 'Are you erm… not into women, Ray?'

Ray raised an eyebrow. 'What do you mean?'

'Well, doesn't she turn you on, at all?' asked Jeff, nodding in the direction of the queen.

'Well, let me see; she's a bald, aggressive, evil tyrant, completely psychotic, and a cannibal to boot. Forgive me for being a little frigid, but no, she doesn't do anything for me.'

Jeff raised his eyebrows. 'So you're not gay then?'

'No, Jeff. I just don't like the idea of fantasising over my executioner, that's all. You must be suffering from "Stockholm Syndrome".'

Jeff was a little put out by his tone.

'Suit yourself. Least I'm gonna die with a smile on my face.'

He thought for a second.

'And I've never been to Stockholm anyway, so it can't be that.'

The queen greeted the two men with a big smile. But the smile looked insincere, almost sinister. It was the kind of smile one sees on air hostesses and speed cops.

'Ello, me old muckers!' said Shelley, ''Ows' it goin'?' she continued, looking both of them up and down.

Jeff spoke first.

'Not bad, your Fine-ness. Well, we both nearly died, but nothing too heavy, y'know?'

He was surprised to hear the amount of sarcasm in his tone. But he put it down to stress.

Queen Shelley was also a little surprised.

'Never mind, eh? Yer back now, ain't'cha? 'Ave you got a little pressie for me, then?'

Ray pulled the handbag off his shoulder and held it out.

'Yes. Here you are. The Universal Remote. It's all yours. Can we go free now, like you promised?'

Shelley shot an arm out, making Jeff flinch wildly. She took the handbag with greed in her eyes, and rummaged around for the object of her desires. Her face lit up with satisfaction and a certain amount of maniacal pleasure.

'Not until I test it, Scump!'

Ray looked at Jeff and Jeff looked back at him. They seemed to be doomed all over again.

'Oi! Guards!' called the queen. 'Take these two inside. Clean 'em up and send 'em back to me in an hour! Off ya go!'

The guards did as they were instructed, and just like before, Ray and Jeff were pushed, cajoled and prodded all the way until they were back inside the castle.

Queen Shelley walked back to her quarters, carefully holding the remote. She stared at it, thinking of all the things she could do now, trying to come to terms with the fact that she was now the most powerful being in the entire universe.

Except perhaps, for Bod.

Underneath the throne room, Jeff and Ray were treated rather well this time around. They still had to undergo the repeated humiliation of the anti-parasite strobe rays, but they were both relieved and surprised to be presented with their own original Earth clothing. It was in fact, a set of sophisticated copies, generated from the royal tailor's fabric-fabricator, but for Jeff especially, to be back in jeans, trainers and a t-shirt was a warm feeling that only served to convince him that their freedom was assured.

The royal chef whipped up a couple of plates of food, but both Jeff and Ray declined to eat Hoppa steaks, and settled for green salads instead. The chef was none too pleased.

As they sat at the wooden table to eat, Jeff tried to cheer Ray up, which was no mean feat, as Ray had descended into another silent mope, which generally meant that things, in his estimation anyway, were hopeless yet again. Jeff too considered the possibility of being double-crossed by the queen and wondered how they could retrieve the remote, escape the queen, return to their ship and escape the Profanian authorities. But hope springs eternal, as they say, and Jeff was just trying to remain optimistic, until hope decided to spring something opportunistic onto them at the right time.

After dinner, Jeff and Ray were escorted back outside. They realised that they were being shown the way to the landing platform where they first arrived.

'See?' said Jeff excitedly, 'she's keeping her end of the bargain! We're being set free!'

Ray was still suspicious.

'Don't count your chickens, Jeff. This mental monarch still holds a major grudge against my father, and by extension, me. And by extension, you too.'

Clearly, Ray was the realist in this situation.

At the end of the thin platform sat their furry little spacecraft, the Marshmallow Penguin. Ray, despite his sour outlook, was pleased to see her looking undamaged. Maybe Jeff's optimism was justified?

Standing at the front end of the ship was Queen Shelley and a handful of guards. She had changed once again, this time into a figure-hugging silver plastic catsuit which gleamed in the sunlight, topped off with a wig of straight golden hair. It was a truly awe-inspiring outfit, (if a little seventies roller-disco), and it reminded Jeff of his strangely compelling dream about the chrome robo-babe.

Jeff and Ray approached her, each with a belly-full of trepidation, unsure of whether this meant freedom or death.

''Ello lads!' called Shelley, smiling one of those, 'I-know-something-you-don't-know' kind of smiles.

Jeff thought he'd better start the conversation off on the right foot.

'Wotcha, babe!'

The right foot was obviously in his mouth.

The queen dropped her smile like it was made of lead. She grabbed a golden staff from one of her guards, and jabbed it into Jeff's ribs. He yelled out in pain as a few hundred volts zapped through him instantaneously. He fell to the floor like an un-strung marionette.

Shelley walked up to Jeff, and without a sound, grabbed him by his left ear, which made him squeal in pain. Pulling him close, but without loosening her grip, she snarled.

'Nobody – but NOBODY calls me "babe"!' She spat the last word out.

'But on the other 'and, you did 'elp me out in a big way, so fanks muchly for that, Jeffrey boy!'

Ray looked over to Jeff.

'Oh well done, that man,' he muttered, accompanied by a metric tonne of sarcasm.

Shelley let go of Jeff's ear and left him whimpering on the ground.

She walked back over to her guard, who retrieved the electro-prod-staff, and handed her what looked like a pink handbag.

Opening the bag, she pulled out the Universal Remote. Jeff and Ray could only look on in semi-curiosity as she examined it.

'Right then!' began the towering amazon, 'fanks to the success of your mission, I'm gonna show you what this fing does... and why it's just made me the most powerful bird in the 'ole bleedin' universe!'

She'd prepared the speech earlier.

Ray felt he had to at least try and reason with the power-mad ruler. He stepped forward gingerly.

'Your majesty, I thought we had a deal? You know, we get you the remote, and in return we get our freedom?'

He was surprised to see that the queen had allowed him to talk without interruption, and she seemed to have a pleasant, patient smile on her face as he did so.

'You're an intelligent woman,' he patronised, making open-handed gestures to accentuate his vulnerability, 'And after all, you have the Universal Remote – what more could you possibly want from us?'

Ray had stopped pacing and gesticulating. He realised that he'd run out of paces and gesticulations. Still the queen looked uncharacteristically smiley.

Then she quickly clouted him on the head with the remote, which Ray had to admit hurt. Quite a lot.

While the lump was forming on his forehead, Ray thought it best to retreat. He shuffled backwards, still curled in a hunchback-like, semi-bowing position. Jeff put a defensive arm around his friend's crouched shoulders.

'He's got a point, you know!' spat Jeff in defiance, 'What else do you need us for?'

Shelley raised a thin eyebrow at the tone. This weed of a man, who first stood before her tremulous and fidgety, was now imbued with a new strength. A new spirit. She liked it.

It was a pity she'd have to kill him.

'You've both got a point, mate,' she replied, 'I don't need yer, either of yer. But I do have a little matter of revenge to sort out. And seeing as ole Scumpy 'ere hasn't got a lot of hair to lose now, I think I might as well vaporise both of yer and yer poxy little spaceship!'

Jeff and Ray gasped. This, surely had to be the end of the road. After all, the queen had the power to rearrange the atoms of the universe in the palm of her hand. Instinctively they stepped backwards, gritting their teeth as the mad monarch pointed the metallic controller directly at them. She pushed one of the buttons, grinning horribly.

There was a click from the remote. A low, almost distant rumble. Then, like a sudden total eclipse of the sun, it went dark.

Up above the landing platform, from out of the clouds, the Furious Anger descended, vibrating the air, the ground and the teeth of everyone below.

Jeff looked up. Was this supposed to be happening?

Then he looked at the queen – she was stabbing the buttons on the remote madly, screaming in anger. It hadn't worked at all. But whether it was providence or something 'miraculaculus', it was an opportunity, if nothing else.

Grabbing Ray by the shoulder, Jeff raced toward the queen and their spaceship. At that moment, the huge scarlet battleship above them opened fire on the palace, its bright blue beams sizzling into the stone towers with ease. Debris and fire rained down onto the platform, punching huge dents into the concrete. The queen's guards scattered in every direction, leaving their leader like rats leaving the proverbial sinking ship.

Ray ran over to the Marshmallow Penguin's side hatch and wrenched it open with both hands. He looked around, and saw Jeff racing over to the insane-with-rage queen, looking like he was going to do something stupid, like rugby tackle her.

Jeff rugby tackled her.

The queen yelled out in frustration and shock as Jeff's shoulder ploughed into her waist and knocked her off her feet. The Universal Remote flew out of her hand and skittered off across the platform.

Up above, the underbelly of the battle cruiser opened up a number of sliding doors and ominous, red armour-clad commandos abseiled down, blasting everything in sight. Some of the Slarg guards joined the battle, firing back with their pulse rifles and throwing gold-plated spears.

In the midst of the chaos, Jeff struggled and grappled with the queen. He'd managed to climb onto her and hold her wrists for a brief moment, knowing that her impressive physical strength would soon kick in, and he'd be pummelled into the ground. If there was any ground left, that is – it was beginning to fracture and split like an ice floe, and as he looked to his right, he could see the Penguin beginning to bounce and shake, with Ray hanging onto the door handle with all his strength.

Jeff saw the enraged expression on the queen's face. He was about to get hurt. Really, really badly. So, taking a deep breath, he stuffed his mouth onto hers and kissed her as hard and as passionately as he possibly could.

Two seconds of confusion later, Jeff pulled away.

The kiss had served its purpose – the queen was dazed, confused and momentarily weakened. She even sighed a little sigh.

'Gotta go, babe. Sorry!' said Jeff. He flung his arm out to grab one of the cattle-prod sticks near him, and jabbed it into her side, pressing the discharge button as hard as he could. Shelley shook and convulsed, trying to yell out, but in a second, she was unconscious. Out cold, she flopped limply.

'Come on, Casanova!' screamed Ray. 'We really have to go!'

Jeff jumped to his feet, scooping up the Universal Remote as he made for the spaceship's entrance. He dived in head first and rolled inside. Ray raced to the cockpit, punching controls to start the launch sequence without sitting down.

Jeff pulled the hatch shut and the Marshmallow Penguin lifted off. It spun about and whizzed off the platform like a rat out of a drainpipe.

Aboard the Furious Anger, Overlord Kelvin noticed the escaping ship.

'Nobody leaves!' he commanded. 'Get them!'

A gunner at the front of the ship swung a pair of evil-looking gun barrels around until they pointed at the ever-accelerating little ship.

'Fire!' yelled Kelvin, clasping his hands together

under his chin. The guns blazed, propelling two superheated balls of plasmic energy across the sky. One missed, but the other found its target, exploding across the stern of Ray's little craft, burning a hole through the outer layer of keratin, and shorting out one of the propulsion systems.

'What the hell? We've been hit!' yelled Jeff in terror.

Ray had strapped himself in and was busy trying to pull the ship out of a spin and back into space.

'I know!' he replied, equally terrified, 'It'll hold for now! Just get strapped in!'

Jeff did as he was told.

At that moment, the Furious Anger was set upon by a fleet of Profanian fighter craft that had scrambled into attack. They provided a welcome distraction, and it was just what Ray needed to make a break.

'Hasto La Bisto, gravy!' yelled Ray, as he gunned his ship's damaged engines into overdrive.

The hairship pointed toward open space, and with a little bit of luck, and a little prayer to Bod, it sped out into the stars and with it, safety, obscurity.

chapter eight

Metal and Mental

Whizzing through the stars as fast as their damaged little craft could go, Jeff and Ray took stock of their current situation.

Jeff studied the Universal Remote. How such a small and simple object could make someone incredibly powerful and cause so much trouble at the same time was beyond him. Then again, the workings of a digital watch were beyond him too. He scratched his head and looked at his friend.

'Who made this thing, Ray?'

Ray was looking intensely at the controls in front of him, trying to work out what the extent of the damage was. He answered without looking up.

'Nobody knows really. Well, the old legend says that a race called the Methuselans were the keepers of it. They're the oldest race in the universe. Immortals, basically.'

He rubbed his beard as he tried different combinations of switches.

'It's been said that when the universe was first created,

it wasn't working perfectly. Well, the major things – planets, stars, et cetera were, but the minutiae needed tweaking. So someone – the "creator", if you subscribe to that theory – put together a tool that would fix certain things at a smaller level.'

'Ah,' said Jeff, trying to make the information fit into his already overcrowded brain.

'So, this, er, tool then, it's got the power to remake things? How does it work? Do you have to choose the settings or something?'

Ray stopped testing the controls and looked up. He held out a hand and Jeff placed the remote into his palm.

Ray pointed to the gold button on the remote.

'I think,' he said, 'that this is the main alteration control. Well, OK, I'm guessing, but this one does look like the most important one, wouldn't you say?' He turned the lozenge shape around, looking at it closely.

'I wouldn't go messing with it though, Jeff. Just in case.'

Jeff shrugged.

'But when the queen tried to zap us both, nothing happened. Why would that...?'

'Eureka!' interrupted Ray. 'I'll tell you why. Look!'

He showed Jeff the underside of the remote. Flicking a small catch, a section of the body slid open, revealing a small compartment about the size of a matchbox. From inside it, a square rusted lump fell out onto the floor. Jeff and Ray looked at each other and in unison, exclaimed:

'Dead batteries!'

They laughed. Something that simple had saved their necks, and the queen of the Slargs wasn't even bright enough to check if the thing had a battery in it.

'So it's useless, then?' asked Jeff.

'For now, yes. Safe at least,' said Ray, 'but we're not. The Penguin took a hit just now, and I don't think we've got the power to get to either the Methuselans or Kangazang.'

Jeff frowned. 'Oh.'

'Oh indeed,' continued Ray, 'apart from that, what about those soldiers in the red battleship that attacked the queen's palace? It wasn't on our side either. I'm betting they're still after us too, whoever they are.'

'Oh,' repeated Jeff. He chose to elaborate: 'Oh bugger. What's the plan then?'

Ray put the remote down safely and touched the windscreen of the ship. It illuminated, projecting a map of the nearby star systems onto the glass.

'This might be handy,' said Ray, enlarging a square section of the map. Jeff leaned in closer to see exactly what he was talking about.

'Repairs. I think we can get the damage sorted out here. It's called Orbitron,' said Ray.

Jeff cocked his head at a quizzical angle.

'Orbitron? Well, if you say so, but if this place turns out to be as hostile as the last planet, you can count me out. I'll stay in the ship, mate.'

'It'll be fine, Jeff. Trust me,' offered Ray. Jeff screwed his face up a bit. Ray reconsidered his statement.

'Don't trust me then. But we're not going to get any trouble from Orbots. They're programmed to help out.'

Jeff's face unscrewed and his eyes widened.

'Orbots? You mean this place has robots on it? Walking, talking ones?'

'Some of them, yes. Orbitron isn't technically a real

planet. It's home to the biggest race of artificial lifeforms in the galaxy. And they prefer to call themselves "Orbots", not robots.'

'We're going to get captured, interrogated and probably killed again, aren't we?' Jeff sighed despondently.

'Will you relax?' said Ray, trying to keep the mood light. 'It's just repairs. A little tech support and we'll be off in no time, honestly.'

Jeff slumped back into his seat, clearly downhearted. Ray noticed his mood and suddenly thought of a way to conserve power and cheer his friend up at the same time.

'Zero-G?' he smiled.

Jeff raised an eyebrow.

'Yeah, go on then!' He unbuckled his seatbelt and made for the gravity control switch.

The Marshmallow Penguin sailed off in the direction of Orbitron with whoops and yells coming from its interior.

The surface of Orbitron gleamed. It was a million differing shades of reflective chrome, brushed silver and plastic, from clear perspex to flawless white polypropylene that could easily be mistaken for porcelain.

The sky was always cloudless and pitch black, speckled with stars, as it had no atmosphere system, no clouds and no polar ice caps. It was an artificially constructed planetoid, but in order to accommodate visitors, the Orbots had placed their world inside an 'Atmo-Sphere' – a massive plasti-glass sphere that could be filled up with oxygen or any other gas that would allow their organic guests to breathe freely.

Dotted all over the relatively flat plain were hemispherical dwellings, like igloos in a variety of different sizes. Roads and paths were perfectly straight and corners were always an exact ninety degrees.

A scream echoed out into the Atmo-Sphere from one of the dwellings.

Inside, a tall man-shaped Orbot called M4 jumped up from his chair and went into the front section of the domestic dome. His resident partner, a pretty female-designated Orbot named M25 was standing up against the wall, shaking visibly, and pointing to the other side of the room, where a tiny hexagonal nut lay on the ground.

'Twenty?' asked M4. 'What is it now?'

M25 pointed again at the innocent fixing on the floor.

'What's that? I've never seen it there before? Make it go away! Please!' she wailed.

M4's facial expression modules slid into a configuration resembling a smile.

'Don't be silly, Twenty. It's a hex nut. You have lots of them. So do I.'

M25 looked up at her companion.

'I know! But I've never seen one on its own before – where did it come from? What does it want? Why is it looking at me like that?' She trembled as if it were a poisonous snake of some sort.

M4 just picked it up and approached her. Calmly putting a gentle hand on her shoulder, he tried to placate her.

'Look – it's fine. It's just a hex nut. See? Nothing to be afraid of.'

M25 tentatively poked the nut with a slim plastic finger. She looked at M4 and smiled in relief.

'Thank you, Four. I don't know what came over me. Nuts.'

M4 sniggered childishly.

'Yes, you are.'

He walked over to the window and saw a small spaceship hovering up above the Atmo-Sphere. Then he fell over backwards, howling with laughter.

'Look at that stupid hairy spaceship! I've never seen such a pathetic thing!' he giggled. 'It looks like a ball of iron filings!'

As he rolled on the floor laughing, M25 walked to the door.

'Come on, Four, it's waiting to land. Time to go to work.'

M4 calmed down sufficiently enough to get back to his feet. He allowed himself another short chuckle.

'Ball of filings... hee hee! Priceless!'

The Atmo-Sphere opened one of its triangular sections, and Ray's ship lowered itself down through the aperture. Once landed, the Atmo-Sphere filled with an oxygen-nitrogen mix that matched the air inside the spaceship, and green lights positioned around the landing pad signalled that the air was breathable.

The hatch opened and Ray stepped out. He took a deep breath and looked around.

'Coast is clear, Jeff! You can come out,' he called.

Jeff insisted on remaining inside until he was sure that nobody wanted to eat him, mate with him or abuse him in any way.

After a few minutes and repeated assurances from Ray, Jeff decided that it seemed safe enough to venture out, so he followed Ray down the steps and onto the surface of Orbitron. It was a strange feeling, like walking on a polished marble floor. There was no wind, nor was there any discernible smell. It was clinically clean and sterile. But it was comfortably warm, and all around there was a low hum of millions of computer systems underneath his feet.

From over to the right, Jeff could see one of the domed houses, its front door sliding open and two shiny figures emerging.

'Ah! Here comes our tech support!' beamed Ray, waving to the two metallic figures in the distance.

Jeff looked around at the strikingly conformist architecture.

'I don't suppose there are any pubs here?' he asked, remembering how much he missed a pint.

'Afraid not, Jeff,' replied Ray, 'but it won't be long before we get back on course.'

Jeff could only sigh.

The two robots arrived. Jeff looked at them in awe. He had difficulty accepting that these were real robots and not people in costumes. Their movements were smooth and lifelike, not the jerky, body-popping movements of 80s robot dancers. The one that looked like a man was a strange plastic-limbed figure, something like a marionette, but it walked with elegance and a kind of half-grin on his face-plate. More interesting than that was the female-shaped one. She looked a little nervous and wide-eyed, but she was so good looking that it made Jeff feel a little embarrassed to look at her. After all, in his mind, she was little more than a toaster. A washing machine. A million light-years away from totty. How dare she be so attractive?

Then he remembered his dream and the poster that he had on the bedroom wall in his teens. Again, it made him feel a little strange. After all, he'd never previously had a fetish for inanimate objects before. Although there was his first car – a lime green Ford Capri. He loved her as much as any woman. Or at least as much as the law would allow. He decided to introduce himself.

'Hello there! Jeff Spooner!' said Jeff, thrusting his hand out at the curvaceous computer. M25 yelped in terror, and hid behind her counterpart.

'Blimey! She's a little jumpy, isn't she?' asked Jeff.

'Yes. One has to be gentle with Twenty,' said M4. 'She's a little nervous around strangers.'

'Oh, I see,' said Jeff.

'And humans,' added the Orbot.

'Gotcha.'

'And spaceships.'

'Erm, OK then.'

'And me. And food. And stars. And noise. And…'

'Is there anything she isn't scared of?' said Jeff.

'Erm. No, not really, Mr. Spooner,' replied M4. 'But she'll get used to you in a minute.'

Ray stepped in.

'I'm Barbaray, you can call me Ray. We need repairs to our spaceship.' He pointed at the Penguin.

'Could you take a look at her?'

M4 looked at the two men. He grinned. Which Jeff found rather disconcerting.

'Of course, Mr. Ray,' said M4, 'I'm designated M4, and this is M25. We'll be happy to…'

He was looking over at the Marshmallow Penguin.

‘Er… happy to…’ he smirked.

‘I’m sorry, Mr. Ray,’ he said, holding a hand over his mouth, ‘it’s just that…’ He began to chuckle.

‘Is that your spacecraft?’ he asked, beginning to shake.

‘Yes. Yes, it is… Why?’ replied Ray, eyeing the twitching android with suspicion.

M4 couldn’t hold it in any longer. He burst out laughing. All Jeff and Ray could do was to look on in total puzzlement. They’d never seen an artificial being laugh so heartily, and it felt slightly offensive. Jeff had never seen an artificial being at all in his life, let alone one that took the mickey out of him.

‘Look,’ said Ray, trying to muster some dignity, ‘I know she’s not much…’ he continued. But M4 was already on his knees, pointing at the ship and clutching his waist, which was an odd thing to do as he didn’t have any feeling in his waist at all. Still, the overall impression was that of someone in paroxysms of hysteria.

‘Oh, for God’s sake, pack it in!’ yelled Jeff, getting annoyed by the giggle-fest.

M25 stepped forward.

‘I must apologise for my cohabitant unit, Mr. Spooner. He has a habit of miscomprehending the serious nature of many things.’

Jeff was already aware of this, but the persuasive tone of the female Orbot’s gentle voice synthesiser helped to ease his irritation.

‘That’s alright. He’s only human… oid.’

M4 had used up all the comedy potential in looking at the spacecraft, and returned to his feet.

‘Yes, sorry about that, Mr. Ray. We both have personality defects. This is indicated by the prefix on our casings.’

He pointed to his forehead which, like M25, bore an embossed letter 'M'.

'Malfunction?' asked Ray.

'Yes, that's right,' replied M25, looking a little ashamed.

'Please don't judge us. We are still hard workers despite our minor defects.'

Jeff took M25 by her gleaming white hand.

'It's alright love,' he purred, 'we're all dysfunctional in one way or another…'

M25 smiled. Then she looked down, screamed at the sight of Jeff's hand and ran off. M4 burst out laughing again.

'Bloody nutters,' said Jeff.

Speeding its way through the stars was the Skraggi battle cruiser, Furious Anger, commanded by Overlord Kelvin. They'd wasted enough time on Profania Alpha looking for the Universal Remote and still hadn't captured it. The lengthy interrogations of the Slargs only revealed some basic facts that served to point them in a pretty vague direction.

For example, they discovered that it had been retrieved from the Yob village. They were also aware that it was briefly in the possession of Queen Shelley, and now it had been pilfered right from under her exquisite hooter by two complete oddballs named Barbaray Sprambladack Fasstalon-Scump and some primitive Earthlet named Jeff Spooner. But from there on, there was little else in the way of information.

Kelvin insisted that his astro-spatial navigators plotted a course that visited all the possible locations that the thieves could seek refuge on. Many planets in the immediate area were inhospitable for humans, so they were ruled out. But there were only a handful of planets to visit, and Kelvin was looking forward to a spot of sight-seeing before returning home anyway. He saw it as an impromptu tour of his new domain. Plus, if he didn't get off the damned spaceship soon, he was in real danger of throwing up his internal organs.

Ray took M4 around the Penguin, showing him the damage they'd sustained. Once he'd had a good giggle at the state of the spaceship, the Orbot seemed to be quite a competent mechanic. He ordered replacement parts and began to fit them quickly and efficiently, stopping from time to time to point out something quite trivial which, to him, was hilarious. Ray managed to bite his lip and not clout the smirking droid with a wrench.

Jeff was doing his best to look after M25, who had decided to prepare some food and drinks for organic consumption. After an initial hour of random screams from her, Jeff was surprised to find that he could handle her odd personality.

'That's what the "M" is for, Mr. Spooner,' said M25. Jeff nodded, as a few pieces of the puzzle began to fit together.

'Malfunction. I remember,' said Jeff.

The shapely synthetic servant picked up a tray of perfectly-cooked food and headed for the door. Jeff followed her towards the parked spaceship.

'Can't they fix you then? I mean, with all the technology down below, they just dump you two up here while they get on with life?'

M25 swivelled her head a full hundred-and-eighty-degrees around to speak to Jeff, while her body faced the other way as she walked.

'They have tried to fix us, to no avail. I suppose you're right, Mr. Spooner. But there are more M-class Orbots up here than perfect ones below. We have formed our own community on the surface. Why should two differing species co-habitate, Mr. Spooner? We are clearly defective and, as such, inferior.'

Jeff couldn't help feeling a little deflated at her naivety. To him it felt like racism, apartheid, segregation. But in all walks of life, the rich and the poor stayed apart – from the affluent Slargs to the Neanderthal Yobs back on Profania Alpha. Perhaps it was a universal characteristic of sentient beings. It didn't mean that he had to like it though.

They reached M4 and Ray, who were making a good job of the repairs. Ray welcomed the food and drink.

'Cheers, Twenty!' said Ray, grabbing a tumbler of water.

'My pleasure, Mr Scump' replied M25.

'Four, do you require power or maintenance at this juncture?' she asked her fellow Orbot.

'No thank you, Twenty,' replied M4. He looked at Ray glugging down his drink and began to giggle.

'He's pouring water into his head!'

Jeff suddenly realised that M4 had a point – when seen from a different point of view, almost anything could be seen as humorous. He laughed too. And it felt good to laugh – he hadn't laughed for what seemed like ages.

'Listen, you two,' said Jeff, 'there's something I just realised. Back on my planet, there are two roads called

M4 and M25. Did you know that?'

This started M4 off again. He rocked as his shoulders bounced up and down in amusement.

'Really? That's fantastic! Hey, Twenty – they've named streets after us! We're famous!'

He went off again, laughing heartily.

Jeff waved a hand to try and cut his laughter short.

'Yeah, well, you two need better names. And just because those snobs underground have stamped you with an "M" as a badge of imperfection, doesn't mean you should accept it.'

Ray wondered what he was getting at. This was a more thoughtful side of Jeff.

'What do you suggest, Jeff?' he asked. 'I mean, Bob and Sheila don't exactly fit, do they?'

M4 screamed in hysterics.

'Ha ha! Bob and Sheila! Priceless!' he howled.

'Well, I had a think, and M4 – from now on, you're "Gridlock", and M25 can be "Tailback". How's that?' suggested Jeff with a smile.

M25 repeated the name tentatively.

'Tail-Back. Tailback. Yes. I like it. Thank you, Mr Spooner!' she beamed.

M4 ran an internal logic algorithm. Then he nodded.

'Gridlock! It's funny, but it's good to have a proper name like you, Mr Spooner.'

'And that's another thing – you can forget the "Mister Spooner" nonsense, OK? Call me Jeff, and call him Ray, got it?'

Both Orbots nodded in agreement. For the first time since their Operation Days, they began to feel accepted. Perhaps this would be the start of the new life that they'd dreamed of.

Ray remembered the Universal Remote, and its missing batteries.

'Take a look at this, if you would,' said Ray. He pulled the remote out of his coat pocket and held it out for the Orbots to examine.

With an ear-piercing yelp, the female droid jumped off the ground and into Jeff's arms, where she sat, trembling in fear.

'Steady on, Tailback!' said Jeff.

For the rest of the evening, Jeff and Ray re-stocked their spaceship with fresh supplies of water, food (in dehydrated biscuit form – not to be confused with hair products) and toilet roll. To be more accurate, the Orbots didn't actually have toilet tissue, but they did have a large stock of perforated printout paper, which although a bit coarse to the discerning derriere, it performed its new task adequately enough.

Ray and Gridlock sat indoors, trying to work out the next leg of the trip. They downloaded some up-to-date galactic star charts, and attempted to plot an efficient course to Kangazang via the distant world of Methuselah.

Jeff, as usual, had no idea what they were on about, so he was excluded from the nerdage. This was fortunate for him, as he rather enjoyed being in the company of Tailback. Alright, so she wasn't quite a 'real' human female, but he found it relaxing to be in the company of a woman who didn't hate him. Despite her random phobias popping up unexpectedly, he felt quite protective toward her.

'Is Gridlock your, er, boyfriend then?'

He was embarrassed to admit to himself that he was actually chatting up a machine.

'Gridlock is designated a male unit. He was the first Orbot that I came into contact with when I was reassigned to the surface. Other than that, I do not quite understand your question.'

Jeff tried again.

'Well, obviously you two have lots in common. No, that's not it. Erm, do you have feelings for each other? No. Um…' he trailed off, trying to think of a way to elaborate.

'Do Orbots know what love is?' asked Jeff, deciding to start with the basics.

Tailback turned her head unit at a slight angle, as she momentarily accessed a long-lost data file.

'Love. Biological models of both sexes tend to view love as a mammalian drive, much like hunger or thirst. Leading human experts in the topic of love, divide the experience of love into three partly-overlapping stages: lust, attraction, and attachment. Lust exposes people to others, romantic attraction encourages people to focus their energy on mating, and attachment involves tolerating the spouse long enough to rear a child into infancy. Is that what you mean?'

Jeff blinked.

'I have no idea what you just said, but I think you've got the gist of it.'

Ray sat next to Gridlock, who had detached his right hand at the wrist and plugged it into a network portal on the wall. A large portion of the wall illuminated with the default opening screen of the InfoHEX. Similar in concept to the Internet found on Earth, the Information HyperEXpressway was a million times faster and more efficient than anything else in the galaxy. Mainly because it was run by mechanical beings who had no interest in writing viruses, sharing pictures of other Orbots in the nude, or living pointless virtual lives in role-playing games.

Grid opened up the InfoHEX search site, which was named SpotBot. Most Orbots referred to it whenever they needed information outside their programming. It contained around a googol of data-saturated pages, but to call it 'googol' would've been, for want of a better adjective, silly. Grid thought it was funny anyway.

Grid thought everything was funny.

Grid thought that gruesome injuries on a battlefield were funny, if you recall.

Once they'd downloaded the relevant trajectory and course coordinates for the journey, Ray asked Gridlock to take a look at the Universal Remote.

It took a while for the giggling Orbot to calm down, but soon they were back in business.

It was indeed missing batteries to make it work.

'Unfortunately, Ray,' said Grid, 'there is only one location in the universe where the batteries are manufactured, and that is the planet Methuselah.'

'Methuselah?' said Ray, 'Oh, that's actually fortunate for us! Better that this thing doesn't work at all.'

'In addition, Methuselah is nearer than Kangazang. You can deliver the Remote first,' said Grid.

'Ah! That's good. We need to get rid of this, because I think we're being followed.'

'By the battleship that damaged your – hee hee – Marshmallow Penguin?' asked Grid, snickering as surreptitiously as he could.

'Yes,' said Ray, nodding solemnly.

'Hey – do you think we could identify that ship? Maybe find out who's chasing us?'

Gridlock nodded and opened up a new site, one that enabled anyone to find a particular spacecraft of any sort.

'Describe the ship as best you can,' said Gridlock.

'Well, er, it was big and red. Like a shark,' said Ray, starting with the basics.

Gridlock fell backwards, howling with laughter.

Ray sighed.

'It's going to be a long night.'

He gazed out of the window at the dark starry sky and the two talking shapes outside.

'So,' said Jeff, still on the same subject, but trying a different approach. 'Are you and Gridlock in love with each other?'

He realised that he was back in the familiarity of being completely out of his depth again.

Tailback accessed her internal servers again.

'In sociology, familial love is a type affinity or natural affection felt between members of a group bound by common ancestry or blood ties. The cultural ideal of familial love is one that is committed, unconditional, selfless, emotionally full, and reciprocally returned by the other.'

Jeff shook his head.

'Er… right. Never mind, eh?'

He turned to head back towards the domed enclosure, but Tailback touched his arm.

'Gridlock is not my "Friend-Boy". He is closer in sentiment to my sibling. A brother, perhaps.'

She smiled, which had the strange effect of making Jeff blush like a twelve year-old with a crush.

'Oh. Oh well, that's fine. I just wanted to know what the situation was, that's all,' he mumbled sheepishly.

Tailback pointed a smooth plastic finger at her smooth plastic face.

'Kiss me, Jeff.'

Jeff's heart and brain went into a fierce battle with each other. As such, neither organ was available for comment.

She asked again.

'Kiss me.'

'Er...' said Jeff, trying to stall for time while his brain fought against an internal mutiny.

Tailback took the initiative, and held Jeff by his shoulders. Pulling him closer, she planted a kiss onto his rapidly stuttering lips. Holding him there for a few seconds for effect, she saw his eyes close and his shoulders relax. Then she pulled away.

'I assume you enjoyed that?' she asked.

Jeff had to admit that despite the smooth and cold sensation, he did, and he smiled embarrassedly to acknowledge it. But Tailback didn't alter her blank expression.

'I felt nothing. I'm sorry, but I seem to lack the ability to experience the feeling of love as you know it. I understand the basic concept, and have a familial concern for Gridlock, encompassing—'

'It's alright, I understand. No need for the sermon again,' interrupted Jeff. He realised how ridiculous this whole situation was. But ridiculous situations, as we have seen, are extremely common in this reality, so Jeff was doing rather well, if truth be told.

Tailback could see that she'd made Jeff feel a bit embarrassed.

'My apologies, Jeff. I would like to be in love, the way humans do, but the implementational data just doesn't exist.'

Jeff smiled.

'I know what you mean. Sometimes I think I'm a few files short of a program, too.'

Jeff and Tailback turned around to see Ray and Grid hanging out of the window of the dome, laughing uncontrollably.

The next morning, all was ready. Jeff and Ray stood at the entry hatch of the Penguin, and bade farewell to the Orbots.

'What a great couple of droids,' said Ray as they watched the two robots leave the platform and enter their domed house.

Jeff had to agree.

'Yeah. Y'know what? I bet they're a lot more human, and a lot more fun than their so-called "superiors" underground. Bloody stuck-up cyber-toffs.'

'They'll be alright. I'll miss them. And I daresay you will too, eh?' said Ray, giving Jeff a playful nudge with his elbow.

'Gerroff. She's a nice girl. Er, I mean robot. I mean Orbot,' replied Jeff, a little annoyed and embarrassed simultaneously. 'Anyway, I'm not bothered what you think. She's tons better than Sarah ever was.'

Ray allowed himself a short giggle. Hanging around with Grid had obviously influenced him to see the funny side of things.

They went to the cockpit area and strapped themselves in. Ray made some pre-flight checks, and opened the intercom channel.

'Orbitron Repair Station, this is the Marshmallow Penguin, ready for take off. Do you read me?'

There was no answer. Ray reiterated his request.

'Orbitron Repair Station, this is the Marshmallow Penguin. Do you read me?'

Still no answer.

'I'll try another channel,' said Ray, switching over. A short static burst signalled that they'd got through to someone.

'Marshmallow Penguin, this is Orbitron Atmo-Sphere Control. Preparing to open in twenty pulses.'

'Thank you, Orbitron Control,' said Ray.

'Wonder what happened to Tail and Grid?' he mused.

chapter nine

The Affluence of Inkohol

Jeff took a final swig of water from a bottle that they'd picked up on Orbitron. Suddenly he realised that he'd still not had a drop of booze since they left Earth. He was beginning to feel all the withdrawal symptoms: his hands were completely shake-free, his breath had no odour, and quite worryingly, common sense seemed to be creeping into his mind. This wouldn't do.

'Ray, I'm sorry to keep on about this, mate,' he began, 'but you promised me a pint somewhere out here. I think we've earned it.'

Ray looked over.

'Yes, and you're completely right. I did promise.'

'So when can we stop for a drink then? Any planets with a pub nearby?' asked Jeff, salivating at the mental image of a cold glass of frothy amber bliss.

'Well, apart from the obvious detriment to your health, Jeff, I do think there are more important issues to deal with at this moment.'

Jeff wasn't impressed.

'You're such a control freak, aren't you? Blimey, Ray

– live a little! Life shouldn't be a journey to the grave with the intention of arriving safely in an attractive, well-preserved body!'

'Really?' asked Ray, eager to hear Jeff's philosophy of life.

'I plan to skid in sideways, Champagne in one hand, strawberries in the other, body thoroughly used up, totally worn out and screaming, "Woohoo! What a ride!"'

So much for deep and meaningful philosophy. Ray took a deep breath.

'Yes, very interesting. Do you want to hear my reasons why neither of us can stop off for a drink right now?'

Jeff folded his arms.

'Go on then. Bet they're rubbish!' he declared.

'Well, for one thing, we're currently carrying the fabled Universal Remote en route to Methuselah, to deliver it to the hands of the only race fit to control such an item of unimaginable power.'

'Right,' replied Jeff. 'That's no reason not to have a drink. Got any more?' he asked defiantly.

'We're being chased by a giant red battleship, belonging to the Empire of Skragg and their Evil Overlord.'

'So you found out who turned up at the palace? They were a great diversion – without them, we might never have escaped from that mental Shelley bird. Why is that a good reason?'

'Because they're right behind us.'

Jeff choked on his tongue.

'Fairy nuff! Get us out of here!'

Not far behind them, the Furious Anger increased to pursuit speed.

Ray set the acceleration to maximum and the Marshmallow Penguin sprinted away like a mechanical hare being chased by a pack of moronic greyhounds.

At the front of the giant Skraggi ship, a large sliding door opened, and two sleek fighter craft, both in the same shade of crimson, emerged, banking and rolling stylishly. The Overlord's best pilots were born for this moment.

Ray, on the other hand, wasn't born for this moment. As far as he knew, he wasn't born for any particular moment, and if he had been, it had most probably passed him by without announcing itself.

The hairy little ship sped on, as Ray tried his best to duck, dodge and weave this way and that, to keep the pursuers from getting a weapon lock on him.

As they got closer, they primed their tractor beams, ready to capture the escaping craft in an unshakable net of molecular energy pulses. After all, their mission was to capture rather than destroy, but Jeff and Ray were not privy to this information, which is why they screamed and yelled as the ship did its best to lose them.

'We're going to die!' yelled Jeff, demonstrating his finely-honed ability to state the painfully obvious.

'I know! What do you want me to do about it?' yelled Ray in answer.

'Avoid it! Stall it! Postpone it if you can!' replied Jeff, gripping his chair so hard that it was beginning to hurt.

'Dammit, Jeff – I'm a barber, not a fighter pilot!' said Ray, attempting another barrel roll.

The fighter craft were in tractor beam range. Both ships released their beams – intense lime green sprays of light fanned out, grasping for any object within their reach. The beams wrapped around the little ship, slowing it down and eliminating any chance of escape.

Inside the Penguin, Ray turned to Jeff with fear in his eyes, and was glad to at least see that Jeff had an equal amount of fear in his eyes too.

'We're caught in their tractor beams! It's the end!' he gasped, letting go of the controls in resignation.

Both men watched as their ship began to decelerate, and the fighter craft moved in, tugging at the hairship from either side with their sparkly green beams of unescapable-ness.

As the red ships dragged them backwards, Jeff looked up and noticed the small pair of furry dice hanging from the ceiling. This sparked off a childhood memory. He used to own a toy called a pair of 'Clackers'. They were simply a piece of string with two plastic balls on either end, and a small square tab at the mid point. The aim of the toy was to hold the tab, and move it rapidly up and down, making the balls 'clack' together as they collided and bounced away.

It suddenly occurred to Jeff that the spacecraft that they were in was the tab, and the Skraggi fighters were the balls at either end of the string.

'Vertical thrusters! Where?' he yelled at Ray, who just looked blankly at him.

'Come on! How do you make this thing go up?' he repeated, with a little more detail.

Ray had by this time, already decided to give up and was well into the process of making mental notes on how his estate should be divided, but he humoured Jeff by pointing at the vertical control stick in front of him. Why shouldn't Jeff have a few moments of fun before they both died horribly?

Jeff lunged forwards, grabbing the stick with both hands.

'Hang on to your lunch!' he said as he pushed the stick forwards.

Both men's stomachs lurched disconcertingly as the small ship dropped like a rollercoaster car. Then Jeff pulled the stick as hard as he could, forcing the ship to shoot upwards.

The Skraggi fighters began to swing and bounce, up and down as the Marshmallow Penguin began to swing them around. The pilots inside, having already experienced the moment that they were born for, soon realised that this moment was not on their life's agenda, and began to fight with their own systems and levers to try and regain some kind of control over their trajectories.

But Jeff kept on. He pushed and pulled and pushed the stick wildly, while Ray gulped back the contents of his stomach. The three ships performed a strange bouncing dance, dragged along by the momentum of Jeff's insanely erratic flight plan.

Suddenly, the two fighter ships found themselves about to collide. Instinctively, the panicking pilots engaged their deflection shields at full power to prevent against total destruction, but the combined effect and power drain on the ships systems served to disable the tractor beams. The string had snapped.

The fighter pilots deafened each other with their cries of terror as their ships collided. Saved from damage by their shields, the two ships bounced away from each other, spinning out of control.

Underneath them, the Penguin, having suddenly been freed from its tethers, flew off in the opposite direction, also spinning wildly as it disappeared into the blackness of deep space.

Jeff and Ray had blacked out during the interstellar tug-of-war. Their ship had stopped spinning, and was drifting gently towards the only gravity source nearby, which was a huge planet, surrounded by a ring of asteroids. The planet itself was a giant. Covered in continent-sized patches of monochrome shades, it looked like a morbidly obese Friesian cow.

Jeff came around first, and sat up. Looking around, he realised that he'd been flung from his co-pilot's seat, and was lying on the floor a few feet from Ray, who was still out cold. Perhaps he'd suffered some sort of concussion.

Crawling over to Ray, he checked that the man from Kangazang was still breathing. To his relief, he was.

Jeff stood up on wobbly legs, and staggered over to the water recycling unit. He grabbed a small plastic cup and filled it. Swigging down two cupfuls, he refilled the cup and went over to Ray, throwing the contents into the unconscious man's face.

Ray sat bolt upright with a scream.

'I'm drowning!'

Jeff crouched at his side.

'You alright, mate?'

Ray looked around.

'I don't know! Where are we? What happened? Are we dead?'

'No, mate. We made it! I dunno how, but we're free and in the clear!' enthused Jeff in incredulous wonder.

Ray got to his feet, assisted by Jeff's arm.

'Oh. Brilliant!' He smiled. 'Let's see where we are then,' he said, sitting back in the pilot's chair.

'So where are we, then?' asked Jeff, staring out at the mottled planet and its asteroid belt.

'Well,' began Ray, going through the screen-displayed star charts, 'I'd say… No idea whatsoever.'

'What? Oh that's just brilliant, that is,' said Jeff, his heart sinking.

'But this might interest you, look!' said Ray brightly, tugging at his sulky friend's sleeve.

Out in front of them lay the huge asteroid belt, composed of millions upon millions of flying rocks of all sizes. One very large one was illuminated by lights and spun slowly, like a mirrored disco-ball. Jeff looked at the twinkling rock and squinted.

'What's that?' he asked.

Ray had begun to pilot the ship towards it, skilfully managing to avoid being hit by the other rocks.

'That, my dehydrated friend, is a sight for your sore eyes.'

Jeff rubbed his sore eyes.

'Meaning what?'

Ray smiled in anticipation of Jeff's reaction.

'Meaning… The first round is on you!'

Jeff jumped out of his seat like a small boy on Christmas Day.

'Woohoo! A pub! A pub!' he beamed.

The ship approached the meteoroid cautiously, and managed to set down in the mouth of a large crater. Jeff and Ray sat and watched as their ship was swallowed by a large hemispherical dome that came up from both sides. Then they saw a row of green lights illuminate the landing platform, just as they had on Orbitron, which indicated that the air was a breathable cocktail of gases.

Jeff unbuckled his seatbelt and raced to the door, hopping from one foot to the other, like a dog that was desperate to be let outdoors. The entire rock was quite large and so the gravity was slightly less than normal. Jeff felt strangely lighter as the door opened and he stepped out onto the platform. In fact, he was only half his normal twelve stones, which meant that the meteoroid that they had landed upon was approximately half the size of Earth.

Looking out, Jeff could see a tunnel carved in the walls of the crater, leading off to what looked like an illuminated subterranean cavern. Ray locked the hatch of the spacecraft, and joined him on the platform.

'Told you we'd be fine!' Ray smiled at his excited friend.

Excited was hardly the word. Especially as Jeff's largely neglected nostrils could detect a faint, but familiar aroma… It reminded him of day trips to the coast, stag parties in popular seaside resorts. The warm and welcoming scent of freshly-baked doughnuts mingled with the delicious smells of malt vinegar on hot chips. And… what else? There was… yes.

'Beer! I can smell the barmaid's apron from here! Let's go, Ray! Come on!'

He tugged at Ray's arm, trying to cajole him into a medium stroll. But suddenly, Ray stopped, staring out into the darkness.

'Ssh! Can you hear that?' he asked, 'Sounds like laughter.'

'Yeah – everyone in there is having a whale of a time, and I wanna be in there, with 'em as soon as—'

'No,' said Ray, 'not there – nearby. Listen!'

Jeff did as he was told. There was definitely someone nearby, having a giggle at their expense. No change there, then.

Ray put a finger to his lips to silence Jeff, and the two men crept around the landing platform. The sound of laughter got louder. It was definitely female laughter, which to Jeff, was definitely nothing new in his life.

As they reached the rear of their ship, they discovered the source.

Clinging onto the back of the ship were Tailback and Gridlock.

'Oh my Bod Almighty!' gasped Ray.

Jeff just gasped silently, as he saw the two recent robotic repair droids. Except something was wrong; Gridlock was shivering in fear, while Tailback was hooting with laughter.

'Come down from there, will you?' called Ray.

Both Orbots climbed down and stood in front of them. Tail had calmed her laughter down to a suppressed giggle and Grid had regained some courage. He still looked shaken up though.

'Well, it's nice to see a familiar pair of face-plates!' said Ray, scratching his cranium in confusion.

'How in the seven shimmering suns of Salsaggora did you two manage to stay on my ship all this time?'

Grid spoke up first.

'We magnetised our casings to your inner hull. I was against the whole idea, but Tailback wanted to get out and see the galaxy. I'm so sorry, Mr. Ray.'

He hung his head in shame.

'Ah well, that's alright,' said Ray comfortingly. 'Why

didn't you just ask for a lift? It would've been much easier.'

'I know! It was the most terrifying experience of my operation period! I thought we were going to be thrown out into space or blasted into our component parts by those fighters that attacked you!'

He resumed his uncharacteristic trembling.

'What about you?' said Ray to Tailback, who was still sniggering quietly.

'It was the funniest thing I've ever seen! We bounced up and down and up and down… and when Gridlock stopped smiling and began screaming, it was brilliant!'

She hooted a loud laugh once more, which made Jeff chuckle.

''Ere, Ray – I think we've sorted their personality disorders out!' he said.

His statement was met by Gridlock bursting out with laughter so loud it made him jump. Tailback responded by screaming and running off away from everyone.

'Nice try,' said Ray with a laugh.

The two Orbots were instructed to stay in the Penguin by Ray.

As they left the docking bay area, they entered a cavern. It was, for want of a better word, cavernous. It was lit with millions of different neon signs, mirror-balls and every doorway was a new nightclub, pub or drinking den, each one crammed to the rafters.

'What do you think of that, then?' asked Ray, to a near-speechless Jeff.

'My God – it's full of bars!'

They walked deeper into the cavern, towards the sights of neon and revellers, the sounds of partying and music, and the ever-present smells of fish, chips, beer, cheap perfume and inexpensive lavatory arrangements. Walking down the high street, one could easily make the mistake of thinking it was a war zone. There were several small fights, with crowds standing around them hailing the combatants to kill each other. Girls of every shape, size, colour, species, and moral persuasion paraded past with arms locked, garishly screaming obscenities, and bottles flying across the path, barely missing people. Truly disturbing images of a society in serious decline.

'Hey!' exclaimed Jeff, looking around wild-eyed.

'Remember you said you'd never go to Swansea?'

Ray nodded cautiously.

'Go on,' he urged.

'Next best thing!' said Jeff, scanning the caverns for a suitable drinking spot. Ray just groaned and kept walking, trying not to get hit by flying bottles as they wove their way into one of the bars.

For Jeff, this was another first among his many new experiences.

He was standing in a pub. OK, no big deal.

A pub where everyone was drunk?

Still no big deal.

A pub filled with a myriad of alien occupants approximately fifty-six thousand light-years from the Red Lion in his home town?

Possibly the largest of deals.

The place was definitely popular. Music played out of an odd-looking moulding on the wall. Patrons would step up to it, place a hand, claw, probe or tentacle upon its sensor pad and the music would change. Just like a jukebox. And yet so unlike one at the same time. It wasn't particularly catchy music, just incoherent tones interspersed with the occasional drum sound. Weird.

As were the patrons. Jeff tried not to stare. He went into a sort of 'don't-mind-us-we're-locals' kind of shuffle, looking mostly at the floor ahead of him. Just like that time when he went through the 'Nothing To Declare' gate at Heathrow with twelve bottles of industrial-strength sangria in his hand luggage.

But as he followed Ray to the bar, his eyes skipped from person to person; some people were tall, thin and scaly – more trout than lizard, while others were grey, squat and thick-skinned. Others looked almost human, save for their translucent skin, beneath which blurry organs pumped pink blood around purplish arteries in a multicoloured display of anatomy. The strangest ones defied accurate description. Some even resembled estate agents.

Ray pushed past two sozzled patrons to claim a place at the bar. The two drunks were short and rodent-like. Large incisors hung over their lower lips and a fine reddish fur covered them all over. Gerbils.

Jeff squeezed in next to Ray as the gerbils muttered quiet curses and slurred references to Jeff's mother. But Jeff let it go, as he was finally beginning to feel like he was on holiday, and after hearing Ray's description of all the wonderful intoxicants available out here in deepest space, he was ready to let his hair down. Plus, he felt like he could take a gerbil in a fight.

The barman was big. Big and red. He stood with his back to Ray.

'Service!' called Ray, tapping the palm of his hand on the wet bar.

Turning around, the barman stepped forward to take the order. Jeff tried to smile a friendly touristy smile, but when he saw the bovine head of the barman – short horns and huge nostrils, complete with a brass ring through the septum – Jeff smirked rather rudely. He tried his best to remain calm, but this place was a menagerie of mixed-up species. The fish people. Rhinoceros things. Gerbils. And now a large crimson cow was serving them drinks.

The barman had seen it all before, and ignored Jeff's tittering. Ray turned to his drinking buddy and pointed a stern finger at him.

'Behave yourself or we're back in the ship, got it?'

Jeff nodded in a suitably embarrassed fashion.

Ray got on with the ordering. 'Two Scuzzmeisters, please.'

The cow snorted at Jeff a little, and turned around to pick up some large-ish glasses. Luckily, evolution had provided him with three digits on each hand, instead of the hooves one would expect. He poured the drinks – identical to lager, thankfully, and placed them in front of Ray.

'Twelve fifty,' grunted the cow. Ray pulled out an octagonal plastic credit card and handed it over.

'Kangazanian Express?' he asked the barman.

'That'll do nicely,' came the reply.

Jeff studied their surly bartender. He looked quite demonic, being a deep shade of scarlet, muscular and with those horns on top. It made sense not to annoy the devil, anyway – they'd had enough near-death experiences to last them a while. But Jeff was possessed by one nagging thought, one tiny impulse to open his mouth and say something puerile. It had to be done.

He picked up his glass and took a sip, waiting for the barman to saunter off, then he winked at Ray.

'Should've asked for a red bull.'

*

Inside the Marshmallow Penguin, Tailback and Gridlock were doing what they did best. Aside from Grid's occasional laughter and Tail's shrieks of fear, they repaired and improved the inner workings of the spacecraft as best they could.

Grid looked at Tailback and smiled. 'This is our dream. We're finally away from Orbitron and existing like real fleshies, aren't we?'

Tailback nodded.

'Yes. Although we haven't really done much since we left. Do you think we should take this opportunity to move on and find our own way?'

'Perhaps. But it would be better to strengthen our companionship with the humans. They've been very good to us, haven't they? Jeff certainly seems to like you.'

Tailback looked a little coy.

'Oh, he's a long way from his home too. Everything's new to him and from what you told me about him, his female cohabitant unit had disengaged their union, so he's clearly a little... what was the word?'

'Lovelorn,' answered Grid.

'Yes. That's it. Does it concern you that he seems affectionate towards me, Grid?'

'You refer to jealousy,' said Grid, his pleasant expression not changing. 'No, I feel nothing of that emotion. We are merely cohabitants, bonded by our similarities and defects, but not emotionally entangled like fleshies are. I think the most efficient description of our relationship would be "free agents". Would that be accurate?'

Tail nodded. 'I suggested that we were siblings.'

Gridlock considered this for a moment. He smiled in acceptance.

'Siblings. Heh. Yes, you're my sister then. Heh! We're practically human!'

'When in roaming mode, do as the Carbon Units do?' asked Tail.

Grid smirked. Then he laughed. Then he laughed some more. Tailback joined in, beginning to feel a little more human too.

Suddenly, both Orbots stopped laughing.

They stopped moving.

They stopped thinking.

Unknown to any organic lifeforms on the asteroid, the entire sector of the galaxy was being bombarded by a powerful electro-neural inhibitor field.

Very similar to an electromagnetic pulse, the field targeted the brain-data-waves of any sentient artificially created humanoids in the vicinity, effectively rendering them blank and open to suggestion.

The waves of energy raced through the minds of both the Orbots, disrupting all their voluntary actions.

New instructions were being piped into them without their permission, and location coordinates were sent back to the source.

And over a light year away, the source of the inhibitor field prowled through the stars, sniffing out the two rogue machines like a shark that had detected a drop of blood in the water.

Only this shark was a big red spaceship called The Furious Anger.

In the noisy lounge of the extraterrestrial pub, which, Jeff managed to find out was named, 'Drunky Balunky's Intoxication Emporium' or more commonly known as 'Drunkies', Jeff and Ray sat at a small hexagonal table near a corner.

Jeff was liking the place more and more. The beer was all that Ray had promised: tasty beyond belief, cold and smooth to drink, yet it still didn't taste like any earthly beer.

'What do they make this stuff out of?' he asked Ray.

'Well, for the most part,' said Ray, settling back in his chair, and holding his litre glass up like a connoisseur, 'Water. But as you know, that's not all. Various other chemicals and natural items are blended using a unique fermentation process that—'

'Whoa, hang on, professor!' said Jeff.

'What?'

'I wanted to know what's in it, that's all, I didn't want a scientific analysis!'

Ray looked affronted. 'Oh. Alright, but put your glass down first.'

'No need,' said Jeff, chugging the remaining half-litre in one go, then burping impressively.

'Well, for generations, brewers have found that in order to achieve the very peak of—'

Ray was off on one again.

Jeff waved his hands in protest.

'Stop! Just tell me what it's made of, will you?'

'No,' said Ray, flatly.

'Why?' asked Jeff, feeling ripped off.

'I'll tell you why, Jeff,' said Ray, leaning forward to get a lot closer. 'Because you've been going on about getting a drink constantly since we left Earth, and now I've managed to provide you with a pub, a chair and a beer, I'm not going to be the one to spoil your obvious enjoyment by revealing the ingredients. I take it you're enjoying it?'

'Yeah! It's lovely, but—'

'Good. Shut up and get another round in then,' ordered Ray, handing him the credit card.

Jeff grabbed both glasses and stood up, shaking his head in bewilderment.

He walked off to the bar, beginning to sway a little. Whatever the drink was made of, it was having the desired effect. *Perhaps*, he thought, *it might be the lower gravity helping the alcohol (or whatever they put in it) to get into his bloodstream.*

Standing at the bar was a pair of girls. They looked like girls anyway. Long silken hair, curves in all the right places, reassuringly familiar chest-bumps and light, pleasant-sounding voices. Unknown to Jeff, they weren't technically girls. In fact they were 'Indies', androgynous beings from that part of the galaxy. The universe has a lot of non-gender-specific people. (The term 'Indie' derives from the word 'Indeterminate'.)

But, as we have established, Jeff was neither in possession of this information, nor was he fussy. Plus he was tipsy, in good spirits, and for all intents and purposes, on the pull with his new best mate.

Locking his features into a smarmy grin, Jeff sauntered up and between the two Indies.

'Evening, ladies…' he began.

Had he received just the one slap, it probably wouldn't have hurt so much.

Ray drummed upon the tabletop with his hands as he

waited for Jeff to return. He looked over at the door, and watched as a tall and thin man walked in. The man was dressed in a colourful cloak, which went down to the floor. His face was deathly pale and his sunken eyes looked watery and somehow sad. This sombre visage was framed by lank straight hair, black as night and greasy as kebab meat. The combined effect looked like the sullen head had been stitched onto the body of a more vibrant and colourful person in a bizarre experiment.

Ray watched as the figure scanned the room, then glided along and sat without purchasing a drink at a nearby table.

At that moment, Jeff returned, bearing two fresh glasses of booze and two red cheeks.

'I just got slapped. Twice,' he said, handing Ray a glass of the lovely liquid.

Ray looked over and saw that the pale man was looking in his direction. He raised his fresh litre in salute.

'Cheer up, mate! Might never happen!' he exclaimed with a smile.

The man's solemn face didn't register the slightest flicker of emotion. Ray noticed.

'Bugger you then,' muttered Ray, chugging back some more beer. He looked at Jeff and smiled.

'I know what'll liven this lot up a bit!'

Ray delved into his coat pocket and pulled out his 'Top Hits of the Eighties' compilation CD.

'Party on, dude!' yelled Jeff.

Back at the Marshmallow Penguin, Tail and Grid sat perfectly still. Their minds were being scanned, interrogated, scrutinised and rogue software – viruses –

were piped in. A great distance away, at the other end of the transmission, the Skraggi cruiser closed in.

Overlord Kelvin strolled into the bridge, wearing his father's scarlet and gold robes of office, complete with an ornate hat, upon which lay a banana. Previously idle soldiers snapped to attention as he passed.

'Commander! Report, please!' he called.

The Skraggi Military Commmander walked briskly up to face his monarch.

'My lord! We've scanned the local wavenet and had a stroke of luck. The planet Orbitron has been broadcasting a missing Orbots message. It seems that two of their surface operatives have left the planet without authorisation.'

Kelvin's eyelids felt heavy.

'Really. Why are we concerned with Orbots again?' he mused.

'Well, the runaway Orbots escaped by stowing away on a small ship – the one that escaped us outside Profania Alpha. We've confirmed that the occupants of the ship are named Barbaray Sprambladack Fasstalon-Scump and Jeff Spooner. We can track the Orbots and they'll lead us to the ship.'

'Excellent work. How far away are we?' asked Kelvin, fishing in his pockets.

'Half a light year, sir. We can be there in twenty minutes.'

Kelvin kept searching his extravagant robes for any possible pocket that he might have missed.

'Good. Make it so, Commander.'

The officer remained there, saying nothing, but looking as if he wanted to say something. Something pretty important.

'Did you not hear me? I said let's go there – now!' exclaimed Kelvin, rather annoyed at the apparent insolence of his commander.

At great personal risk, the officer spoke out.

'My lord, there is a problem. The fugitives are in the vicinity of Emo Prime. Possibly on the planet as we speak.'

Kelvin's expression screwed up, denoting his total non-comprehension.

'Sir, Emo Prime has the largest space armada after our own. It wouldn't do to upset them, as they might possibly destroy us in a conflict.'

Kelvin, being less of a strategist and more of a coward-ist, understood.

'Oh. Well, that's a problem. What do you suggest then?'

'We're currently establishing a remote control link with the refugee Orbots. They'll do whatever we tell them to. I thought we could use them to try and retrieve the fugitives from the Emos, rather than cause an intergalactic incident?'

Kelvin patted his chest and thighs, still looking for something.

'Yes, good idea. Erm, before you go, commander, one question.'

'Yes, my lord?' replied the officer.

'Have you seen my banana?'

'It's on your head, my lord,' replied the officer, with all seriousness.

Kelvin felt his hat, and retrieved the banana.

'Excellent work, commander. Now – to work!'

The bar at 'Drunkies' was busier and noisier than before.

Cheers and laughter rang out. The unmistakable sound of mid-1980's pop music also rang out, courtesy of Ray's compilation CD, which had somehow been forced into the jukebox and miraculaculus-ly, it played perfectly.

Most of the patrons were standing now, gathered around the corner table, where Ray and Jeff had been sitting.

Now, they were standing too, but they were atop the dangerously wobbling table, both men completely smashed and singing badly. The crowd cheered and waved their arms in encouragement.

Jeff was belting out his slurred rendition of 'Especially For You', the chart hit for Kylie Minogue and Jason Donovan, with Ray taking the Donovan role in the duet:

'And now we're back togeeeeeeether… Togeeeetherrrr!' they wailed, trying and failing to maintain a coherent melody.

Jeff slipped on a damp beermat, and fell off the table into the assembled throng. Luckily, they caught him and he found himself crowd-surfing, held aloft by the crowd's hands, claws, tentacles and fins.

Ray saw Jeff whooping in delight as he bobbed along on the crowd, and thought, rather dizzily, that he'd follow suit.

He leapt off the table, spinning around in mid air, so as to land on the crowd back-first.

The crowd had other ideas and parted like the Red Sea, allowing Ray to crash unceremoniously onto the floor.

The pain was minimal, as the gravity kept him from landing as hard as he would have done had he been on Earth, so he lay there for a moment, giggling in hysterics.

Some of the party people helped him to his feet, and he looked around the room, noticing that Jeff had surfed all the way to the bar, and was now standing upon it, attempting to upstage Elvis with his own rendition of 'Jailhouse Rock'. He also noticed that the sullen, white-faced man in the multicoloured cloak had been joined by some more of his species, about twenty in total. Like the first man, they stood watching in silence, with a look of disgust on their faces.

Ray thought it best that he address the situation. He stumbled through the swaying crowd, burping and hiccupping, until he got to the group of pallid party poopers.

'Come on, fellers! Let your hair down!' bawled Ray, wobbling uncontrollably. He noticed that their hair was already let down.

'Oh – brilliant! Come on then! Who wants a drink? I'm buying! Scuzzies all round, is it?'

The group dispersed. Two went to the door, closing and locking it. Then all the coloured cloaks came off, revealing black, functional outfits. Each man drew a gun from a side holster.

One of them raised his aim and blasted the wall-mounted speaker, killing the music instantly. The crowd settled down just as quickly.

The first of the pale men addressed the crowd.

'This is a police raid! All of you are under arrest, under the anti-joviality act of Emo Prime law. Anything you do or say to have further fun will be used in evidence against you.'

Jeff looked at the police officers from his vantage point at the bar.

'Oi, Dracula! Whadda you doing?' he called out to the arresting officer, and was promptly shot with a stun beam. He toppled off the bar and crashed right through a table underneath him.

Ray saw this and grabbed the arm of the officer who'd blasted Jeff.

'You can't do that!' he protested.

They could. And they did.

Ray hit the deck face-first.

chapter ten

Don't Worry...

Jeff regained consciousness and realised that he was lying on his back. He opened his eyes and looked around. He saw nothing. Black.

Nothingness. Blackness.

He tried again. Still nothing. At first, he was sure that he'd gone blind. It was a possibility, as nothing was visible at all. The ground upon which he lay was hard and cold. He sat up and began to crawl around, reaching out for a wall or door, but found nothing.

'Ray?' he called. His voice echoed in the emptiness of the dark.

A disembodied voice echoed out: 'Are you happy?'

Jeff got to his feet, which wasn't easy in total darkness. He wasn't drunk anymore, he was certain of that. Thank goodness the beer was hangover-free, just as Ray had described it.

The voice asked again, 'Are you happy?'

Jeff looked up, which was pretty pointless. He had no idea where he was, where the voice was coming from, or even where Ray was.

‘Where the hell am I?’ he asked.

‘Answer the question. Are you happy?’

‘No! Of course I’m not! What is this?’

The voice seemed mildly pleased at this. ‘Would you prefer some light?’

Jeff rubbed his eyes, preparing for the sharp pain of light to assault his optic nerves.

‘Yeah, actually I would.’

The light came on. For a long moment, Jeff looked around. He was standing in the middle of a grey room, perfectly round, with no visible doors and walls that stretched up hundreds of feet, where a light source was located. But still no sign of the owner of the disembodied voice or his friend.

‘Are you happy now?’

‘Yes thanks,’ said Jeff.

The light went out again, prompting Jeff to grunt in annoyance.

‘Oh, for God’s sake! Stop messing about!’

‘I take it you’re not happy now?’ asked the voice calmly.

‘No, I’m bloody not!’ yelled Jeff.

The light came on again.

‘How about now?’ asked the voice.

‘No – I’m still not happy!’

‘Excellent. Remain that way and we’ll all get along splendidly.’

Not too far away, Ray was experiencing the same treatment. He stood in an identical cylindrical room which was the same unappealing shade of battleship grey. For him, the light was switched on.

‘So what you’re saying,’ he continued, pacing around

in thought, 'is that we've been arrested for the heinous crime of enjoying ourselves too much?'

'Not too much,' replied a similar sounding and equally disembodied voice, 'At all! And you shall be tried in a court of law for this crime.'

Jeff sat back down on the floor. At least the light remained on. As long as he seemed angry or annoyed, he noticed that the voice was willing to talk.

'Tried in court?' he asked. 'Having fun isn't a crime!'

'It is here. It is a virus. One that you carry deep within your brain, ready to infect our people. And you will be punished for this. Dealt with before you can hurt anyone!'

The voice seemed a little emotional. Maniacal, even. Jeff raised an eyebrow.

'I am a fairy, my name is nuff…' he muttered.

'What did you say?' asked the voice. Jeff repeated it louder.

'I said – I am a fairy, my name is nuff! It's a joke!'

'A Joke? Blasphemy! Let the trial commence!'

The light went out.

Ray looked rather worried as the light in his cell also went out. Jeff, on the other hand, was sure he'd had a little accident.

When the lights came on again, Jeff was pleased to see himself standing beside Ray. He was even more pleased to find his underpants reasonably clean. But he was far from pleased to see that he and Ray had somehow been transported into a large room full of sour-faced people. Both men had experienced no sensation of having travelled anywhere, yet they looked around the place and they were in a large grey courthouse of some sort. They noticed that they were both standing in the dock. Which was never a good place to be standing, in general.

'Ray!' said Jeff, happy to be reunited with the barber. 'Are you alright?'

Ray nodded. 'Yes, I'm fine. I think we're in trouble again, though.'

'No kidding,' said Jeff. And he wasn't.

The room was populated by about fifty white-faced Emos. At the front of the room, facing them, was a raised dais, with a lectern placed on it. The entire courtroom was drably decorated in uninspiring shades of grey, as were the occupants. The thin, sad-looking group of Emo witnesses huddled together in their collective depression, and looked over at the accused with sorrowful eyes, half hidden by black fringes.

'All rise!' called a voice. It was the same disembodied voice that Jeff had heard in his cell. Everyone in the room instantly stood up.

The huge grey door on the huge grey far wall slid slowly open, to reveal a very tall man in flowing black robes. His craggy, colourless face showed very little emotion, just a sort of deep sadness. *For a race called Emos, they seem awfully emotionless*, thought Jeff.

The High Priest glided in and took his seat at the end of the room. Before sitting down, he addressed the assembled group in front of him.

'Mood: apathetic,' he said dolefully.

'Mood: apathetic,' replied the Emos in unison.

Then he sat down, prompting everyone else to do the same. Ray tugged at Jeff's sleeve to encourage him to take a seat and stop gawping.

'Members of the jury,' began the High Priest. 'This is a case of the highest importance. Look ye upon the faces of the accused, and know that they are sent across the universe on a dread mission to destroy all that our very existences stand for.'

Jeff's eyes turned to look at Ray, while his head remained still. He whispered out of the side of his mouth.

'That's a bit much!'

Ray hummed a 'yes' sound.

The Priest continued with his opening speech.

'Know ye all this: a crime of levity such as these two detestable parasites have committed is reprehensible enough, but there is more. Much more to this than ye may be aware.'

He pointed an accusing finger out at the two frightened men. Jeff flinched. For a second it looked as though his twig-like digit would snap off and fly at his face like a dart.

'The planets are in alignment, as the Great Prophecy says. And here before ye stand the Evil One and his accomplice, also as it was foreseen!'

A ripple of nervousness ran through the assembled Emos. The Priest had successfully put the fear into them.

The dusty old books in the gothic archives of Emo Prime's Chamber Of Records had indeed told of a time when the planets would line up, bringing with it the arrival of a being so evil, so corrupt to the core, that the countless years of po-faced peaceful but drab existence would be shattered forever. In some circles, it was known as 'The Coming Of The Joyfulness-ness'. In others, it was referred to as 'The Age Of Pleasure', but most lowly

Emos had got used to calling it 'Happy Hour'.

'Happy Hour': a time when, for one tumultuous hour in their history, life would become the total opposite of all they knew. Colour would fill their vision, music that dared to transcend the higher end of the musical scale, dabbling with the evil forces of high-pitched, cheerful tunes. A time when all of the millions of poor victims of this plague would see their faces disfigured by twisted, gruesome expressions known as smiles. It was a horrible thought. Not because the experience was particularly traumatic, but the very thought of being thrust into this hour in the unknown frightened them. And the High Priest had kept them this way, bound and captive in a life of servitude and depression.

The truth was that this frightening, albeit wholly untrue, legend was dreamt up by the long-dead Powers That Be, who outlawed positivity so many years ago. Like many religious doctrines, it began with one person in a position of power who decreed that something was wrong, and that everyone should agree with him, her or it. If someone were to ask why, the Great Decider had to come up with yet another lie – another frightening (and still just as untrue) story or punishment to dissuade anyone from disagreeing with them. And so on. The stories were passed down through word of mouth, Hieroglyphics, Hand-written Scroll, Printed Page, Wax Cylinder, Vinyl seven-inch Single, Cassette, Compact Disc, MP3, E-mail, Text Message, Tweet, Holo-Speak, YadaYadaFone, and PsychiBlip and the resulting story had by then taken on its own unique personality which was, in every instance, more terrifying and totally unlike the original text. A little bit of nonsense goes a long way.

Or in other words, bad news travels fast.

Needless to say there were no Boddist temples on Emo Prime.

The case for the prosecution stood up and looked over at the accused.

'My fellow Emos, look upon these accused heretics and see that they stand for all that we strive to avoid. See – how the colour of their hair deviates from the divine blackness that we share. Their strange garments in aberrant tones that seek to poison our vision. Are these colours not the work of the Evil One?'

At this point, Jeff couldn't help but smirk at the ridiculousness of it all. These sad and pale idiots were trying to condemn them for daring to seek happiness.

Bad idea. The prosecutor saw Jeff's smirk, and pounced.

'Aha!' he yelled, pointing to Jeff's grin. 'Look how he mocks us even now, practising the forbidden expression here in our room of sombre justice. He tries to spread the poison that—'

'Oh for God's sake, give it a rest, will you?' blurted Jeff. He'd had enough of the pantomime.

The crowd gasped at the outburst, then mumbled to themselves in apprehension. The prosecutor too was a little shocked, but still Jeff ranted on.

'You lot could do with a little happiness in your lives. Look at this place! Look at yourselves! I've had more fun in an abattoir!'

The crowd gasped.

What kind of sick individual would think of such an activity? Their minds tried not to conjure up images of

Jeff having deplorable kinds of 'fun' in a slaughterhouse.

Clearly getting a little enthusiastic, Jeff stood up, gripping the front of the dock.

The High Priest raised an eyebrow.

'The accused will be silent!'

'No he won't! Make me!' answered Jeff defiantly.

Bad idea number two. The Priest pushed a grey button on his black desk and the dock in which Jeff was standing was infused with high-voltage electricity.

The current raced through Jeff as if it were dental floss made of barbed wire. Jeff grimaced as he felt his every muscle tighten against his will. The pain was excruciating. He had no choice but to endure it, shaking violently, as Ray could do nothing but look on in horror.

After what seemed like an age, but was in actuality a few seconds, the current was shut off. Jeff fell back into his chair, twitching and wondering how close he'd come to death.

Jeff turned his head gingerly to look at Ray.

'Not… Not one of me best ideas, eh?'

Ray looked tenderly at his frazzled friend, tears welling up in his eyes.

'You bloody idiot. Shut up and let me do the talking.'

'I can smell bacon,' mumbled Jeff.

The prosecutor looked uncomfortably eager to proceed.

'Perhaps now we may continue uninterrupted? Excellent.'

He turned to face the jury and paced slowly and deliberately along the line, fixing each member with his avian features, looking as though he might peck at one of their faces any second.

'As despicable and evil as these followers of joviality may be, let us not forget that we are a decent and honourable race. As is the law on Emo Prime, we shall provide these miscreants with a defence counsel, so that they may be tried fairly and justly. Is that not our way?'

The jury mumbled nervously, but the overall impression was one of agreement.

'Send in the defence counsel!' called the High Priest.

Ray looked over at Jeff, who was still twitching and smoking in his chair, like a twitchy, smoky thing.

'There – you see? We're being defended! It'll be alright, just you watch!' he whispered optimistically.

The door opened, and in walked another identical scarecrow of a man, pale and sombre, dressed in every shade of black and carrying a piece of black paper the size of a postcard. Ray regarded the stick insect with not insubstantial shock.

'We're screwed, Jeff.'

The defence counsel approached the bench. Looking up at the High Priest, he began his opening statement.

'My lord, as is our way, I hereby declare that I am to defend the accused in accordance with the law, to the best of my ability.'

The High Priest nodded slowly.

'Very well. If you must. Proceed.'

'Thank you my lord.'

The scarecrow turned and approached the dock, where Ray and Jeff eyed their only saviour with quickly dissolving confidence.

'Members of the jury and my learned friend, I stand here today to provide a defence for the accused. Look at their misguided attempts to live a righteous life. Their un-frowning features, their unknowing eyes. I put it to you that they are not truly evil, but merely ignorant of the truth. Dumb animals, fit for nothing more than menial labour. I say to you that they be taken from this court and indoctrinated in the ways of the holy ABC, so that Apathy, Boredom and Complacency forms a new and righteous core to their meaningless existences.'

Jeff whispered to Ray out of the side of his mouth again.

'Blimey. If that's the best he's got to say, we are screwed!'

Ray offered a calming thought.

'Listen, if it gets us out of the death penalty, isn't that an improvement?'

'S'pose. Let's see what this bloke can do then, eh?' said Jeff. Ray nodded, although the main reason for it was not to let Jeff see that he'd lost all confidence by now.

The High Priest looked over at the accused. He straightened the bones of his back, which made a jarring crunchy sound, and addressed his captives.

'What say you, the accused? Are you willing to accept salvation and deny your sinful ways?'

Ray blinked, thinking deeply.

'Will you surrender your very lives to follow the holy ABC, in its ultimate wisdom?' the creaking judge continued.

Jeff just sat there, staring. His thinking had become rather transient and shallow after being semi-fried.

The High Priest coughed one of those false coughs that could be read as 'Excuse me, I'd like an answer…'

Ray blinked again, still trying to put some mental jigsaw pieces together. Something was missing here, but he couldn't think what it was.

Jeff's somewhat shallower thoughts got to the point quicker than Ray's did.

'Evidence!' proclaimed Jeff loudly. 'Where's the evidence? If we've committed these so-called crimes, any trial should have evidence against us!'

Ray looked at Jeff in admiration and confusion simultaneously, which made him blink speechlessly. The defending attorney looked at Ray for some sign of agreement or denial.

'Er, that thing what he said,' mumbled the befuddled barber.

Turning to the right, the High Priest regarded the counsel for the prosecution.

'Is there any evidence to support or deny the charges?'

The prosecutor nodded solemnly, and the corners of his slit-like mouth twitched. Had smiling not been outlawed on Emo Prime thousands of generations ago, he would have beamed a sinister grin.

'There is, your Honour. I submit to the court Exhibit A – an audio device that the accused willingly brought with them into the bar. This proves their intentions to corrupt the minds of our citizens and thus prove their guilt beyond a shadow of a doubt.'

'Proceed. Play exhibit A,' said the High Priest.

The prosecutor strode over to the High Priest's dais, and handed him the compact disc. The High Priest eyed it suspiciously, as if it were a forged banknote, and read the hand-written title: 'Top Hits of the Eighties'. He gave a little shiver, then carefully slid it into a thin slot on his desk.

The pale occupants of the pale courtroom mumbled nervously, until they heard a faint crackle coming out over the room's PA system. Then silence reigned. For five long seconds.

The unnerving sounds of a synthesised drum fill tumbled out of the speakers, signifying the opening beats of a classic Stock, Aitken and Waterman hit. The audience grimaced in obvious discomfort as Rick Astley launched into his debut single.

Ray began to jig about in the dock, unable to ignore the infectious rhythm. Jeff noticed this and while he tried to throw an advisory glare at the dancing fool, he couldn't help noticing that he too was bobbing up and down in time to the beat.

The prosecutor noticed this and pointed his prosecutor's finger at the humans in his most dramatic and prosecutey way.

'See!' he bawled. 'See how the accursed music of levity possesses their souls! Are these not the actions of the guilty?'

The High Priest regarded the accused with disdain, and Jeff looked down at his own guilty feet, which, in their movement, were just as accusatory as their prosecutor. Guilty feet have, indeed, got no rhythm. The defence counsel rolled his eyes and dropped into a chair, utterly defeated.

Ray looked across the faces of the audience in shock. He'd expected the stony sneers of hatred, intermingled with twitchy grimaces of discomfort, but there were none. Everyone seemed to have had their facial expressions wiped of all discernable emotion.

He looked over at Jeff.

'Jeff! Look at them – something's happening!' he hissed, trying to be subtle. Indeed, something was happening, and it was happening on a widespread basis.

The Great Prophecy was for all intents and purposes, law on Emo Prime, and as the capture and trial of the two humans was perhaps the most important event to have happened to their civilisation since the prophecy was discovered aeons ago, the High Councillors had decided to broadcast the trial live to every home on the planet, encouraging the public to tune in to see the perpetrators get their just desserts.

Unfortunately, their plans had backfired. Every single inhabitant of the joyless sphere was listening intently as the irresistible musical masterpiece bounced around their auditory canals, and in a unique way, infused their very thought patterns with the previously unknown feeling that was optimism.

Optimism became happiness, happiness became joy and joy became bliss, as billions of people turned to one another and bared their teeth in a new expression: The Smile.

Pete Waterman, had he known, would've been so proud.

In the courtroom, things were no less dramatic. Only the High Priest looked unaffected, but even he showed the signs of panic, as he swung his head from left to right, trying to comprehend the impossible.

Emos were rising from their chairs and swaying in time, twirling and waving their arms in unabashed ecstasy.

And then something even more incredible happened.

White, pallid skin warmed, filling with revitalised, enthusiastic blood flow. Lank hair, that had once hung like glossy black spaghetti, lightened and formed into waves as the chemical change forced their follicles to move. A monochrome, monotone planet was bursting into bloom like a garden of poppies.

Ray saw his chance and grabbed Jeff by the arm.

'Come on! Now's our chance to get outta here!' he said, clambering out of the dock. Jeff, trailing bacon-flavoured smoke, followed him as they weaved through the beaming throng of revellers.

A few yards behind them, the High Priest called out.

'Stop the infidels! Somebody help me!' but his time had come. As the first song had begun to fade out, another took its place.

A song so utterly determined in its optimism, so unstoppable in its rhythm and a cast-iron guarantee of bringing a warm, thawing glow to the hardest of icy cold hearts:

'Here's a little song I wrote,
You might want to sing it note-for-note;
Don't worry… Be happy…'

The High Priest's mind soaked up the jolly sentiment like a dry sponge. He was lost forever. His cheeks cracked audibly like the mud of a sun-dried riverbed, as they forced themselves into a smile, and he bobbed up and down in joyous accompaniment to the jaunty melody.

Ray pushed past some more shiny happy people as he made his way to the courtroom doors. Jeff stopped him.

'Hey – why don't we hang out for a bit now? We aren't in any danger any more, are we?'

Ray looked deadly serious as he produced a paper envelope from his pocket. It was the track listing of the

CD currently revolutionising the planet's population.

'Read it,' said Ray, still serious of face.

Jeff did so, scanning the list of mid-to-late 1980's hits.

'Er, Rick Astley, Bobby McFerrin... What's your point?'

'Track three,' said Ray, urging Jeff to concentrate.

Jeff read it and looked up at Ray, finally realising the gravity of the situation.

'Oh my God – The Smiths!' he gasped.

'Exactly,' said Ray. '"Heaven Knows I'm Miserable Now" – number ten in 1984. The most depressing song in the entire universe. If they hear that, it'll totally reverse the current effect and we're back in deep doggy doings! We've got just under four minutes and fifty-one seconds before the song finishes! Now let's get out of here while they're still smiling!'

Jeff was through the door long before Ray.

chapter eleven

Frying Pan Vis-á-vis Fire

'Wait for me!' yelled Ray as he struggled to keep up with Jeff Spooner's impressive sprintage. Jeff looked back and saw the bedraggled barber trying his best to catch up, but he looked rather like an albatross attempting a running take off; determined but darn funny with it. All his years of standing around cutting hair had provided him with reasonably toned legs, but they were built for support rather than speed. So Jeff stopped and waited for Ray to arrive.

'We've gotta get back to the Penguin before they get to track three! Which way?' asked Jeff, looking around like a meerkat.

Ray pointed upwards.

'There!' he called, as the familiar rowing-boat shape descended. Jeff let out a whoop of victory.

'Good old robots!'

The hatch opened, and both men rushed inside, just as they heard the end of track seven on the CD.

Racing to the flight controls, Ray saw Gridlock in the pilot's chair.

'Well done, Grid! Now get off this world as quick as you can go – there's a bunch of Emos out there about to come down with a big bang!'

Gridlock pushed the thrusters, sending the ship upwards and outwards, toward the safety of Emo Prime's upper atmosphere. Ray slumped in the co-pilot seat, and attempted to get his breath back.

Jeff went over to the back of the ship, where he saw Tailback looking out of one of the portholes.

'Ello, sweetness!' he purred, truly happy to see the attractive androidette.

Tailback looked at him and refused to smile, which Jeff thought was odd. Even odder was the complete absence of abject terror on her faceplate.

'What's the matter, babe?' asked Jeff in total puzzlement.

Totally out of character, Tailback made a fist and whacked Jeff firmly across the temple. His face had the look of a betrayed man as he flew across the cabin, collided with the far wall and collapsed unconscious on the floor.

Ray heard the clang of head against metal and looked round to see Jeff in a heap. Then he heard a deeper clang; that of human head against a metal head, as Gridlock rammed his shining dome into Ray's.

Like Jeff, Ray collapsed unceremoniously onto the floor, as Gridlock took his pilot seat again, and directed the little craft upwards and outwards. Heading: the huge scarlet battle cruiser, currently in orbit.

On board the Furious Anger, Overlord Kelvin was awaiting the news of the capture of his newly-appointed mortal enemies. He sat in his impressive bone-throne and tried to look especially Overlord-ly, as the huge sliding doors opened and the Military Commander strode in.

'My Lord! We have captured the Marshmallow Penguin and its occupants. They are being held in the docking bay, and await your arrival.'

Kelvin stood up and straightened his robes.

'Excellent, commander. I told you it was a good idea to use the robots to do my bidding!' He grinned and strode past the quietly groaning soldier.

The cavernous docking bay of the Skraggi ship easily held the Penguin, a dozen fighter ships and a hundred armed soldiers, who stood stock still, waiting for their leader to enter. They snapped to attention as the elevator doors hissed open, and Kelvin emerged, looking focused, regal and committed to victory.

In front of the captured haircraft sat Jeff and Ray, manacled to blocky metal chairs. They twisted and groaned as they regained consciousness and felt the cold steel seats bully and chill their aching bodies. Jeff felt a shiver of impending, expectant fear. It meant only one thing:

He needed to use the lavatory pretty soon.

A distant cackling echoed around the hangar. Both men turned their heads to see where the feeble yet mocking laughter was coming from.

'Excellent! So – we finally meet!' declared Kelvin in the most authoritative tone that he could muster. He stood in front of his prisoners and scanned the small spacecraft that sat behind them.

'And this is your vessel, then? Crude, but surprisingly evasive. I'm impressed, gentlemen!'

Over the far side of the hangar, there was a large window, through which the Galactic Tax Inspectors watched the proceedings. They took notes silently, assessing Kelvin's performance. Waiting for a slip – one slip – and they'd depose him and take it all for themselves...

Kelvin knew this and so he had put on his most dictatorial robes and black gloves of office. He'd resolved to putting on a good show in order to save his authority and his father's reasonably good name from shame.

'And now, my helpless worms, you will give me the Universal Remote, before I have you executed!' he declared, gesturing dramatically.

Jeff, like Ray, had had quite enough of being tied up, lectured, imprisoned and chased for one lifetime and decided to speak out. Except Ray knew better, and kept silent.

'Listen, mate,' began Jeff, trying to sound nonchalant, 'I dunno who the bleedin' 'ell you are and frankly, I don't give a monkeys.'

Ray shut both of his eyes tightly. No good could come of this.

Kelvin looked as surprised as everyone else in the room at this scruffy human's impudence.

'You DARE to speak to me without permission?' he hissed in anger. 'Do you not know who I am?' he added, pointing at his own face to underline the statement.

Jeff looked Kelvin up and down with distaste.

'No, mate. And like I said, I don't give a monkeys. Fact is, you don't know who I am either, do you?' he said, as if spoiling for a pub fight. In all honesty, Jeff had no idea what he was trying to achieve by this posturing, but he thought it would at least buy him some time until he or Ray thought of something.

Kelvin was appalled by this outburst, this total lack of respect. He cast a rapid glance over to the window in which the Inspectors were standing, and realised he was in danger of being undermined.

'Hah!' mocked Kelvin, trying flippancy as a new approach. 'I know for a fact that you are Barbaray Sprambladack Fasstalon-Scump, and your hairy friend is Jeff Spooner! But before I—'

'Other way around, mate,' interrupted Jeff.

'Ah. Well, that's what I meant,' continued Kelvin, 'so before I reduce you both to your component molecules, allow me to tell you who your captor is.'

He stepped closer to Jeff, totally ignoring Ray, who had decided to watch the proceedings with just the one eye, and took a deep breath.

'I am Kelvin – Lord Rancydd the Third, Supreme Overlord of the Skragg Empire, and you will kneel before me!'

Jeff ignored the spittle that had rained onto his face, and shook his head in defiance.

'Sorry, pal, no can do.'

'What?' screamed Kelvin, losing more and more self-control by the second.

'Are you so eager to die, human?' he asked, finding himself completely confused by the prisoner's insolence.

'Oh yeah. I'm not afraid to die, but how am I supposed to kneel when I'm chained to this stupid chair, you nutjob?'

'For your defiance, I shall…' Kelvin stopped. He looked at both the chairs.

'Good point. Untie the prisoners at once!' he commanded.

A soldier tried to intervene.

'But, my lord…' he stammered.

'SILENCE!' bawled Kelvin. The word "silence" had become his favourite over the past week. The louder the better, ironically.

'Untie them, so that they may prostate themselves at my feet!' he declared.

Jeff sniggered at the word "prostate" and sat back as the soldiers unclipped the metal bindings on both chairs.

Ray had decided that stereo vision would be needed, so he opened another eye. Looking up at the red-armoured guard silently freeing his hands, he smiled a genial smile.

'Oh! Brilliant! Very kind of you!'

'And now,' continued Kelvin. 'You will both kneel!'

Ray looked at Jeff, expecting more taunts to come tumbling out of his mouth, but to his surprise, Jeff crouched down and knelt as he was told.

'Listen!' whispered Jeff from the corner of his mouth, 'I'm gonna try and get to the ship, just follow my lead!' he added.

Ray still had no idea what to do, and as he too was waiting for time to pop a workable idea into his head, he decided it was best to follow suit.

'Now, the matter of last requests,' said Kelvin.

'Actually, yeah, I could do with—' said Jeff.

'SILENCE! No last requests!' asserted Kelvin gleefully.

'And you, my hairy friend,' he continued, striding over to Ray, 'are no mere Earth man, are you, Barbaray

Sprambladack Fasstalon-Scump?' he grinned.

Ray realised that his reputation had preceded him once again.

'Er, yes. You must've known my dad, I suppose?' said Ray.

'Nope. But I heard the story of what he did to Queen Shelley of Profania. Very funny actually. Anyway, I have decreed that—'

Kelvin stopped mid-sentence. He looked around.

'Alright! Who's let one go?' he asked, scanning the lined up soldiers carefully.

Ray coughed gently, and Kelvin looked back at Jeff, grinning madly.

'Sorry, I couldn't help it. I was trying to tell you that I could do with popping into the ship to use the toilet, cos—'

Kelvin was dumbstruck.

'That's disgusting! Kill them both!' he ordered.

'Brilliant,' muttered Ray. 'You're a genius, it has to be said.'

Jeff ignored the sarcasm and carried on regardless.

'Whoa whoa! Hang a banger, mate! You kill us now, and you'll never get the Universal Remote! Isn't that right, Ray?' He nudged his friend with an elbow.

'Ah, yes, the Remote. Hand it over, Spooner!' said Kelvin, pinching the end of his nose just in case.

'It's hidden in our ship, back there,' said Jeff.

Kelvin looked over at the Penguin's open hatch and realised that it was an obvious hiding place. He turned to his soldiers. Every one of them had a vacant expression. This confirmed Kelvin's suspicions.

'Why didn't anyone think of searching their ship? You

useless cretins! I mean, what is the point of having a task force if I have to do every sodding little task myself?'

He was clearly losing his authoritative cool. As if to confirm this, the three Tax Inspectors strode into the area. They had seen more than enough of this farce and were stepping in. Kelvin jumped when he saw them.

'Ah! Good! Erm... It's all going splendidly, as you can see... erm...'

'This is the last straw,' said the head of the Inspectors, pulling out a freshly sharpened pencil to make some fresh notes. 'You're obviously quite incompetent.'

'Agreed. Totally unfit to rule,' said another.

Kelvin gasped.

'We're taking over from here,' said the third Inspector.

The first inspector pulled out a laser pistol and shot Kelvin's commander.

'Locate the Universal Remote, then kill everyone!'

Kelvin watched his commander fall down dead at his feet, and realised that they'd just shot the closest thing he'd ever had to a friend. Finally realising that one really doesn't appreciate the good things in life until they're gone, his heart sank. He knew deep down that he wasn't really Overlord material, and though he'd tried his best to be evil, the game was pretty much up. Now the matter of simply surviving the day seemed to be the main issue.

Ray and Jeff looked at Kelvin's expression turn to utter despair, and they could tell that he was no ruthless dictator, just a frightened young man trying to fill his father's cavernous – albeit fabulous – shoes, inadequately. He watched as his authority was systematically dissolved by the tall suited men. Then he regarded the still-kneeling

Jeff and Ray and through teary eyes, whimpered, 'Help me?'

The three Inspectors marched in unison over to the Marshmallow Penguin, and climbed in, preparing to search for the hidden remote.

Within Jeff's brain, his underworked, overpaid neurons saw this opportunity to postpone their work-to-rule, and decided to spark into action. He finally had the idea that he'd been waiting for, and against his better judgement, he called out to Kelvin, feigning desperation.

'Alright! I'll tell you where it is! Please! Have mercy!' he wailed, sounding hammier than a ham sandwich without the bread and butter. And extra ham.

Kelvin looked bewildered as Jeff approached him. As soon as he was face to face, Jeff whispered to the frightened ex-dictator.

'You help us right now, and I'll solve all your problems. Deal?'

Kelvin knew there was no real choice. Everyone was in danger of losing their lives at that moment.

'Alright.'

The Inspectors had begun to throw items out of the hatch in their search for the remote. The chemical toilet bounced across the floor, mercifully clean and recently emptied. Jeff's rucksack was emptied out, scattering clothes, coins, toilet roll and socks everywhere.

The head Inspector was getting frustrated by the lack of progress.

'Keep searching!' he barked. 'The sooner we find it, the sooner we eliminate these incompetents!'

'Ahem – perhaps I can help?' said Kelvin, stepping away from Jeff. He approached the ship's hatch.

'The human has told me where it's hidden. In

exchange for my life, I could…'

'Tell me. Now,' replied the head inspector, clearly not in the mood for any nonsense, levity or indeed, mercy.

Kelvin pointed up at the interior ceiling of the craft.

'There's a hidden compartment. For smuggling, I believe.'

The Inspector noticed the small hexagonal panel in the ceiling, which swung open when he pushed it. A T-shaped handle hung from the ceiling.

'Turn that handle clockwise to open the safe, and the Remote will be yours!' said Kelvin, slowly stepping backwards.

Kelvin watched as the Inspectors gathered around their superior as he took a firm grip on the handle.

Kelvin ran away as fast as he could, as the Inspector twisted the handle around as far as he could.

Ray turned to Jeff, finally realising what was happening.

'No touchy?'

'NO touchy!' replied Jeff with a grin.

The Inspectors felt heavy for a brief moment, but this momentary discomfort didn't last long as the gravity field pressed them into the floor in a split second, crushing them to puree, with a sickening crunchy sound.

Jeff and Ray turned their heads in disgust at the carnage, and Kelvin threw up all over his dead commanding officer, which everyone thought was a rather disrespectful thing to do.

'I don't think they understood the gravity of the situation,' said Jeff, raising a Bond-like eyebrow.

Then he released the last vestiges of his earlier flatulent outburst, completely shattering the coolness of the moment.

'Wait a minute,' said Ray, 'where is the Remote?'

Jeff looked at his friend dumbly.

'You mean you haven't got it? Oh blimey – I thought you had it last!'

'Don't blame me! I haven't seen it for...' began Ray, but then he noticed the crafty grin creeping across Jeff's face like a crack across a frozen pond.

'Oh, nice one, Jeff. You had me there,' said Ray. 'Where is it, then?'

'Down me pants.'

Later on that afternoon, Jeff and Ray had been freed, and given a tour of the Furious Anger by Kelvin, while their spacecraft was thoroughly cleaned of all remnants of the doomed Tax Inspectors.

As they gazed out of giant windows in the great Skraggi Imperial Palace, Jeff and Ray noticed a change in the very landscape of the once mighty world. It still had breathtaking views of giant spiky mountains that curved and twisted, like the spines of a porcupine that had experimented with crimping tongs. But they seemed almost graceful as they pierced the clouds now, no longer hostile and irritable. The sky, once boiling red clouds, had relaxed to gently swirling candy floss. It was almost as if the elements had realised that Lord Rancydd was no longer watching them. Down on the surface, even the acidic oceans had ceased their thrashing, and the Great White Megasharks that swam in it, took a day off, gliding around in relative comfort, like tranquilised dolphins. It was the dawn of a new era. An era of congeniality, friendliness, niceness.

Which was nice.

Kelvin was overjoyed. It felt as though a great weight

had been lifted off his shoulders. Now free of any responsibility to his father's memory, or a faceless bunch of bean-counters, he pondered his future.

'You see,' said Kelvin – who had decreed that from this moment on he should be addressed as 'Kelvin the Reasonable' – 'I'm not really a bad person. It was just that being my father's only son and heir, I was sort of press-ganged into the family business. I'd rather be more of a laid-back king, not an evil overlord.'

Ray patted a friendly hand on the young monarch's shoulder.

'And so you shall, my friend. So you shall.'

At that moment, a sliding door opened, revealing the Orbots, now fully back in control of their faculties. Jeff smiled at Tailback, who smiled back coyly. Gridlock waved at Ray, sniggering quietly.

Jeff took a deep breath.

'Well, now that's all sorted, we'd better make tracks then, eh, Ray?' said Jeff, rubbing his palms together, eager to move on.

'Wait!' implored Kelvin nervously. 'What about me? I don't know what I'm going to do from now on!'

Ray looked at Jeff standing impatiently by the newly-cleaned and repaired spaceship.

'I have just the thing, your majesty. Wait here a moment,' said Ray, walking over to the hatch and reaching inside.

He retrieved a small cardboard box, checked its contents visually and proceeded back to Kelvin. Handing him the box, Ray smiled.

'There you go! Your own small business: Skragg's first royal hairdressing salon!'

Kelvin pulled out a comb and a hairdryer from the box, tears welling up in his eyes.

'Oh! I can't thank you enough – I just don't know what to say!' he whimpered in bliss.

'You'll pick it up in no time, I'm sure,' added Ray. 'And now, we'll be off.'

Kelvin nodded repeatedly, still gazing at the hairstyling products.

'Thank you. Thank you, my friends.'

He paced around Gridlock in a circle, trying to get the hang of the jargon.

'Yes, sir? Certainly, sir. A little off the top? Lovely. Something for the weekend, sir?' Et cetera.

Gridlock did his best to stifle a smirk.

''Ere, Kelvin,' called Jeff, 'what about those tax inspectors? Won't they be sending some more out?'

Kelvin stopped pacing and considered the possibility of another visit.

'Oh, I doubt it,' he replied. 'They only come around at the beginning of every new reign, and us Skraggi rulers have rather a lengthy lifespan, so they won't bother me for oh, I dunno, four hundred years. Something like that.'

Jeff was a little jealous, but pleased for the new King.

'Don't go all evil on us again, OK? 'Cause if you do, and I find out, I'll be back to have words, alright?'

Kelvin put both hands up.

'You have my word. I wasn't much good at it, to be honest. I just wish I hadn't executed so many henchmen, now. And my poor commander's gone too. Did you know his name was Kenneth? I only just found out. Poor Kenneth. I miss him, you know.'

Ray stepped in.

'Well, look – I'm not sure how it works, but if the Universal Remote can rectify it, I'll see what I can do, OK?'

'That'd be awfully sweet of you chaps, if you could…' said Kelvin gratefully.

'Take care, matey,' said Jeff. He took Tailback by the arm and lead her towards the ship.

Ray shook hands with Kelvin the Reasonable, and followed his friend into his craft.

Kelvin had a last thought.

'Come back for free haircuts, any time!' he called.

'Thanks! I will!' said Gridlock, before bursting into laughter. 'I don't have any hair! Hee hee! Priceless!'

chapter twelve

The Old/Young/Old Folk's Home

The Marshmallow Penguin lifted off from the spacious palace grounds, and glided out into open space. Ray brought up the galactic star charts and programmed a course to the Methuselah system, as supplied by the Skraggi galactic navigation team. Gridlock sat in the co-pilot seat, quietly sniggering at random unfunny occurrences. Needless to say, Ray realised that this journey would not be helped by the giggling android, and put on his headphones to block out the offending noise. Unfortunately, Ray no longer had his 'Top Hits Of The Eighties' CD, as it had been left on Emo Prime, so he had to make do with white noise.

At the rear of the craft, Jeff and Tailback stood at the porthole, watching the huge red planet of Skragg get further and further away.

'Y'know, its funny,' said Jeff, 'that Kelvin bloke reminded me of me when I was a kid, in a way…'

Tailback turned to him.

'How do you mean?'

'Well, my dad forced me into the family business, you

know, doing up houses etc., where I really fancied doing something else instead. Still, I suppose Liverpool have done alright without me.'

'If you say so, Jeff,' replied Tailback, 'what's Liverpool?'

'Football team. Back home. It's a sport,' said Jeff.

Tailback nodded.

'I think I understand. What's Earth like?' she asked, genuinely curious.

Jeff realised that it was probably one of the hardest questions to answer. He rubbed a hand across his three-day stubble.

'Well… I suppose it's a nice place. OK, well, there's a couple of wars, pollution, a bit of terrorism, crime is a pain, injustice, racism and dishonesty… and obviously, millions of starving people, but the views are nice. Generally, it's alright.'

He stopped to reconsider his statement.

'I didn't paint a very good picture really, did I?'

'No. I'd be terrified of it. Can we not go there, Jeff?' said Tailback, with a shudder.

Jeff noticed something about the female Orbot: she hadn't freaked out once since he'd returned from Emo Prime. He tested his theory.

'BOO!' yelled Jeff unexpectedly.

Tailback hardly flinched.

'Steady on!' came the voice of Ray from up front.

Tailback cocked her head in that cute way.

'What was that all about?'

'I wanted to see if it'd frighten you,' said Jeff. 'It looks like you're cured!'

Tailback took a second to process the idea.

'Cured? Oh! This is… illogical! It's wonderful!' She beamed, and made off to tell the guys up in the cockpit. Suddenly she turned and came back to Jeff, who watched, intrigued.

'I'm sorry that I hit you before. I was under the influence of the virus that the Skraggi ship uploaded to me.'

'Hey, it's OK. I'm alright. Mostly. I mean, I think I'm getting used to it now,' said Jeff, remembering the many recent attacks that his bonce had been subjected to.

'I think it was the virus that removed my phobias, in all probability,' said Tailback, trying to smile sweetly.

Jeff smiled back. 'Well a bang on the nut was worth it then – to see you straightened out, babe.'

In answer, Tailback leaned forward and kissed Jeff. She didn't know quite why she did it, as she previously saw it as a pointless exercise. But after their shared experiences of life, death and altered states of being, she calculated that it would be an appropriate thing to do. As for Jeff, he was a little taken aback, but it didn't put him off enough to reject the kiss. As before, it felt unlike a real kiss – just cold and smooth to him, as if he'd kissed a marble statue. But he could tell there was more to it than just a physical act. And that was what made it special. A kiss with a reason behind it made all the difference.

'Thank you,' said Tailback, breaking away, and resuming her walk towards the cockpit.

Jeff stood entranced. Unblinking. His fingers touched his cold lips.

'Oh my God. I'm in love with a robot.'

While our fantasmic foursome are undertaking the lengthy yet uneventful journey across the Galactic disc to reach the Methuselan system, it would be a nice idea to fill in some previously unfilled-in blanks for you. It's the least I can do to reward your enthusiasm. If you've got this far, you're either very interested, a glutton for punishment, or clinically insane. But I still appreciate it – you're only human, after all.

Remember the life-changing chaos on Emo Prime? Course you do. Well, life had changed forever, just as prophesied in their legends. And it did so in four minutes and fifty-one seconds, the exact running time of the song, 'Don't Worry, Be Happy'.

When the dreaded track three came along on the CD that was being played, fate, luck, providence – or perhaps an act of Bod's divine intervention (call it what you will) – had interrupted the track list, having spectacularly dramatic results.

The facts were these:

Track two, McFerrin's serenade to serendipitous satisfaction, had finished as planned, and merely the opening chords of, 'Heaven Knows...' were heard, but the CD was so scratched and damaged by beer and food stains, that the track skipped, missing the entire song, the disc forever altered so that no one would hear that dreaded song again. Instead, it went directly onto the next song, which was 'Walking On Sunshine' (by Katrina And The Waves – UK no. 8, 1985), another recklessly happy ditty that only served to cement the currently joyful disposition of all the people who'd been listening. The damage had been made permanent. And then it multiplied in the same exponential way that human cells do when they divide upon conception. Then again, bacteria might be a better analogy. Bootleg copies of the

CD were quickly duplicated and distributed, and are to this day, it is said, being spread like the proverbial wildfire across the entire planet, and, some say the whole Milky Way Galaxy itself.

So the great (albeit nonsensical and fabricated) Prophecy of the Emo people finally came true: two 'evil ones' had totally usurped their age-old society, and inspired a revolution, a new happier existence. The surface of the planet is now rumoured to be a multicoloured ball, spinning happily in space, accompanied by a great soundtrack. Jeff Spooner would later be astonished to learn that Bobby McFerrin's joy-inducing tune did save a life or two, and it was indeed declared a public holiday, celebrated every year, across the planet by the now happy population of Emo Prime.

Oh, and by the way... If, and maybe when the American Voyager probes (As of March 2007, Voyager 1 was at a distance of approximately 9.5 billion miles from the Sun, making it the most distant Earth-made object from Earth) do ever find their way back to Earth in the far future, the Human Race will no doubt be extremely surprised to discover that at least one of them will no longer contain a golden audio disc containing facts about life on Earth, but a compilation of *Top Hits of the Eighties* will be found, whistling its joyous melodies right back at its creators.

Imagine having to explain that to your superiors at NASA.

'Here it is, folks!' announced Ray to his three crewmates, as he saw the very, very large and grey planet come into view. He got no reply.

'I said – here we are!' he repeated.

No reply again.

Ray sighed. He wasn't the best star pilot in the Galaxy, but he felt pride at managing to locate and reach their destination without help. So it was a little disappointing that no one was there to congratulate him on a job well done. At least hairdressing provided a constant source of gratitude and small talk, neither of which he'd had for over two hours.

He put the ship into braking mode, making sure that it was floating in the general direction of their destination, unbuckled his seatbelt, and climbed out of his chair to see where everyone was.

Everyone was sitting cross-legged on the floor of the ship, engrossed in an enthusiastic and almost rowdy game of cards. The only game Jeff could think of to teach the two robots was 'Snap', but everyone seemed to be having a good time, much to Ray's added isolation and disappointment.

Jeff looked up and saw Ray watching. He patted the floor beside him.

'Come on, matey! Join in for a bit!'

Ray declined.

'No thank you,' said Ray stiffly, 'some of us have got a ship to pilot.'

Jeff realised that perhaps they'd had enough fun for now, and that they'd left poor old Ray to do the work.

'Come on you lot, let's go and see where we are, eh?' said Jeff, throwing his cards down.

'Snap!' yelled Gridlock, slamming his hand down on the deck, then rolling around in hysterics.

'Wish they'd cured you too mate…' mumbled Jeff.

Gridlock looked up at Jeff, looking a little sheepish. He was finally realising that despite his inability to control his annoying habit, he was being annoying from time to time.

'Sorry, Jeff,' he mumbled, unheard.

Tailback took the co-pilot's seat, and stared out at the colossal globe in front. Serious grey and beige clouds waltzed over its surface like dirty net curtains in a bowl wash.

'Lovely inviting place, innit?' said Jeff, sniffing aloofly.

Ray remained optimistic for once.

'Oh, it'll be fine. Give it a chance. What can possibly go wrong?'

'Would you like a list?' asked Jeff.

Gridlock was still considering his annoying habit, and thus remained strangely silent. Jeff tapped him on the shoulder.

'You alright, Grid?'

'I've got a bad feeling about this,' said Gridlock solemnly.

Coming from Gridlock, this put everyone on edge. If he couldn't find something funny about the situation, there was definitely something to be wary of.

The ship began to descend into the cloudy atmosphere of Methuselah. Layer after layer of icy, crystalline altostratus gave way to wispy cirrus, which in turn revealed familiar Earth-like cotton wool of globular cumulus. Then, finally the surface of Methuselah was visible; continent-sized cities, stretching from horizon to horizon, consisting of ornate cathedral-styled buildings. Spires and ramparts decorated every wall, elegant and rather gothic in their splendour.

The crew of the Marshmallow Penguin stared silently in awe as they zipped past the impressive structures. If this is the home of immortals, what wisdom, what beauty, what secrets lie within?

The ship's computer homed in on the coordinates given to it by Kelvin's galactic navigators, and as the little flying hairball touched down in a large stone courtyard outside a huge castle, the crew wondered what incredible sights and knowledge would be found within. A race of immortals – perhaps the only immortal beings in the universe – would surely have a lot to teach those poor unfortunates lumbered with painfully brief, finite lifespans. It was truly an awesome prospect. An awe-inspiring thought.

Jeff finally articulated the feelings of everyone on board:

'Out the way, I need to use the bog.'

Ray unclipped his seatbelt and went to the hatch. He picked up his small bag containing the Universal Remote, and checked that it was intact. After all, not many things could survive an hour or two down Jeff's trousers.

Jeff emerged from the toilet cubicle, buckling up his belt.

'Alright, everyone?' he said enthusiastically. 'Let's go meet the locals!'

Ray opened the hatch, and a dusty breeze wafted into the ship. It smelled of old wood and leather. But then it had a hint of disinfectant about it too. New plastic. Bubble wrap. Curiously and cautiously, the four travellers clambered out of the ship and stood before the castle.

They approached the humungous wooden drawbridge, and noticed that there was no moat for it to lie across, just flat and sandy ground.

'That's weird,' noted Ray, 'I suppose this is just to keep out intruders.'

'Ha ha!' giggled Gridlock. 'Careful you don't fall in the moat!'

'Fairy nuff,' said Jeff, 'but we still need to open it to get in there, don't we?'

Both men looked around, until Jeff noticed that Tailback was staring up at something high above the drawbridge. She pointed at a tiny window, where an old man with a white beard was looking down at them.

Ray gave the man a friendly wave.

'Er, hello! I say, could you open the drawbridge for us, please? We're here on a matter of great imp—'

He stopped, as the old man seemed to duck out of view.

'Oh. Charming!'

Just then, a small boy popped his head up into the window and stared at them in the same way.

'I was just saying,' said Ray. 'Could you open the drawbridge please?'

The small boy giggled mischievously and dropped out of sight.

Jeff was still looking at the drawbridge when suddenly he heard a slight creak, and saw dust fall from the edges of the wooden slab.

'It's opening! Move!' he yelled, as the drawbridge came thundering open, casting a long shadow onto the group. Ray rolled sideways, while Jeff dived to his left, taking Tailback with him.

Gridlock was right in the middle and opened his mouth to laugh when the five tonne drawbridge smashed him right into the ground, crunching horribly.

The dust cloud began to settle, and everyone had got back to their feet when they realised that Gridlock had been under the drawbridge when it fell open. Tailback noticed first and ran to the edge of the fallen door.

'Grid! Grid!' she wailed, trying to lift the huge slab. It was no use.

'Tail, I'm sorry,' said Jeff, putting his arms around her and helping her back to her feet, 'I think he's gone, love.'

Tailback looked up into Jeff's eyes and cried without tears.

'He was my friend, Jeff. He was… my brother.'

She put her head on Jeff's chest, whimpering softly.

Jeff felt his blood boiling.

'Right, whoever's in there had better hope they're bloody immortal, 'cause I'm gonna kill whoever did this!'

He strode off into the shadowy castle, clenching his fists as he went. Ray and Tailback followed, a lot less confident than the angry Earthman.

As they cautiously stepped into the darkness, the echoing sounds of the little boy giggling, mocked them.

One of the strangest animals on Earth is the jellyfish. Apart from being composed of 94–98% water, and lacking major organs and a brain, one type of jellyfish, called Turritopsis nutricula is blessed with a life cycle in which it reverts back to a child (the 'polyp stage') after becoming mature. It does this through the cell conversion process of transdifferentiation. This cycle then repeats, rendering it effectively immortal. Clever and rather handy, isn't it?

The aeons-old civilisation of the Methuselans share

this form of immortality. They are neither indestructible nor immune to disease, but if they remain reasonably healthy and undamaged, they too, like the jellyfish, will never die.

Unfortunately, as we will soon see, this has its disadvantages…

Jeff reached the end of the darkened corridor, and stopped to study the foreboding wooden door that stood in his way.

Ray and Tailback caught up with him, and they too wondered what lay beyond the door.

'Well?' asked Ray. 'Do we knock again?'

'I'm done knocking, mate,' said Jeff angrily. 'The next thing I'm gonna knock is somebody out.'

'Be careful, Jeff,' said Tailback, placing a hand on Jeff's shoulder, 'they're still powerful beings. Who knows what abilities they have?'

Jeff seemed to calm down at that point. He realised that aside from a lucky swing in a moment of rage at Reverend Wilson, he hadn't fought anyone since he was eight years old, and as such, his hand-to-hand combat skills were still those of a child. He was still quite angry at the destruction of his robotic friend though.

'You might be right. But I don't think what happened back there was an accident.'

'We can at least make sure first, eh?' offered Ray, still quite nervous.

'Yeah, well… we'll see,' said Jeff. 'Now – let's have a butcher's behind this door!'

Jeff lifted his foot and launched an almighty kick at the door as hard as he could. It was at that exact moment that someone on the inside had pulled the door open, forcing Jeff to tumble forward onto his face. Ray and his two remaining upright friends looked through the doorway.

It was a huge, wooden panelled conference room, with forty or fifty people standing there in shock. There were old men with beards, in white form-fitting outfits, wrapped up in togas, looking for all intents and purposes like Greek philosophers, and there were some old women too. They stood and stared, clearly offended by the rude entrance.

Running around the room, and paying no notice whatsoever, were a large number of ten year old children, dressed in similar robes. They hopped, screamed, rolled and jumped around, clearly having the time of their lives.

Jeff and his trembling companions walked into the room. The old man nearest him raised a withered arm in his direction.

'I say there! How dare you just barge in like that, eh?' he declared in a paper thin, tremulous voice, 'What are you playing at, young man? Hmm?'

Jeff felt an unusual sense of bravado.

'Alright, Grandad, don't have a Connery,' he said, sizing up the occupants of the room to see whether anyone was physically a match for him.

'Me and my mates are here in peace, alright? We've come all the way across the bleedin' galaxy, just to bring you lot a present, and the first thing you go and do is let one of your kiddies kill my friend!'

The old man looked dumbfounded.

'Eh? Kill your friend? Oh! I see – the robot outside?' he asked, stepping forward.

'He was my brother,' said Tailback tenderly, 'and your drawbridge destroyed him. Why?'

‘Oh! Another robot, eh? Very nice. Well, I’m sorry, young lady, but it was an accident. I couldn’t help it, you see.’

Jeff held his hands up.

‘Wait a minute, gramps. It wasn’t you, it was one of these little brats here. They opened the bridge without any kind of warning and…’

Jeff’s words ran out of volume, and his mouth ceased to move as his eyes took in the scene before him. Finally he regained the power of speech, and put his vocabulary to good use.

‘Bloody hell!’

The old man in front of him began to shrink. But as he did so, his skin tightened up like a blanket being pulled at each corner, and his hair darkened, every strand of it being sucked into his head. Watery eyes cleared and shone brightly and liver spots faded away, as the man turned into a ten year old boy.

Ray and Tailback gasped in amazement at the transformation.

‘Bloody hell!’ repeated Ray.

‘Now that does not compute at all!’ said Tailback.

The little boy looked shocked.

‘Ooh! You swore! I’m telling!’

The stunned onlookers turned their attention to the rest of the people in the cavernous room. Every one of them were undergoing the same change; elderly women regressed into energetic girls and screaming toddlers aged like drying leaves into doddery pensioners.

The white form-fitting outfits stretched and shrank to accommodate the change in size and shape. Luckily that saved their embarrassment, but the togas fell off the newly-formed kids, while the recently-aged grabbed fallen sheets and wrapped them around their thin and wiry bodies.

The boy in front of Jeff looked up and smiled.

'I 'mashed your robot! I 'mashed your robot!' he sang in a familiar playground chant.

Jeff looked at Ray for some kind of explanation, but there was none. Ray shrugged.

'Beats me!'

Jeff tried to reason with the kid.

'Right, listen matey, what's your name, eh?'

The kid began to dance on the spot, singing nonsensical songs.

'Big frog, Barvle-frog! Old and grey with a big fat gob!'

Jeff felt one eyelid twitch in annoyance.

'Oi!' he yelled, grabbing the dancing child by the elbow, 'I said, what's your name?'

'BARVLE!' yelled the boy, kicking Jeff in the shin.

'Where's my pressie? You said you had a pressie! Gimme gimme!'

Jeff resisted the temptation to kick him back, as he realised that he was finally getting somewhere.

'Right, Barvle,' he said as calmly as he could, 'I've got your pressie. It's called the Universal Remote, OK? Remember that?'

Barvle stopped dancing. He looked up at Jeff and then over to Ray.

'Uni-Mote? You brung it back?' he asked, smiling. 'Yay! Ev'rybody! They brung the Uni-Mote back here!'

Everyone stopped and cheered. One of the other old men hobbled over.

'Did I hear that correctly, eh? Did you say you've brought back the Remote? Hmm?'

'Yes,' said Ray. 'Actually, we've all gone through great hardship to retrieve it and all we want to do is drop it off safely. Erm, is that alright?'

The old man put out a hand in greeting. Ray shook it.

'My name is Blutekablab. I'm so glad to meet you, Mister…?'

'Scump,' said Ray, 'Ray Scump. And these are my friends, Tailback and Jeff.'

The old man nodded a weak acknowledgement.

'Excellent! Come with me. Come, come!'

He tottered off in the direction of another door, beckoning the travellers to follow him.

Jeff let Barvle 's elbow go, and the boy raced away, running around the perimeter of the room, singing more nonsense songs.

As they got to the door, Blutekablab turned around to Jeff and looked rather embarrassed.

'Oh, excuse me, please…'

Then he shrank, morphing into a short youngster, just as Barvle did a few minutes ago. Everyone watched in renewed astonishment as the life and vitality flooded back into his body.

Barvle had finished his lap around the room, and reached the door, growing in size, and aging rapidly until he became recognisable as the old man they had first spoken to. He grabbed his toga and carried on as if nothing had happened.

Looking down at the youngster, he patted the child on his head.

'Come with us, Blutie. We're going to the archives.'

Blutie clapped his hands happily, and the group left the room, closing the door behind them.

The walk took everyone down a very long and straight corridor, lit from the sunlight outside, which shone multicoloured beams of light through ornate stained glass windows. It took just under ten minutes to walk through the corridor, during which time Barvlefrog and Blutekablab continued morphing from young to old and back again. It seemed to be quite regular; three minutes between each change, and as Barvlefrog got older, then Blutekablab got younger.

Jeff began to realise that the two Methuselans were known as 'Blutekablab' and 'Barvlefrog' while elderly, and their names were truncated to just 'Blutie' and 'Barvle' when in their younger state. Confusing, but still, it seemed to work.

Between the two of them, they managed to keep their attention on their duties, although Ray was a little creeped out by the whole odd business.

'So, you're a human, eh?' said Blutekablab in his elderly form, 'from Earth, no less! Well, well… you're a privileged man, Mr. Spooner. Privileged, yes.'

Barvle tugged at Jeff's sleeve annoyingly.

'Spoonie! Spoonie! Spoonie you're a loonie!'

Jeff forced a smile.

'Bless his little cotton socks.'

He looked at Ray with a big smile that hid the murderous intent in his eyes.

'I swear – I'm going to kill the little git.'

'Humour him,' replied Ray. 'We'll be gone in no time.'

Blutekablab indicated Tailback, who walked alongside Jeff, holding onto his arm for safety.

'Is this female robot your companion? We could probably use the Remote to convert her into a human, if you'd like?'

Tailback shuddered, which when you think about it, was an odd thing for an Orbot to do. Although she'd lost her phobias, there was something not quite right about these immortal imbeciles.

'No thank you, sir,' said Tailback. 'Jeff – would you prefer me if I were an organic?' she asked.

Jeff had a think, and although the Pinnocchio-like concept was appealing and mind-blowingly crazy to comprehend (given all the ethical, moral, theological, physical and downright lewd implications), if it meant his synthetic sweetheart was afraid, he decided he'd defend her.

'Listen, you can be anything you wanna be, as long as you're you, alright?'

It was a cheesy line, but true all the same. Tailback gave his arm a little squeeze in appreciation.

'No thanks, chief, she's perfect,' said Jeff.

They reached the door at the end of the corridor, and waited for the still-infantile Barvle to catch them up and settle down a bit. Blutekablab handed a large iron key to the boy, just in time for the age change to begin again.

Barvlefrog, now withered and shaky, put the key in the lock, and twisted it. The door opened, and little Blutie raced into another room, this one more of a living room, with sumptuous armchairs and fine rugs on the floors. He leapt into the air, screaming like a banshee, to crash spectacularly into a large brown settee, where he giggled madly.

'Please, take seats, all of you, yes, sit. Sit,' said Barvlefrog, gesturing to the chairs. He looked around and hobbled over to the main desk, and sat down.

Ray looked around at the décor. It was clad in the

finest dark wood for the most part, looking like a mansion or stately home, but there were lots of plastic items dotted around, an eclectic mix of old and new, just like the inhabitants.

The old man pressed a button on his desk and a large holographic projection manifested itself before the startled audience. To Jeff, it was reminiscent of an old wartime newsreel, with the obligatory cheesy marching band music over the top.

The projection flickered, showing an entire galaxy, spinning slowly; its billions upon billions of stars twinkling prettily.

'Since the dawn of creation, and probably long before, lifekind has searched for the Universal Remote,' said the fossilised fogey, trying his best to keep up with the images.

The picture changed to a fly-by of hundreds of planets. As each one appeared on screen, a pictorial representation of a typical inhabitant appeared next to it. Jeff recognised a few of them from Drunkies bar, back at the Emo system. The gerbil people, the fish ladies, even the big red bartending bull was there. He noticed also that there were very few human beings, which made him realise how rare his species was.

'Searched for?' interrupted Ray, 'I was always told that you chaps had owned it, made all the changes you wanted and then somehow it got lost.'

Barvlefrog was about to answer, when he regressed to being a youngster again. Still, he did the best he could.

'Nyaah! You smell, hairy face man!'

He skipped off, giggling. Blutekablab stepped in to complete his colleague's reply.

'Sorry about that. Well, yes – we had a bit of a problem when we were visited by a group of pirates, you see. They ransacked the place, and made off with the Remote, but the batteries were almost empty.'

Ray smiled at Jeff.

'Ha har! We worked that out, didn't we, Jeff?'

'That we did, mate!' said Jeff, feeling very proud.

Blutekablab paused the showreel, and went over to join the travellers. At that point, Barvle came racing past him, and Jeff, who was getting steadily more and more irritated by the dark-haired little brat, couldn't help but stick his foot out to trip the running child.

Barvle yelped and went tumbling along the carpet, where he sat dazed for a moment, then burst out crying.

'You tripped me on purpose! Horrible Spoonie!' he wailed, and ran out of the room. Jeff shrugged in mock innocence.

'Nothing to do with me.'

Ray cast a glare at Jeff that said, 'Yes it was and we all know it', and Jeff instantly glowed in shame, acknowledging that he'd got the message.

Blutekablab coughed.

'Where did you find it, then, hmm?' he asked.

'Profania Alpha,' said Ray. 'It was in the hands of a bunch of nutters called the Yobs, in fact. To be honest, I don't even know if they knew what it was.'

The wizened old face lit up.

'Profania Alpha! Ah! This explains a lot! Yes! Very interesting!'

Everyone sat up to hear the 'very interesting'-ness, but it was not forthcoming, as Blutekablab shrank back to child form. Without Barvlefrog to take over from him,

(He was, at that moment, having his grazed knees seen to by a nurse) they had to wait until he morphed back into his elderly self. So they sat and waited, while Blutie ran around, threw books all over the place (Ray did his best to tidy up after him) and played worms by wriggling under tables and chairs. Finally, after the longest three minutes they'd ever endured, the old man was back.

'My apologies. Anyway, where was I? Hmm?' he asked.

'Profania Alpha,' said Jeff.

'The Yobs, remember?' added Ray.

Blutekablab snapped his fingers triumphantly.

'Yes! That was it! The pirates stole the remote over half a million years ago, you see…' he began. Jeff gasped, being totally unable to comprehend that this old duffer had been around for at least half a million years or so.

He went on. And on, as old folk tend to do.

'Well, after that, the story goes that they set up their base of operations on Profania Alpha, and their limited experiments with the Remote provided them with a place to live, food, shelter and the one thing they really wished for – female company.'

Jeff looked at Ray, to see Ray already looking back at him, both men displaying the same expression that said, 'Ah-ha!'

'Ah-ha!' said Jeff. 'So the pirates created the Slargs?'

Blutekablab nodded.

'Very good, my boy. They weren't the cleverest of beings, it has to be said, but they managed to create a small number of physically perfect females, for companionship, and, well, er… you know. All that awfully primitive pro-creation nonsense. I think the term they used was "man-eater" or something.'

Ray was enjoying being one step ahead of the old fossil, so he decided to postulate another of his theories.

'Hence the cannibalistic tendencies! Aha! So the Slargs took control of the remote and destroyed the pirates then?'

Blutekablab changed back to a ten-year old at that moment.

'You're funny, hairy man!' he yelled, attempting to jump on Ray's foot. Ray side-stepped it.

'Slargs turned pirates into Yobbity-Yob Yobs!' yelled the little boy, spinning around until he fell down with dizziness.

Blutie sat giggling for a second and then got up, staggering like a drunkard.

Tailback leaned over, and picked the wobbling boy up by his arms and despite his initial protestations and attempts to break free from the lovely Orbot, he soon calmed down.

'Now, behave yourself, Blutie,' said Tailback, as gently and as motherly as she could. The child looked into her glassy blue photoreceptors and smiled contentedly. Even Jeff was touched by her manner, and at that point, his heart and mind banished all thoughts of having an organic girlfriend again. He sighed a little sigh.

'Isn't she great?' he said, to nobody in particular.

Ray sighed too, but in impatience more than anything.

'Yes, wonderful, but what happens now?'

'Now, I tell you the final part of the story.'

Everyone turned round to see Barvlefrog enter the room, wearing bandages on both knees.

'Trip me again, Spooner, and you'll be sorry,' he added, as he passed Jeff.

Ray thought it best to avoid the awkwardness of the moment and get to the point.

'So what happened to the pirates then? Blutie there said the Slargs turned them into Yobs.'

'Yes, that's correct,' said Barvlefrog.

'The Slargs had had enough of being treated as mere property, so they stole the remote and regressed the pirates back into their primitive states. Dumb animals, basically. Then the Slargs escaped across the desert and set up a kingdom with a large palace. And there they stayed, safe and secure, free and peaceful for centuries. I can only assume it was then that the batteries ran out.'

'But we found the remote at the top of a tree, in the middle of the Yob village,' said Jeff.

'Really? Oh, well, I can only assume the Yobs made an attempt to retrieve it... Or something. Hmm...' said Barvlefrog.

The change happened again, leaving Barvle free to hop and skip around the room, while Blutekablab found himself embracing the pretty Orbot. He coughed in embarrassment and stepped away.

'Oh! I'm so sorry, my dear,' he mumbled.

'Yes – so, as my friend was saying, the Slargs had no alternative but to live a relatively peaceful existence, and that's how it was. Unfortunately, they were visited by an alien. A bitter, vindictive one. A scorned woman with a hatred for men unlike anything they'd ever known.'

Ray's heart turned into icy debris.

'Oh my Bod. Shelley Bakerloo.'

Blutekablab raised a quizzical eyebrow.

'You mean to say you know this woman?'

'We only met recently, but she used to go out with

my father. Long story. Tried to kill us. A lot.'

He turned to Jeff, who looked eager to continue.

'Remember you said that Shelley went off across the galaxy when her hair fell out? She must've got to Profania Alpha and set herself up as their queen! Bloody hell! Your old man's got a lot to answer for, Ray.'

Ray looked suitably ashamed. 'I suppose so. But how was he to know?'

'Don't worry about it,' continued Jeff, 'I guess it's all over now, right? We beat the Slargs and the Yobs, stopped the Overlord of Skragg and delivered the Remote! All we gotta do now is get back to Kangazang, and we're sorted, right?'

Tailback tapped Jeff on the shoulder.

'We lost Gridlock though,' she said sadly.

Jeff considered this.

'You're right. Listen Booty-kebab,' he said almost correctly, as he approached the old man. 'Your little mate killed one of our friends when you dropped the drawbridge onto him. You said you could make Tailback human, so what about bringing Gridlock back with the Remote?'

Blutekablab rubbed his beard.

'Yes. Yes, I'm sure we can do that for you. My apologies.'

He turned to look at Barvle who, for once wasn't running around. Instead he was bending over, baring his naked bottom at the visitors, in particular Jeff, his new enemy.

Then the wonder of transdifferentiation kicked in again, changing the youngster into his older self, and vice versa for Blutekablab, now Blutie.

Barvlefrog quickly realised what he'd been doing and stood up, grabbing his baggy trousers to cover himself up as quickly as he could.

'Ahem. Sorry. Come along, everybody, let's put right this terrible wrong.'

Everyone followed the old man as he made his way out into the long corridor again. Jeff, Ray and Tailback walked slowly, while Blutie screamed as he hopped, skipped and jumped around the group, whooping and giggling madly.

Ray looked intently at the Methuselans for a second, then whispered to his friend.

'Here, Jeff. I'm not sure that these are the right people to be trusted with this Remote. They're intelligent enough, but when they turn to kids, it's a bit of a dangerous thing to leave with them, wouldn't you say?'

'Good point,' nodded Jeff.

'I've been thinking – these people must have done this stupid age-reversal thing to themselves, just so they could stay as the owners of the Remote for all time.'

'What – you mean like wishing for more wishes from the Genie of the lamp?'

'Exactly,' said Ray. 'They used the Remote to get immortality, but I think they hadn't really thought it through, and this ping-ponging from young to old and back again is the result.'

Jeff scratched his head.

'That'd explain a lot. What do we do now then?'

'I'm not too sure, to be honest,' said Ray, 'I suppose we play it by ear and be careful.'

Tailback adopted a similar whisper.

'Logically, the Remote should be in safe hands, and this is clearly not a safe place. We should take it back and ensure it's in a safer location than this.'

'Er... well said, love,' said Jeff, trying to work out what Tailback had just said.

'It's up to us to do the logical thing, the right thing. After all, we're fine, upstanding people, right?'

Ray and Tailback nodded in agreement.

Jeff smiled.

'So – first chance we get... We nick it.'

Tailback stood at the edge of the drawbridge. It was still open and still on top of the crushed remains of Gridlock.

She attempted to lift it up, slipping her fingers underneath the huge wooden slab, but it was far too heavy for her servo-motors to handle.

'Come away, love,' said Jeff gently, 'let them lift it up.'

Barvlefrog looked up to the castle wall where Blutie stood waving. Blutie was clearly better behaved as a child than Barvle, and he managed to keep his mind on the job as he operated the mechanism that pulled the drawbridge up.

Slowly the bridge creaked and rose up to its closed position. Ray and Jeff tentatively crept towards the crumpled Orbot, keeping one eye on the vertical drawbridge.

'Keep that thing open, Blutie!' yelled Jeff.

They scraped together the plastic and metal debris that used to be Gridlock, and dragged it all out of harm's way. They stood and looked at the heap of remains, shining in the sun. Jeff put a comforting arm around Tailback, who looked horrified at the vision. It made her think of her own mortality. True, being an Orbot came with a longer lifespan than a 'fleshy', but she now realised that everyone – and indeed everything – had a finite time in which to live.

Blutie came running into the courtyard, morphing into the old man as he went. Again, Barvlefrog shrank down to his mischievous younger self, and lost all interest in the proceedings. He began to run away, but Blutekablab caught the youngster by his arm.

'Now, just a minute there, Barvle,' said the old man. 'You owe these nice people an apology, eh?'

Barvle looked up at the faces of Jeff, Ray and Tailback, and with an embarrassed mumble, finally admitted his guilt.

'Sorry I 'mashed your Bot.'

Blutekablab patted the child on the head and took the Universal Remote from him. Then Barvle skipped off, singing another of his nonsense songs:

Bing, bang!
A-bingy bang bang!
You'll never get to
Kanga-zang!

Ray heard the song, and it didn't make him feel good. He watched intently as Blutekablab reached into his toga and produced a new cuboid battery, which he placed into the Remote.

Ray stepped forward.

'Um, sorry. Just before we get started, I remembered something.'

'Eh?' said Blutekablab, 'what's that then, young man?'

'Well, as Jeff said, we met the Overlord of Skragg, and I promised him that I'd try and undo some of the mess that he made. Mainly all the staff that he vaporised. And Kenneth. Can you do that kind of thing?'

Blutekablab had a think.

'Ah, yes. I think so. I suppose it's the least we can do in return for all your help. Just concentrate hard on the result, and let me do the rest.'

Ray closed his eyes and Blutekablab placed a wrinkly hand on his head. He pointed the remote directly upwards and pressed a button.

Nothing happened. Blutekablab smiled.

'I think you'll find that all's well now.'

'Really?' asked Ray. 'How can you tell?'

'Well, you can't – from here anyway. But trust me, everything is back as you wanted it.'

Across space, a small number of Skraggi generals and soldiers suddenly popped back into existence again. This convinced the general population that Kelvin The Reasonable was indeed a mighty and benevolent king after all. And a rather good barber too. Kenneth, the Skraggi Commander, was especially impressed when he appeared all of a sudden, to see Kelvin, arms outstretched, saying, 'Ta-daaah!'

Back on Methuselah, Blutekablab turned to Jeff, waving the remote.

'Is there something we can do for you, Mr. Spooner?' he asked. Jeff looked at Tailback again and realised that he'd got used to her as she was. If she suddenly became organic, it wouldn't be the same. Then he realised that he was starving, and wondered if the remote could rustle up a feast for him. No, that was too tiny for such an object, but the thought of his last meal reminded him of something important.

'Yeah, actually. I made a promise to a little hero a while back. I can think of something that needs fixing, quick sharpish.'

Blutekablab put his hand on Jeff's head, just as he did Ray. Jeff squeezed his eyes shut and wished for all of the Slargs and Yobs on Profania to become strict vegetarians, saving the Hoppas from persecution, genocide and the pitta bread of certain doom.

So it was wished, so was it done.

Finally, Blutekablab pointed the remote at the bits and pieces of Gridlock and closed his eyes in deep concentration. Then he pressed the main button, while mumbling some incoherent incantation.

This time, a bright blue beam of light shot down from the clouds above. Everyone jumped back in surprise, as they were expecting the same bland response as before, or at least the beam to emanate from the remote itself. Like focused, perfectly straight lightning, it hit the robotic remnants and disappeared as suddenly as it arrived, leaving Gridlock's parts glowing softly.

Then there was a faint, crackling sound. It grew louder and louder, as everyone watched the plates, wires, tubes and circuit boards begin to reassemble themselves.

To Jeff it looked like reversed footage of a building being demolished, which essentially was what it was. Finally, a buzzing sound, much like a radio being tuned in, could be heard coming from within the newly recreated Orbot.

Tailback gasped.

Ray stood in silent awe.

Barvlefrog aged rapidly, and Blutekablab regressed once more.

But Gridlock stood silent and still.

Tailback stepped forward to her synthetic sibling.

'Is that you, Grid? Are you alright?'

She looked into his face for a sign of the old Gridlock that she knew. Silence greeted her.

Ray tried.

'Hello, Griddy! How do you feel? Not every day you get brought back from the dead, eh?' he said cheerfully.

Suddenly, Grid tilted his head. He swivelled it to face Ray.

'Dead?' he said flatly.

'Yes,' said Tailback, 'you were completely destroyed by the drawbridge, and we lost you. How do you feel?'

Gridlock seemed nervous, hesitant, as he tried to think of the right words to say.

'I... was... destroyed? Dead?' he asked again, looking up at the wooden slab that crushed him.

'That's right, mate. But you're back now. We've sorted you out,' said Jeff. 'Great to have you back!'

Gridlock looked down at his body for signs of damage. He could see none.

He turned his hands over. Clean and new as the day he was assembled.

Then he looked up. Everyone gazed intently at his face. Even Blutie stopped cavorting and waited for Gridlock to say something.

Gridlock trembled. It looked like he was about to cry.

Then he laughed out louder than he'd ever done before. Everyone jumped at the sound, but they were relieved to hear the Orbot in hysterics once more.

'Hee hee! Priceless! I was dead? Oh, stop it! You must

be joking! I'm a machine! I was never alive! Good one! Ha ha ha!'

He held his sides as he got a great deal of laughter out of his system. Tailback hugged him in joy, while Ray and Jeff smiled at each other, happy that the gang was back to relative normality.

Suddenly, Blutie grew up into Blutekablab, and Barvlefrog shrank down to Barvle. He still had the Remote, and pointed it at his Methuselan friend.

'Time to shootie, dumb old Blutie!' he sang, pressing the button. Once again a blast of focussed ethereal light flashed down from the sky, hitting Blutekablab. The second it stopped, Blutie was no more. At least not as everyone had known him. His atoms had been re-engineered into a rather impressive and lumpy toad, who sat blinking and inflating his throat sac.

Everyone gasped in terror. Except Gridlock, who pointed at the toad and broke into laughter.

Jeff tried the gentle approach, holding up both hands to the crazy kid.

'Now, come on Barvle… We're all friends here. Just pass me the Remote, and…'

'Shurrup, Spoonie!' cried Barvle, pressing the button again. Lightning flashed down, hitting Jeff right on the head. A sickening second later, he was replaced by a life-sized plastic doll of Jeff Spooner, complete with jointed limbs and frozen confused expression.

'That's for tripping me up, nasty man!'

The doll lost its balance and fell onto the floor next to the confused toad.

Gridlock found this hilarious too, and laughed accordingly.

Tailback looked at Ray.

'What are we going to do?' she cried in desperation.

Another flash of lightning later and Tailback became a chrome-plated sunflower.

Gridlock stopped laughing. He suddenly realised that he did in fact die not too long ago, and it was about to happen again.

Ray stepped back in fear, as Barvle eyed his last two victims menacingly.

'Five little people, standing in a row. Three gone bang, two left to go!' he sang in glee.

Gridlock pointed to Ray.

'Shoot him! He hasn't had a go yet!'

'Oh cheers, Grid,' said Ray in disgust, 'I go to all this trouble to save your skin – er, plating, and this is how you repay me? Charming!'

Barvle found this amusing, and levelled the Remote at Ray.

'Hairy man, hairy man, stupid long hair, I can make you funnier, like a teddy bear!'

He blasted Ray, who yelped in pain as he turned into a six foot teddy bear, and rolled onto his back, lying there uselessly.

Gridlock looked over at the fallen bear, the sunflower, the toad, the 'Action Jeff' doll, and the hyperactive youngster dancing with glee, then he realised he was the only one left.

'That's not funny.'

A blast of lightning later, and Gridlock joined the newly-created menagerie, in the form of a balloon tied to a stick.

Barvle giggled for a moment. Then he looked around, trying to find another target.

As there was none, he turned around, bored with his new toy. Seizing the moment, the toad shot out his sticky prehensile tongue, and grabbed the remote. He pulled it back into his mouth and held it there, as Barvle dived onto him, kicking and screaming in a fit of rage.

The toad shook him off and hopped away, avoiding the boy's oncoming assaults. Then finally, the aging process began, and as Barvle grew old and withered, the toad spat out the Remote, and regressed into a tiny tadpole, that lay on the sandy ground, wriggling and gasping.

Barvlefrog, now older and wiser, realised what he'd done in horror. Quickly, he picked up the remote, and wasted no time, zapping the odd collection of random objects back into their original selves once more. Blutie lay on the ground crying.

Jeff ran over to Barvlefrog and snatched the Remote from him.

'You bloody idiot! You nearly killed us all!' he barked, 'This is way too dangerous for you lot. I'm taking charge of it from now on, alright?'

Barvlefrog looked genuinely sorry.

'I'm sorry, Mister Spooner. I had no idea that would happen. You see, when we were first given the duty of guarding the Remote, we weren't immortal.'

'Yeah, we worked that out, mate,' said Jeff, still angry.

Ray checked himself all over, and was relieved to find himself back to normal. He joined Jeff and the Orbots.

'I think,' he said, 'that Jeff here's got a point. This is no place for an item of such power. We'll have to keep it. Sorry and all that, but you lot could easily unmake the universe if we leave it with you.'

Barvlefrog nodded sadly.

'I know, I know, Mister Scump. I'm sorry. You're right, of course. But I feel you should leave soon, before anything bad happens again. The change is coming in a few minutes.'

'Too right mate. We'll be off then,' said Jeff.

'But what will you do with the Remote?' asked the old man.

'Never you mind, Grandad,' replied Jeff. 'It's better you don't know. I've got an idea…'

Ray knew instinctively it was a good one.

chapter thirteen

The Big Bounce

Down on the dusty surface of Profania Alpha, the Marshmallow Penguin landed gently.

Jeff and his friends were greeted by the entire village of Hoppas, who bobbed up and down in excitement, eager to see their heroic friends again.

Jeff stepped out of the ship and looked at the gathered crowd. At the front was Fnar-Fnut, the elderly chief Hoppa, and balancing on his antennae was little Pon-Pon, smiling broadly.

'Ello, little 'un!' said Jeff warmly. Pon-Pon bounced up and Jeff caught her in his arms.

'Hello, Jeff! Me big happy to see you again!'

'Me too. How's it going then? Any more trouble with the Slargs and the Yobs?'

'No trouble now,' replied Pon-Pon, 'they not bother us no more. They know we fight back now.'

Jeff remembered that he'd converted the Slargs and Yobs to vegans, and guaranteed the survival of the Hoppas, but he kept it to himself, happy to let the bouncing animals retain a sense of pride.

The crowd made their way to the village. During the journey, Jeff regaled the listeners with his account of the events that had transpired since he last saw them. This served to confirm without a doubt that he and Ray were indeed great heroes, the stuff of legend.

The sun began to set, casting long shadows across the plains, and the Hoppas watched as Jeff and Pon-Pon made their way to the centre of the village. Jeff took out the Universal Remote, and removed the battery. He placed the Remote down on the ground and took a few steps back.

Pon-Pon signalled to the onlooking Hoppas to get into position, just like they'd done before. The Hoppas dutifully lined up in a row, ten of their strongest and best. On the other side of this row were the rest of the villagers, tightly packed together like a living crash-mat.

Pon-Pon hopped over to Ray, who was holding a suit of armour, made for a Hoppa, out of wooden plates, slabs of stone and woven ropes. Pon-Pon bounced into it, and Ray tied it tightly around her.

Then, just as before, the line of Hoppas began to bounce up and down, like a Mexican wave. Pon-Pon bounced onto the top of the end Hoppa and up into the air. Along she went, gaining altitude each time, until she reached the other end of the line.

When she came down again, her plate armour protected her as she smashed the Universal Remote into millions of useless pieces.

The group of villagers caught her expertly, (they'd been practising the trick), and delivered the little Hoppa safely back to Jeff.

'Great job, Pon-Pon. Your mother would be proud.'

He looked over at Ray.

'Think we've done the right thing?' he asked.

Ray put a reassuring hand on his human friend's shoulder.

'Absolutely. What was it you said? "With great power comes great responsibility"?'

'You bet,' replied Jeff, 'I have just one question, Ray,' he said.

'What's that then?'

'What do they make that "Scuzzmeister" beer out of? You never got around to telling me.'

Ray shrugged, and whispered into Jeff's ear. Jeff screwed his face up in utter revulsion.

'Oh. That's just wrong.'

epilogue

The Other Prophecy

The gentle melody of 'Don't Worry, Be Happy' wafted through the air.

The sea itself, was bright yellow. Viscous like custard, but warm and inviting, it bubbled and flopped over in thick rippling waves. The beach sparkled, made up of billions and billions of tiny ball bearings that rattled when you walked upon them. Exotic purplish trees sprung up all over the place, providing cool patches of shade under their long leafy fronds. Between two of them stretched a hammock, in which Jeff lay, dressed in a Hawaiian shirt and shorts, sucking the last of his cocktail through a straw.

This was the life.

This was the best holiday he'd ever had.

This – at long last – was Kangazang.

'Ere, Ray! You want another drink, matey?' called Jeff.

Ray was playing table tennis on the beach with Gridlock. Both players had a paddle in each hand, and even though Grid was a computer with lightning sharp reflexes, Ray was by far the better player. Grid didn't mind though; the more he lost, the more he laughed.

Watching the game avidly beside the table was a fluffy pink and yellow penguin called Tania; The original Marshmallow Penguin. She would periodically waddle off to retrieve any ping pong balls that flew off the table, and fetch them back to Ray in her beak.

Ray looked up.

'Yes please! I'll be over in a minute!' replied Ray, serving another devastating salvo of ping-pongness.

Jeff turned round and called to the straw beach hut.

'Tail – couple more of these, please love!'

'Coming up, sweetie!'

Tailback emerged from the hut, wearing a coloured sarong and sporting a set of new bronze body plating. She thought it'd resemble a human tan more than her usual white and chrome, and she was right – she looked like a golden goddess. She handed Jeff his drink and planted a kiss on his lips. The sun had warmed her up a treat.

'Ow! Hot lips!' said Jeff with a chuckle. Tail went off to hand Ray his drink, and Jeff couldn't help but watch as she shimmied across the silver sands.

If someone had told him a week ago that he'd be drinking cocktails served to him by an android, who was also his new girlfriend, lying on a hammock on a beach that was a thousand light-years from Earth, he would've laughed his head off. But there he was, with everything he'd ever wanted, and it felt good.

Ray took his drink and walked back over to Jeff, followed by the marshmallow penguin.

Swaying in his hammock, Jeff removed his shades as he saw Ray approach.

'So – how are you finding it then?' asked Ray. 'I told you it was a nice place.'

'Awesome, mate. Just perfect. Got me a drink, got me girl, and got me friends around. What more could a bloke want?'

Tailback indicated the beach barbecue, which gently smoked in the distance.

'I think the kebabs are ready, too.'

Music to an Earthling's ears. Jeff sighed in utter contentment. He raised his drink.

'Cheers, everybody!'

Suddenly, the custard-like sea began to bubble ferociously and erupt. Everyone spun around to see a huge metallic lozenge emerge from the liquid. It was covered in small indentations, and Jeff recognised it as the shape of a monkey nut shell. Only this nut was over a hundred feet long.

A loud voice boomed out over the bubbling sea, shaking the trees as it rumbled.

'People of Kangazang! You are now prisoners of the armed forces of Macadamia! Your land and riches are now our property, and any resistance will be crushed. So says our Great Prophecy!'

Ray was far from intimidated. After all he'd been through, a giant talking nut shell wasn't going to frighten him easily. He grinned a confident grin.

'Oh, I don't think so. How 'bout we show these nutjobs who's boss around here, eh, Jeff?'

'Jeff?'

Ray turned his head to see Jeff running away across the beach as fast as possible, with Tailback following after him.

Ray sighed.

'Wait for me!' he yelled.

the end

Almost…

And there you have it. At least for now. The tale of Jeff Spooner and the Universal Remote. I hope you enjoyed it. If you didn't then, unfortunately, you seem to have wasted a sizeable portion of your life reading all of this, just to decide it wasn't worth the effort. Never mind. The journey is what counts. Perhaps you avoided some minor catastrophe while reading this. Who knows?

Oh, I suppose you might still be wondering who I am? Well, my name is ErHuer, and one day, perhaps sooner than you think, you'll know the reason why I've told you this story. Just keep an open mind, that's all I'm saying…

About the Author

Terry Cooper was born in London in 1969 and moved to South Wales in 1980. After a brief period in the music industry with his band Best Shot, who supported East 17 on tour around the UK, Terry went back to his artistic roots and worked for various film and television companies. He has since graduated from the University of Glamorgan with a degree in Computer Animation. Terry released his first book *Kangazang: Remote Possibilities* through Candy Jar in 2010 as the beginning of the now-complete *Kangazang* trilogy.

During May 2012, Terry travelled to the Tunisian desert to restore Luke Skywalker's home. He can often be found impersonating Captain Jack Sparrow all over South Wales, and is currently completing his first feature film, *OFFWORLD*, which he wrote and directed in 2017.

Also available…

Kangazang! Star Stuff

Kangazang! Small Cosmos

From Candy Jar Books and all good retailers.